Crime

I0630530

Family

PT. 1: THE SACRIFICE

Copyright ©2022 by Eugene Day

All rights reserved. No part of this book may be reproduced or transmitted in any form or by any means, electronic or mechanical, including photocopying, recording, or by any information storage and retrieval system, without the permission in writing from the copyright owner.

This is a work of fiction. Names, characters, places, and incidents either are the product of the author's imagination or are used fictitiously, and any resemblance to any actual persons, living or dead, events, or locales is entirely coincidental.

Library of Congress Cataloging-in-Publication Data available upon request.

ISBN: 979-8-9877579-0-1

Cover design by Maria Ingram

This book was printed in the United States of America

ACKNOWLEDGEMENTS

Again, here we are another fantastic work of art, and you are still with me. So, I must salute all of my followers and supporters. My family and true friends. NSIP456 and all we represent. I love you all regardless of what we go through. Let us keep pushing for something if nothing else. Thank you to my parents and ancestors. Kurtesy Kuts barbershop for the great platform it has made for me. I'd like to thank Maria, my graphic designer and her partner Chante for introducing us. I'd like to give a super acknowledgement to my biggest dedication and motivator my son Khalfani a.k.a KD I love you to the ethers and back. You came into my life at the most pristine time. When I felt pressure and turmoil you give me reason to push on. I see nothing but greatness for you.

Nothing much else to say being that I covered most in my last two publications just stayed tuned for more greatness.

<u>PROLOGUE</u>

What is the price you're willing to pay for loyalty and love? What extremes are you willing to go to protect those you care about? Are there any limits? Is there any wall too tall to climb? Any road too rough to travel? Waters too deep to swim in? Most importantly, is there a life too precious to spare?

These are the questions Ecclesiastes Knight aka Stacks is faced with. Wanting out of the game, but not wanting to leave those close to him behind. He must come up with a way to do just that. But there are those who need him to stay put more than those who wish he'd leave.

Sacrifices are in order. In order to save everyone he loves. Yet not everything happens the way it is planned.

CHAPTER 1

Stacks stood by the apartment door on Terrell St. watching out for his partner Piko as he shook down one of his workers. This was their normal routine as they rode through the city of Greensboro checking on the progress of their numerous spots.

Standing at 6'3" 185 pounds, Piko was a little on the slim side. His oversized clothes fooled a lot of people into thinking he was bigger than he actually was. But due to his leathery skin and menacing glare most were intimidated by him whenever in his presence.

Stacks was the complete opposite. 5'7" 175 pounds with a light complexion he was what they called stocky. He kept his haircut, nails neatly trimmed, and was well groomed. Everyone looked at him as a pretty boy and therefore not a threat. His colorful eyes didn't help prove otherwise. Even though he was only twenty-four years old and nonchalant he carried it like an old head. Still as the saying goes 'never judge a book by its cover'. That fully applied to Stacks.

"Nigga, this the second time you've come up short, you better have my motherfuckin' money tonight nigga!" Piko stated as he held the worker by his shirt collar.

Stacks looked at the scene unfold and knew that Piko was wasting his breath. The worker had lost respect for Piko when he let him get away the first time. He had to remind him all the time that these youngsters weren't as easily intimidated like they were back in the day. Stacks never said what was on his mind in public. People considered him to be shy because he didn't do too much socializing. But his tight lip demeanor was his advantage. He didn't have to utter a word, but he heard everything. Even the things that weren't verbalized.

Piko let the worker go and turned to leave. "Let's go," he said walking pass Stacks who didn't move. "What's up?"

"Go 'head, I'll be there in a second," Stacks said pulling off his coat revealing the chrome .357 snub nose in his waistline.

Piko looked at him and shrugged his shoulders as he walked out the trap house. He learned a long time ago not to question him. He just went along with whatever plan he had because it usually worked in their favor.

As soon as Piko walked out the door Stacks reached down to his ankle and pulled out a hunter's knife. He walked over to the worker and didn't wait to hear any excuses, nor did he ask any questions. He listened to the piercing scream as he plunged the knife into the worker's upper thigh and twisted the blade. "Now, where's my money? And don't tell me you not stashing it. I'll torture your ass until you tell me what I want to hear," Stacks stated putting pressure on the knife.

"It's, it's behind the speaker," the worker winced.

Stacks knew the place he was speaking of. It was a beginner's usual stash spot. He went directly to it, slid the back of the speaker wall off and saw the stacks of money. Taking all of them out he turned and walked over to the worker. "I take it there's a g in each stack?" He asked without taking his eyes off of him.

"Yea" he answered with a nod of his head.

Stacks looked at the ten stacks then went in the kitchen too grab a grocery bag. He put eight of the stacks in the bag and placed the remainder on the couch. "Take that and move to the other side of town. I know you got a mouth to feed that's the only reason I'm not taking everything. All I have is what you owe, but if I see your face around here again, I'll kill you, you hear me?"

"Ye-Yea man.

Stacks pulled the knife out of the workers leg and wiped the blade on his shirt. "Now go clean yourself up and disappear," he said grabbing his coat as he walked out the door.

He considered himself a businessman as well as an enforcer. It was a conflict of interest when you had someone like Piko as a partner. Piko liked to drag people along and keep the pressure on them. Stacks would rather get rid of the problem immediately than worry about a dishonest worker. He knew that stubborn people only understood one type of language and that was violence.

Stacks opened the passenger side door to Piko's Jeep Cherokee and hopped in. "Here bruh," he said handing Piko the plastic bag over to him.

"What's this?" Piko asked looking into the plastic bag.

"What it look like?"

"That nigga says he ain't have my money," he exclaimed moving to get out of the Jeep, but was stopped by Stacks. "What up?"

"Let it go, I already handled everything."

"That nigga still breathing?"

"Yea so what?"

"Then you ain't handle everything,"

"Man, you betta come the fuck on. And I said I took care of it."

Piko let go of the door handle and started up the Cherokee. It was good to have people like Stacks around. It kept him from having to live up to his actions and tough talk. That was one thing Stacks didn't do. Front.

"Plus, we got better shit to do," Stacks mentioned.

Piko patted the bag of money and smiled as he pulled off. "You right bruh."

CHAPTER 2

His government was Ecclesiastes Knight. His mother gave him the biblical name in hopes that it would bring some type of godliness into her home. He began going by Stacks for the obvious reasons. He didn't like living flamboyant or spending carelessly. He was a good money manager, as his mother use to remind him to put something away for a rainy day.

He steered his '22 BMW 228i down Bessemer Ave. then turned into the driveway of one of the houses right across the street from Irvin Elementary. Stepping out of his car he took a deep breath of the North Carolina air letting it fill his lungs as if it was his last breath. After grabbing two grocery bags out of the back seat he closed the doors and proceeded to walk up the front stairs.

Even though he no longer lived at the residence he still made it his thing to go grocery shopping and pay the bills when needed. The strong aroma from the kitchen immediately reached his nostrils as he opened the door then kicked it shut behind him.

"Tony is that you?" his mother yelled. She refused to call him Stacks, I she wasn't going to entertain anything that had to do with the streets. But she did realize that his name was a little too long to always be yelling it out. So she succumbed to calling him by his middle name as did everyone else in their family.

"Yea, it's me ma," he said walking into the kitchen and placing the bags on the table. "I brought some food too," he added as he hugged her from behind and placed a kiss on her cheek.

9

"I have enough as it is, it might get spoiled," she mentioned in reference to the fully stocked pantry, refrigerator, and deep freezer.

"Then cook more or give it to Eve. I know her begging ass'll be happy to get anything for free," he stated as he began putting the food away.

"Boy be nice, you know she has Destiny to take care of."

"Is that her excuse? Tell her to quit acting like she doesn't have a little one and she'd have some doe to spend," he made known before leaning over her shoulder to peep what she was cooking.

"Quit it," she said swatting at his reaching hand. "And you can tell her that when she comes by." Ms. Knight cut her eye at her son to see his reaction to her statement.

"I ain't trying to argue wit her. She already knows what she needs to do to get her shit together. I've tried to help her but she's more hard-headed than I am.

"Like I said, tell her when she gets here which should be any minute now," she said as she walked out of the kitchen. "And watch my food, I'm going to rest my feet a little."

"Aight," he replied grabbing the paper bag he left on the table and headed to his old room. Once he got there he closed and locked the door. He went to the nightstand and slid it to the side. Running his hand along the floor's edge he felt the latch that caused a piece of the wall to pop out. He pulled it out to its full length then opened the paper bag. He had placed the money he had gotten earlier in the bottom of the grocery bag with the groceries on top. The only reason he didn't split the eight stacks equally was, because even though it belonged to Piko, he considered the three he got a collection fee. He placed the three grand along with the other piles of money he had stashed there. Returning everything to its proper position he got up and headed to the kitchen to check on dinner.

"Now what was that you were telling me earlier Tony?" Ms. Knight asked slyly as she took a bite of garlic bread. They were eating baked spaghetti with turkey meatballs topped with Parmesan cheese. The light sprinkle of barley and oregano in the tomato sauce brought out its rich flavor. Cream corn and a Caesar salad completed the meal.

"What you mean ma?" he asked playing dumb while stuffing a fork full of spaghetti in his mouth.

"You know, about Eve, "she threw back not letting him off the hook that easy.

"What about me?" Eve asked. Her attention was quickly redirected from the TV show she was watching as soon as she heard her name.

"Ask your brother."

"What's mama talking about?" Eve asked looking at Stacks while raising her eyebrow questionably.

"Ain't nothin'," he answered taking a sip from his cup of sprite.

"He said you need to quit partying and manage your money better."

"Is that right Mr. Money Man? Let me tell you something. I can take care of my responsibilities. And you ain't my daddy so don't tell me how to live my life," she scolded while rolling her neck for added effect.

"See ma that's what I was talking about ain't nobody trying to argue with her dumb ass."

"Dumb?!Why, 'cause I don't drive a Beemer like you? Or keep money on me? Shit, I got a mouth to feed. I ain't out here running the streets like you think I am or like you are?"

"You got some of the craziest excuses. You chose to lay down and get pregnant. Then soon as you ready to go out you call on mama. If you weren't my sister, I wouldn't do half the shit I do for you. You steady trying to make your way in this city, but don't know how to go about doing it. Why you think Dev' went back up north? That was probably the best move he ever made," he said knowing it wasn't even close as to why his brother left.

"Well, I like it down here or else I would've been left."

"Yea right. Just like you said something about moving to Florida."

"You know what Tony, Stacks, or whatever you go by. You need to look at your own life before you start judging mine."

"I'm good, that's why I ain't complaining. I just want you to be good too. Quit letting these fuck boys feed you dreams like they care about you."

"Aye you cut all that cussin' in my house now," their mother said having put up with enough free talk.

"I'm just speaking the truth ma. She should know how the game go. At least I thought she did."

"Whatever."

"Ma, I'm out. I gotta get home and get some rest I have to get up early in the morning," he said grabbing his dishes and heading to the kitchen.

"I don't know what for, it ain't like you got a job or nothin'," Eve mentioned sarcastically.

"For your information if you must know dumb ass. I have an interview at Belk's. See, unlike you, I know what it takes to survive. Maybe one day you'll follow in your little brother's footsteps," he said bending to kiss his mother on her cheek. "Dinner was good as always."

"Thank you sweetie. Thanksgiving is in a couple of months you going to Charleston with us?"

"Don't I always?" he stated going over to his niece Destiny to give her a shy self a kiss. He always had a time trying to explain why she couldn't go with him whenever they parted ways.

"I was just checking."

He went over to Eve, who was looking out the corner of her eye not knowing if he was going to bypass her on his way out. She thought he was when he finished hugging Destiny and kept walking. It was her own guilty conscience that made her feel that way. She knew that she wouldn't want to talk to anyone after having words with them. Her shoulders sagged with disappointment. She loved her baby brother more than any of her siblings even though he gave her the hardest time. He was very transparent and held no punches. Straight raw and uncut. Yet, she knew he was just looking out for her best interest.

"You know I love you girl," he said causing her to jump before giving her an over exaggerated kiss on her cheek. "I'm just trying to give you some brotherly advice. Spend time on something you like that's beneficial instead of blowing your hard earned money on getting other people rich. Just know that regardless of what you do I got your back," he stated giving her another kiss before mushing her head and walking away.

"Who's gonna wash my dishes," their mother yelled out.

She is mama, ain't like she paying for anything."

"Whatever."

"Ma, come here for a second," he asked stopping at the front door.

"What is it?" she walked up whispering.

That's one thing he loved about his mother. She always had his back no matter what lifestyle he chose. She always told him, 'If you're gonna be a drug dealer, be the best at it.' That's why he refused to nickel and dime. He didn't sell breakdowns, only weight. He entered the game at the low level and didn't want to leave unless he was on top.

"You need anything?"

"No baby I'm ok, why?"

"Here, give this to her," he said handing over $500. "And tell her she better not spend my shit at no club either. Also, to let me know when she's ready to pursue any of her dreams."

"Okay."

Stacks gave her one last hug before walking out the house. He paused to hear the locks turn then headed to his car. He thought about the only woman in his life that he considered important. One who stood at 5'4" and a bit on the heavy side that had to be watched because of her diabetes. He was the baby of the family. That alone made his mother hold him close to her heart. Even though she was lighter than him, damn near white, you still could see the strong resemblance between them. His sister was only two years older than him and despite the height difference they could easily pass for twins. He knew just as easily as he attracted women, she attracted men, and he didn't like it. That was only because being a man himself he knew how they thought. Most were only after one thing and one thing only. He had to remind himself that she was grown and lived her own life. Yet, if anyone ever laid a hand on her there's no telling what he'd do.

He didn't have a permanent lady in his life. Not because he didn't want one. He just couldn't find one to meet his standards. Plus, he felt he was too young to settle down. His focus was on money and his family.

CHAPTER 3

"Do you have any experience in sales?" the interviewer asked.

She was a middle-aged lady that you could tell spent hours getting ready for work in the morning. She was more than likely single or divorced and in need of some excitement in her life. This was the simple evaluation that Stacks came up with and he usually wasn't wrong.

"Not to sound arrogant, but I feel given any situation or circumstance I am great at selling just about anything," he stated knowing he never held any type of legal position in his life. He did know what it took to win people over. If you didn't believe in yourself no one else would either. He learned a few interview techniques at the Goodwill help center on South Elm-Eugene St. He learned about the place from making frequent stops on the south side.

"I like that. That's the type of attitude we need around here. The holidays are coming up and we need to reach a certain sales demand."

"Ah, that's not a problem. Well for me it wouldn't be, because if I'm here they will more than likely make a purchase. And that's the thing *I* have to be here," Stacks made known in a joking but confident tone.

"Well Mr. Knight, if everything on your application che4cks out ok I don't see why you can't be."

"Then I guess I'm your new employer," he stated rising out of his chair. "Will there be anything else Mrs.Losman?" he asked as he straightened his polo shirt that was neatly tucked inside his brown khaki pants. His leather Rockports were only a shade darker. His freshly cut hair showed off his 360 waves. He had a small diamond earring in his ear to give him a polished gentleman look.

"Please, call me Phyllis," Mrs.Losman demanded coming from around her desk with her hand extended. "And yes, that'll be all. I'll more than likely be getting in touch with you soon."

"Okay Phyllis," he said taking her hand while staring deep into her smoky grey eyes.

He already scanned her slender body through his peripheral and wondered how he could even toy with the idea when he never been attracted to white women. He saw the color rise in her face as held eye contact then let her hand go. "I'll be waiting."

That was two weeks ago. He had gotten into the routine of his 9 to 5. It wasn't that he needed it, but like he told his sister he knew what it took to survive. One of those things was having legitimate income to account for the money he accumulated.

He stuck a piece of gum in his mouth to keep his breath fresh as he waited for the customers to roll in. He kept his word to Phyllis by talking any customer he approached into buying something. His mind began to drift with thoughts of his future. He was getting on his sister about doing what she liked when he wasn't even taking heed to his own philosophy. It was never really about him. He was content with seeing his family happy and making money. He snapped out of his daydream in time to see a fine lady cross hos line of vision. He quickly jumped to attention and made his way towards her before one of the other salesmen approached her.

He easily slid to a clothing rack next to hers and pretended to be looking through the outfits. He watched as she placed blouses against her body as if that would distinguish how they might look on her. He spied something when she turned and headed toward the dressing room. He glanced at her swaying ass in her tight seven jeans. All he could do was shake his head in disbelief as he continued going through the rack of clothes. The lady's toffee complexion gave her an appealing look. He figured she was either Hispanic or mixed with it. It really didn't matter which he just knew that he had to have her.

As he waited on her to emerge from the dressing room, he saw two more nice looking women moving through the store. After about five minutes of observing their movements, he caught on to what was going on and laughed to himself. Once the lady came back out, he moved towards her as she stopped at another rack.

"Excuses me miss, but I've been having trouble picking put something for a special lady friend of mine," he stated. She was about the same height as his sister as he looked down at her.

The lady jumped a little bit from being caught off guard. "Oh my, you scared me," she said putting her hand to her chest. "Now what was that?"

"I was trying to figure out what to get for a lady friend of mine and wanted to know if you could help me," he repeated.

"Who is the lady friend, and don't try to say it's a family member because I know guys always use that line on women."

"Truthfully the only lady in my life is my mother."

"Come on now who're you kidding? I *know* you got a girl."

"And if I did why would it matter to you? I just asked for your opinion not your number," Stacks stated losing patience. He began to think maybe pursuing here was a bad idea.

"I'm sorry, I was just complimenting you, but if that's how you feel that's fine with me," she said looking into his green eyes. She grabbed the few items she had picked out and headed to the empty register not knowing that the guy she was talking to was supposed to be behind it. "Damn, why can't I get any service when I need it?"

"I got you," Stacks said walking behind the counter.

"Oh, you's a slicksta huh?" she smiled. "Trying to game me. I should've known."

"Nah, I was for real. Can't nobody in the 'Boro claim me," he stated taking the items out of her hands.

"So, you an out of town playa?"

"Nope. I told you only woman in my life is my moms. Oh, my sister and niece too," he added as he rang up the clothes.

"What's your name?"

"Does it matter? 'Cause if this the last time seeing you it really doesn't."

"It depends," she said handing him a credit card.

"On what?"

"How interested I am, but at least I know where to find you at when and if that time comes."

"Well, what's your name?"

"Monica," she said quickly not realizing how he had just caught her off guard.

"Okay, *Monica*," he laughed as he handed her the card back.

"What's so funny?"

"Nothing."

So, you not gonna tell me yours?"

"Like you said, 'If you're interested you know where to find me."

Monica took one last look at him then shuffled off confused.

'She'll be back,' Stacks said to himself. At least he hoped she would. He watched as the two women from earlier exit the store not too long after her. All he did was shake his head. He was from the streets and easily picked up on all the hustles. Too bad Phyllis and her other employees couldn't.

CHAPTER 4

Piko reclined in the driver's seat with his eyes closed and head layer back on the headrest. His mouth was wide open as if he couldn't breathe without it being that way. He was parked on the dead end part of O'Henry Blvd getting sucked off by one of the neighborhood fiends. That was his thing. He never hesitated to trick off being that the smokers in this particular area looked more like call girls than drug users. It didn't matter that he had a girlfriend at home. Nor did it matter that they've been together off and on since elementary school. It was just his pervasive nature. That's another thing that his partner didn't agree on. If he was going to trick, he'd rather snatch one from the club, fill her with some pills and liquor then slide to the hotel.

Piko just loved how a fiend went all out on the dick to get that fix. "Yea bitch suck that dick. Lick them nuts too. You know how I like it. I'll throw you two grams if you get me off in five seconds," he said raising his head to look at the juicy fat lips that were wrapped around his dick. With the mention of the two grams, instead of the normal bump, the chick pulled out all of her tricks.

"Yea, that's it. Do that shit. Get them nuts too," he gritted through his gold covered teeth. He grabbed the back of her head and forced his dick further down her throat. It wasn't long before he released in her mouth. "Swallow that shit its protein," he said trying to catch his breath. He pulled his pants up and reached for his trick bag. "Aight Chocolate I'll see you around," he said handing her two grams as promised.

"Thanks Piko," she threw back as she hopped out of the Jeep.

"Yea yea," replied before pulling off. His phone went off just as he'd turned on the highway. "Yo yo."

"What's good nigga?"

"Ahh, if it ain't the white collar nigga," he said jokingly into the phone picking on Stacks since he now held down a regular job.

"Whateva nigga. You need to be doing the same thing before they come snatch *your* ass up."

"Nah bruh that's why everything's in Iris' name."

"Aight Mr. Know it all. You hitting the club tonight?"

"Just asking. I'll probably breeze thru around one or something."

"That's a bet. Ayo you better find you a jump off or a freak for tonight. I'm tired of seeing your lonely ass wit out someone. Shit, when the last times you had some pussy anyway?"

"Yo, don't be keeping tabs on me nigga. You need to keep an eye on your girl before I slide in that," Stacks came back knowing he was for real. Iris was a freak, but Piko had her gone.

"Man, that bitch ain't going nowhere. On some real tho, we gonna get some bitches tonight and you better not say no."

"I don't even give a fuck. Just be at the club at one."

"Aight yo," Piko replied before hanging up.

Stacks knew Piko was right. He needed to find him a freak for the night to get the Jones off his back. He was thinking of Monica and how the vibe she gave off was intriguing. He wondered if he'd ever bump into her again.

Stacks parked doesn't the street from the club in a neighboring parking lot. He did that because whenever liquor was involved people would become reckless. He didn't want to end up with busted out windows or some other type of damage. He was dressed in a black and red Polo shirt with a red tee underneath. Black Levis along with black with red bottom Jordan's covered his feet. He opened his car door and paused for a second to light a blunt before getting out. Walking towards the club he placed his Red Sox fitted cap on top of his waves. He saw Piko's Jeep as he made his way towards the entrance wondering how long he'd been there. He knew people were trying to figure out who he was as he headed to the front of the line. He didn't believe in waiting in line as he handed the doorman a few bills and stepped inside.

He stopped at the bar to get him a glass of Patron and cranberry juice. He referred to it as a gentleman's drink. Popping a pill, he leaned back against the bar and scanned the room. He saw Piko's tall ass in the crowd grinding on a big booty chick. He wondered how he got away with all the bullshit he did regarding his home and living style. He guessed when you danced with the devil the song never ended. He turned to order another round and immediately felt the presence of someone behind him. He quickly turned back around tensed not knowing if the person was an unwanted guest or not. Once he saw who it was, he started smiling.

"Excuse me can I get by?" Monica asked not recognizing Stacks outside of his work clothes.

"Sure *Monica.*"

"How you know my... Oh, its you from the store. Isn't this a coincidence?"

"Could be."

"So, I guess you still no gonna tell me your name?"

"They call me Stacks."

"And why's that?" she asked reaching around him for her drink.

"Yup oughta be able to figure that out since we kinda in the same field."

"What you mean by that?"

"Come on now, why you think I started laughing when you slipped and told me your real name instead of the one on that credit card?"

"That was my aunt's."

"Don't insult my intelligence. And I guess you gonna tell me them two females weren't with you either?"

"Who?" she asked looking around as if not knowing who he was talking about.

"Those two right there," he said pointing at the two females he saw moving through the store the day they first met. "The ones who came through acting like they were pregnant. I found it funny because ya'll were obvious as hell. I could've turned ya'll in, but I respect all hustlers."

"Okay, you got me. Dang we were that obvious huh?"

"Yea if you know what to look for."

"Gotta tell my girls. Hey maybe we can work something out."

"Nah I got my own thing, but I do ask that you show me some respect and don't do that store anymore, at least not while I'm working."

"Maybe. What's in it for me? Shit, you already said you respect the hustle so why not go back?"

"Because I asked you to show some respect. I ain't trying to lose my job 'cause of your carelessness."

"What kind of hustle are you if you need a job like that?"

"So, you don't have one?"

"Yea but I'm not sweating it like that."

"Look I came here to have some fun not argue. If you trying to see what I'm about then that's what's up. If not, then ease to the side and let somebody else occupy my time."

"Are you serious?" she questioned not believing that this due had the nerve to talk to her like that. Nobody just brushed her off so easily. She liked his cockiness though. It was something different. Something that actually piqued her interest.

"As fuck. You cute and all, but I ain't with nobody questioning my stand on things. If you think I'm the type to bend over backwards or jump when you snap your fingers. I'm sorry, but I ain't him."

Monica just stared at Stacks. She was past interested. His ill demeanor had somehow turned her on. She realized she wasn't dealing with your average weak nigga. This was a man with a strong backbone. And that's exactly what she needed in her life.

"I feel you, but what you mean I'm *cute*? All this woman in front of yo and I'm just cute?" she asked seriously. She knew she looked good but liked hearing it from a man every now and then. You tell a baby that there were cute not a grown ass woman.

Stacks laughed. "You right luv, but you know what I meant. I just don't go around telling women that they fine as hell. That shit be going to ya'll head and be thinking niggas be bullshittin running game. Plus, you know what you look like unless you don't have any mirrors at home."

"Exactly the reason I ain't trying to hear that *cute* shit. Shoot I spend too much time keeping myself up for anyone to tell me I'm just cute."

"Don't fuck it up for yourself by being too arrogant. You were doing alright up until that point. Matter fact don't even say nothing else about it. You and I know you look good so let it go."

"You right, you right," she said waving for another drink. Stacks did the same paying for both of them.

Lyfe Jennings "Must Be Nice", blasted through the speakers as they sipped on their drinks.

"Damn that's my song. Come on Stacks, dance with me," she said pulling him onto the dance floor.

Stacks wasn't no official dancer, but he wasn't a two-stepper either. He couldn't get down like he wanted to being that he still held his glass of liquor. Monica was grinding on him while holding onto her own glass. Her soft bottom pressing against him sent a tingle through his body causing a semi-erection. He wondered if he didn't pop the E pill would he still be having this sensation.

Monica knew what she was doing to Stacks, but really couldn't help it. She was attracted to him and wanted to crack through his shell. She turned and faced him, glancing down for a second before looking into his eyes." I knew you thought I was more than cute," she said smiling.

"So what. You gonna help get this off me or keep teasing me all night?"

"Uh-uh baby, I don't sex on the first night."

"Then what night?"

"I don't know you like that, so it definitely won't be tonight."

Stacks looked at Monica and started to put her on blast, but knew it wasn't worth it. He had to respect her mind though. Most females wouldn't hesitate to bust their legs open whenever he pursued them. He figures he'd give her some time before he had her open like the rest.

"Yo fam, I got something for you bruh!" Piko yelled busting through the crowd with all thirty-twos showing.

"What's that?"

27

Piko leaned in to whisper in his ear. "I got a couple of freaks dying to meet you. So, dump this Selena look alike and come get that jones off you. Looking like you bout to bust through your jeans and shit."

Leave it to Piko to crack jokes at any given moment. Stacks agreed wit Piko though. Monica wasn't trying to do nothing, and it had been too long since he had some pussy. "Then fuck the small talk I'll be outside," he said back.

"My nigga. I'll be right back."

Stacks glanced at Monica who had a questioning look on her face." I gotta go handle some business. I enjoyed your company, even though it wasn't how I wanted it to end, but hey," he said shrugging his shoulders.

"I know you gonna at least give me your number?"

"Yea, I can do that," he said grabbing her phone and programming his number into her phone. He hit the send button so that he'd have hers as well." And don't be afraid to use it either."

"Oh, I won't," she grinned then watched as he left the club. She saw as the guy who spoke to him earlier leave as well. Two broads followed behind him. She already knew what that was about. She was surprised to be feeling a tinge of jealous come over her.' I ain't worried about it. That nigga gonna be mine soon and ain't none of these bitches gonna be able to come around then,' she thought to herself then made her way to the table that her home girls were at.

"Damn Mo', who that fine ass nigga you were all up on?" her girl Misty asked.

"You don't remember him from the store a couple of days ago?"

"Oh word? What's up with him?" her other girl Cassie inquired.

"Said ya'll were slipping on ya'll hustle. But ya'll get him off your minds because that's all me."

Stacks drove down W. Gate City Blvd. with one of the chicks Piko introduced as Joy. She was dark skinned with a medium build. Curly shoulder length hair. She seemed to have a knack for chewing her gum loudly and talking non-stop. When Piko introduced them, he acted as if he really had a choice between the two. "You can have either one you want, but Mimi's mine." He remembered him laughing.

"It doesn't matter my nigga. They say the blacker the berry, the sweeter the juice."

"You ain't never lying," Joy stated walking forwards him.

"Yea, yea nigga. Whatever yo. Just follow us unless you got other plans?"

"Nah, where you headed?"

"To the Econo. I know what you thinkin', but not here dawg. I'll blow one of these fuckas to the moon word up."

"Aight, let's go," Stacks said heading to his car. He wished he never made that comment regarding Joy, because now she felt that she could be also up under him.

"I like this," she said rubbing her hand over the pearl white car before getting in. Her bugged eyes gave her an over-excited look hence her name. "So, what is it you do Stacks?"

"I know you not about to hit me with the twenty-one questions 'cause I ain't trying to blow my high answering them."

"Nah, I was just making small talk."

"You can still do that. Matter fact tell me about you."

"Oh okay. Well, I just graduated college. Thank God that's over with."

"What was your major?"

"Art and film production."

"So you want to do movies?"

"Yeah, something like that."

"What else?"

"I'm twenty-two, single. I basically just like to have fun," she stated shrugging her shoulders.

"Yo, get that out the ashtray and light it if you don't mind," Stacks asked cutting her off before she started ramping again.

He watched as she lit the blunt and pulled on it. He began smiling as she kept toking not even knowing what she was getting herself into. "Hey, hey, don't be hogging my shit. I said light it not hotbox that motherfucka," he made known snatching the blunt from out her mouth.

"My bust. I forgot to tell you I'm a weed head too," she smiled widely.

"I hope you got a bag to replace what you just inhaled ol' iron lung ass."

"Damn, why you so mean?"

"I'm just fuckin wit you. Smoke what you want. But I don't know why all those questions I know Piko had to tell you something about your boy."

"Not exactly, just that you his right hand man. And when he pointed you out, we were like we wanted to meet you. What kinda weed is that it got me feeling funny."

"It's called Xbox. You good tho it ain't gonna fuck your life up or nothing," he stated then grabbed his phone and called Piko.

"What up bruh?"

"Yo, you got some drinks right?"

"Of course. What up with chocolate girl wonder, you like?"

"She good. Just tried to finish my XBox," Stacks laughed then cut his eyes at Joy who started rubbing on herself.

"Word! I already know what's up then."

"Just make sure you have some more Kush we finna have the game system on all night."

"That's what I'm talking 'bout."

Stacks hung up just as he turned into the hotel parking lot. Getting out he locked the doors and hit the alarm. He headed to the front desk and started to get separate rooms but remembered that these were nothing but some jump offs. With that in mind he got the double. While he waited on his room key he took time to peep Joy's attire. Her body hugging dress left one to wonder what was underneath. Everything seemed to be in order until he checked out her shoe game. One inch open toed heels with straps that wrapped around her ankles and up her calves. The shoes were mediocre. As if they were worn one too many times. Probably her favorite club shoes. He automatically labeled her a hoodrat.

Once Stacks had his key, he headed to the elevator. The door wasn't even all the way closed before Joy was trying to shove her hand down his pants.

"Hold on ma, be easy. We got all night, ain't no need to rush."

"I gotta have it. I'm so hot right now I can't wait." she exclaimed pushing against the elevator wall. He hit the emergency stop button as she unzipped his jeans and pulled his dick through the slit of his Polo boxers. He watched as she dropped to her knees. She didn't put him straight in her mouth, but sniffed down its length as if she was savoring the smell. She slowly slid her tongue out for a taste before leaving a trail of kisses from the base to the tip. As soon as her mouth began to widen to take him in it hi phone rang.

"Yo!" he barked not trying to hide his anger from being disturbed show.

"Calm down nigga, it's me. What room we in?"

Stacks looked at the key. "Two-twelve."

"Aight, I'll be up in a minute."

"Yea, yea," he breathed as Joy continued doing her as if the call never came through. Her bugged eyes reminded him of Monique, one of his favorite porn stars, as her lips stretched over him. She kept her sight on his face as she worked her magic. He tightened his grip on the rail and raised on his toes as she sucked on the tip of him. "Shit that feels good."

Joy continued moving her head back and forth while humming deep in her throat. She slid her hands up to his chest to massage his pecs. She was showing off as she slithered her tongue out to rub the thick vein underneath his dick. Reaching down to fondle his nuts, she felt them tighten up.

Stack as grabbed the back of her head as he shot. Long stream of backed up cum down her throat. "Aaaaahh! Sssss! Mmmm!" he yelled out.

As soon as she finished swallowing his cream, he quickly pulled up his pants and released the hold on the elevator.

When the elevator opened on his floor there were a couple of people waiting to get on. They eyed him and Joy with wonder as to what actually was holding the elevator up.

Once they got to the room Stacks went straight to the TV and cut it on. He kicked of his shoes then laced back on one of the beds. Joy went to the bathroom for a quick second then came back out and laid beside him. He was rubbing on her ass when there was a knock at the door.

"That's probably Mimi and Piko," Joy stated.

"Then let 'em in," Stacks said then reached for his coat. He kept a .357 snub nose in the lining. Like he told Piko when he mentioned the Econolodge, he wasn't out to get marked for nothing. He still remembered reading about to guys found dead in their rooms. It messed the hotel's reputation for a while, but since the coliseum was down the street people weren't trying to drive to far after attending one of the big named concerts. Especially if they came from out of town.

"Yo, where Stacks at?" Piko yelled out making his way into the room.

"Laying down," Joy answered.

"Oh. Yo, Stacks!"

"Man, why the fuck you yellin'?" We ain't at the club no more."

"Fuck that shit, here. I know you said get a fifth, but you also said this was gonna be an all-night thing, so I got a half a gallon and some G13 Haze," he smiled widely as if saying 'Yea this gonna have you wasted.' He placed the bottle on the dresser and threw him the ounce of weed.

'Word. What you waiting on then?" he asked standing up. He went back in his coat and grabbed the bag of pills. He put everything on the dresser and busted open both bags. "Yo, where the gars at?"

"In the bag."

Stacks opened up the brown paper bag, pulled out the half gallon, and saw the blunt wraps underneath. He busted open four of the cigars and laid them on the dresser side by side. He didn't bother with breaking up the buds as he put the Haze on the four wraps then crushed the x pills on top of them. He was a master blunt roller, so it took him no time to roll the four blunts. He handed two to Piko then cracked the bottle of Dulce. He wasn't trying to get drunk just tipsy as he took a couple of shots before passing the bottle to Joy. He cut off the room lights and let the TV illuminate the dark as he fired up one of the blunts.

"What's this," Mimi asked.

Piko laughed before answering. "X box."

"What the fuck is that?"

"That's what I've been trying to figure out," Joy chimed in taking a hit of the blunt.

Ecstasy and weed," Stacks finally let it be known.

"Oooh, y'all motherfuckas think y'all slick," Mimi quipped.

"Quit fronting like you don't like it." Piko maintained.

"I'm just saying I never had it, but its aight."

Stacks didn't say nothing he took a few more shots of Dulce then turned to Joy. He knows she was down for whatever after their elevator episode. He reached out and grabbed her titty through her dress then slid his hand down her stomach. She didn't really seem to into all the preliminaries as she stood up and pulled the dress over her head and plopped back down on the bed. He didn't hesitate to slide his hand into her thong to feel her wetness. He made sure to take all of her clothes off, because you could never be too careful. Sticking a finger in her pussy wasn't only to get her ready, but to see if she had anything stuck inside of her like a razor or something to that effect. After going through his slick examination and old school finger sniff, he relaxed. After taking off his clothes he laid back and let Joy once again her thing.

She began giving him the wonderful head job that she gave on the elevator. He quickly pushed her head off of him as he reached over to grab a rubber out of his pants. He had to see if her bottom was as good as her top.

Joy must've wanted to get him inside her as bad as he did as she grabbed the condom and tore it open. As soon as she rolled it down his shaft, she slid right on him.

"Hold up, be easy baby," he hissed feeling how tight she was causing his dick to bend.

"I got this just let me work," she threw back easing all the way down on him.

'Damn this bitch tighter than a rat's ass,' he thought. He started to enjoy himself as she loosened up. "Yea, that's it right there," he whispered as he picked up her rhythm.

"You like that huh?" she asked leaning forward to kiss on his neck and lick the inside of his ear.

"Yeah, do your thing," he answered reaching down to squeeze her butt as she rotated her hips with each downward motion.

Joy raised back up and continued to do her rodeo style movements. She reached up to squeeze and pinch her nipples while grinding on him. The move was bearable only because Stacks had a rubber on. She felt herself about to cum and leaned wall the way back placing her hands on Stack's knees. She kept thrusting her hips causing Stacks to raise up and palm her butt. She kept going until he came himself. He wrapped his arms around her waist to catch his breath when all of a sudden, the lights popped on.

"Man, what the fuck y'all over there doing, raping each other?" Piko said standing at the end of the bed in all his glory. "Sounds like a fuck flick and shit," he laughed.

Stacks forgot where he was at for a second as he looked at Piko standing there naked smiling. He would've spazzed on him if this was their first time doing this. He already knew what his next move was as he let Joy get up and pour another drink. He looked over at Mimi in the dresser mirror as she sat with the comforter pulled up over her breasts. She wasn't inhibited enough like Joy to just expose herself as she smoked on the other blunt he handed Piko. She must've felt him staring as she locked eyes with him through the mirror and smiled. She gave a suggestive motion to him as she traced her lips with her cherry red tongue. That was all he needed to see as he filled his cup up and headed over to her. He didn't care that he was swinging in the air it was just them and they already saw each other naked.

Her honey dew complexion had him over excited as his little man sprung back into action. She easily replaced the blunt with his erection. He reached down to pull the cover off of her, revealing the prettiest c-cups with thumb sized nipples he had ever seen. He quickly pinched them and felt her moan vibrate through the length of him. He reached down to play with her middle before grabbing one of the rubbers Piko left on the table. He didn't hesitate to jump in the bed with Mimi and kicked the covers on the floor. The concoction kicked in some more putting him in rare form as he placed her knees by her ears and pounded into her.

"Oooh shit, Stacks. I can't breathe," she gasped seriously trying to push him up a little bit so she could get some air in her lungs.

Stacks didn't want to stop, but eased up a bit as he raised up on his knees. He grabbed her by the ankles and held them together as he continued his stroking. He glanced over at Piko, who had Joy's head damn near twisted to the side as she tried to hold on to the headboard for support. Piko looked up and gave his famous grin. Stacks gave him a nod then stopped what he was doing.

"Why'd you stop?" Mimi asked bewildered.

"I'll be right back," he said getting up. "Finish smoking that L." He went over to cut off the room light, which except for the glow from the TV, put them in total darkness. He poured another drink and grabbed two pills as he headed back to the bed.

"Get up," he told her and sat on the edge of the bed facing Piko and Joy. He brought Mimi around and had her sit on him backwards. As she got into position and started moving up and down, he leaned back on one elbow. Sipping on his drink he popped another pill and began rubbing on her ass. The way she was riding him was remarkable. She had bent all the way over placing her hands on the floor as she bounced and rotated on him. Even in the dark he knew that her brown eye was right there winking at him, so he decided to take poke at it. Once he got his thumb in, she went wild. He took the other pill he had and stuck in place of his thumb knowing that in a few minutes she'd do anything. He leaned back again to enjoy his drink and blunt and wait for her reaction.

They had cut the TV off making the room pitch black. All you could see was the glow from the blunt tip. Stacks felt Mimi lift up a bit and stop. He wondered what the problem was as he reached over and cut on the lamp. Mimi and Joy were face to face kissing and Piko was behind Joy flashing his gold fronts. Stacks quickly raised up and continued stroking Mimi from the back. 'This shit is bizarre', Stacks thought as he watched the girls get into the sexcapade. This was going to be a long night.

CHAPTER 5

Monica woke up with a serious hangover. She wasn't use to that, but after listening to her girls Misty and Cassie beat her in the head about Stacks, she couldn't get him off her mind. She tried by downing glasses of Blue Motorcycles and Thai iced tea. She now was paying for it.

Lifting up off the rubbing her temples she looked around and wondered where she was. It took a few seconds to realize it was Misty's place. She headed to the bathroom to take a much needed piss. When she finished, she rumbled through the medicine cabinet for anything that would calm the headache she was suffering from. She found a bottle that just said aspirin. "Cheap ass bitch. All the money we getting and she buying generic shit," she mumbled to herself.

"Hey girl," Misty said when Monica came out of the bathroom. She was picking up the blanket Monica knocked to the floor. "Giiirrrl, you were assed out last night. I don't know how many drinks you had."

"I know right. I lost count myself," Monica mentioned heading to the kitchen. "I know you got something to eat in here. I gotta get something on my stomach. And why the fuck you got this cheap ass aspirin in your bathroom?"

"Shit, I don't know. My mama put that in there. You worried bout names and when they all work the same.

And there should be some waffles in the freezer, turkey bacon too."

"Well hook a sista up."

"Bitch, you know how to cook."

"That's how you treat your guests?"

"Ain't nobody tell you to get drunk," Misty said then saw the ill look on Monica's face. "You better be glad you're my girl."

Misty went in the kitchen and grabbed some food out of her refrigerator. She put a frying pan on the stove before continuing where she left off. "Why were you drinking like that anyway, that ain't like you."

"I had a lot on my mind."

"Probably that guy from the store."

"Girl please, dick is secondary money is always necessary."

"I know that's right. So, what was on your mind?" she asked flipping over the cheese omelet she was making.

"I'm not sure. Oh boy said y'all slipping. Maybe we've gotten too comfortable."

"That nigga a square he don't know what he talking about."

"Nah boo, he ain't no square trust me."

"How you figure that? 'Cause he was in the club dressed in some street gear?"

"You ain't talk to him I did."

"And?"

"His name's Stacks and he told me 'I oughta know what it means since we're kinda in the same field, plus respects all hustlas.'"

"I still say he's a square trying to play a hood nigga."

"Well, he'll be my square."

"You digging him like that?" Misty asked putting the food on two plates

"Honestly? Yea. It's something about him. I don't know what it is. I'm a find out tho."

"Well call him. You do have his number, don't you?"

"Yea, but I don't wanna seem thirsty."

"Then give me the number, I'll call his ass unless you scared he might be with another chick?"

"I already told you to fall back. Plus, he ain't our concern right now so quit trying to get off the subject at hand," Monica said putting a fork full of the omelet and turkey bacon in her mouth. She wasted it down with a few sips of orange juice. "Cassie ain't here, so we'll just fill her in later. But we have to stop doing this in our backyard."

"I've been told you that M."

"Yea, yea, but we were just talking then. It's time we put things in motion."

"So where do we start?"

"You know what? That's where Cassie comes in. She stays on top of all hottest spots and people popping in the street."

"I know right."

"We might need to call her now and tell her to come over here."

"She gonna be mad. You know she ain't no morning person and be going hard in the club. as more fucked up than you."

"So what. We either gonna be about our business or *you* missy will be back wearing wranglers and Capri pants," Monica laughed knowing neither one of them would be caught dead in those cheap clothes. At least not anymore.

"Oh, hells nah. Not in this lifetime," she said back picking up the phone. "Shit she might be able to tell us about your Mr. Stacks," she threw out there sarcastically.

"Whatever ho. Get. Your own nigga to sweat. I don't need none of y'alls help. I'll find out about him by myself."

CHAPTER 6

Piko walked into his apartment off of Lawndale Drive. There wasn't any need to creep, because it was almost seven in the morning and Iris was sure to be up. He smelt the aroma from the sausage links as soon as he shut the door. He saw Iris standing over the stove in her night shirt and bandana tied around her head. He even watched as she scratched her panty covered butt. They were a worn out pair where you could see the little lint balls forming that came from being constantly washed.

"Don't just stand there, breakfast'll be ready in a few minutes."

Piko walked up behind her and kissed her on her neck while rubbing her up and down.

"Get off me boy. Go take a shower and brush your teeth, you stink."

Piko laughed then smacked her on the ass before heading to the bathroom. It was funny how Iris acted like she was raised in the hood when her parents were rich staying in a mansion on the outskirts of Greensboro. Messing with Piko she started smoking weed and partying. He wouldn't say he ruined her life, he just out a bend in it.

"Why you coming in at this time of morning huh?" Iris asked sitting across from Piko as they ate breakfast.

She was waiting to hear what kind of lie he was going to come up with this time.

"Me and Stacks were out handling some business."

"At seven in the morning?"

"You know this hustle a twenty-four hour thing."

"Well, you need to start cutting back on your hours, 'cause I'm tired of going to sleep and waking up by myself. We supposed to be living *together* not whenever you feel like coming around."

"Damn baby, where's all this coming from?"

Iris looked at him but never raised her voice as she spoke. "It's coming from you trying to play me like I'm stupid. I've been knowing you damn near my entire life, but you act like we just met."

"How's that?"

"Hmm, let me see," she said giving him a thinking pose. "Well, I can start with the smell of another woman on you. Or the constant calls from anonymous numbers. Especially when *I* know you don't talk on phones. So, like I said, 'I'm not stupid' Jakeem."

"I didn't say you were, but you got your thoughts twisted."

"I ain't got shit twisted, you do," she said pointing at him to emphasize what she was saying. "I ain't these other hoes out here you trying to impress. I was here when you ain't have shit and I'm still here because I love you just remember that. Don't let that money go to your head," she mentioned as she got up. "I gotta get ready for work, some of us do have to make an honest living around here."

'Ain't this some shit' he mumbled watching Iris head to the bathroom. He stopped eating. His appetite was gone after hearing what Iris made known. How did he come to this? He'd been living it up. The fast life got them whatever they wanted. She never complained before, but he *had* been neglecting her lately. He never thought what life would be like without her and wasn't trying to either. He knew he had to tighten up or risk losing her.

CHAPTER 7

"Four ninety-nine, five hundred," Stacks counted his last sit-up then jumped up off the floor. He was into keeping his body in shape with extensive calisthenics. He didn't want the stiffness or bulk that came with lifting weights. He headed to the shower with only forty five minutes left before he had to be at work. Sometimes he wondered why he even bothered with the job. It was boring and he didn't know if he could take anymore of Phyllis' advances. He had to keep reminding himself that it was a must to balance out his income. He had opened a bank account when he first started hustling and accumulated close to half a mil. Another two hundred was stashed at his mother's house so he was straight. In his eyes he had enough to eat good, but not enough to retire from the streets. He knew that he could have more, but there were reasons he didn't. One being his brother, who was on the lam.

Stacks pulled out of the parking lot of his apartment chewing on a piece of apple he just bit into. He checked his cellphone to see if he had any missed calls. There were three. One was from his mother reminding him about thanksgiving. Which was a good thing because he had been close to forgetting. The second one was Piko complaining about his girl getting on him. 'I told that nigga,' he thought to himself. The last message was from Monica.

"Uh, this is Monica. I know it's early and all, but I just wanted to call and let you know that I haven't lost interest. When you get a chance call me at 336-555-6061."

"I knew she couldn't resist," he said to himself and decided to call Piko back.

"Goddamn bruh you can't answer your phone or something," Piko barked into the phone.

"I told you I have a job to handle. You act like I just be laying around bullshitting. So, what's good?"

"You got my message right?"

"Yea, but you ain't telling me shit. Iris always getting on your ass."

"Not like this bruh. Not like this," he started shaking his sadly. "She basically told me she knows I be fucking around."

"So, what's the problem? Quit bullshitting with these silly ass broads and spend time with your main. Shit, take her on a cruise or something."

"It's brick as fuck outside who the fuck going on a cruise?!"

"Nigga you know what I mean. You don't do shit wit her like you use to. Get her pregnant. That'll keep her busy *and* quiet."

"Bruh I ain't ready for no little crumb snatchers."

"You better do something, 'cause I ain't your pastor or your mother and I ain't gonna let you keep crying on my shoulder every time ya'll fall out."

"Man, this shit's crazy."

"And it's only gonna get crazier if you don't tighten up."

"Yea, you right."

"Man, I'll get back at you later. Don't stress that shit tho bruh. Just handle your business before baby girl leave you for another nigga. And you know that's all a motherfuckas waiting on"

"Nigga's ain't crazy but I get it. One."

Stacks hung up as he pulled into the Four Seasons parking lot. He got out hit his alarm and headed inside. Towards the John Taylor clothing store. He went to clock in and figured he tell Phyllis that he needed the week of Thanksgiving off. He walked to her office door and tapped lightly on it since it was partially open.

"Come in," Phyllis said. She was standing at a filing cabinet going through some papers.

"Uh, Phyllis can I speak with you for a brief second?"

"Oh, Tony it's you," she shockingly said as if she was expecting someone else. "What can I do for you?" she asked looking over the top of her glasses.

'What was that look?' he thought to himself as he saw the smile spread on her face. She had her hair up to showcase her elegant face. "My family gets together every thanksgiving and I was wondering if I could get that week off?"

"You've only been working here a little over a month now and you already asking for time off." She said closing the cabinet drawer and turning back around to face Stacks.

"I understand where you're coming from, but even though I like my job I'm more dedicated to my family."

"So, you telling me you'll quit if I don't give you those days off?"

"Truthfully," Stacks paused as if he had to think about it. "Yea, I promised my mother and I've *never* let her down."

Phyllis smiled. "I admire that. The unemployment rate is so high nowadays I can't see how someone can so easily be willing to give any type of job up."

"I'm not your average Joe. I won't disrespect you and act like I don't need this job just want you to understand where I'm coming from."

"And that I do. I've taken into consideration all of what you've done since you've been employed in such a short period of time," she mentioned as she walked towards him. "The sales are up, the losses are down, but that's not enough to gain you off time," she added as she passed by him on her way to the door.

Stacks turned to see what she was doing. He hoped she wouldn't up and fire him for his blatant statement of quitting. "So, what is enough? Maybe I can do some over time or makeup for it on the weekend?"

"That's possible, but it might not have to go that far," she said locking the office door. She walked back to her desk and leaned on the edge facing him.

Stacks saw that her blouse had a few more buttons loose than before and figured what she was suggesting. He knew it wouldn't take long before she'd quit hinting at what she wanted. "What are you telling me?"

Phyllis placed her glasses on the desk then pulled out the pins in her hair. She shook it loose just like you see on TV. She obviously watched too much of it or it was just a white girl thing. "Convince me that you need a few days off," she proclaimed.

Stacks didn't have to think twice. He knew he could turn Phyllis out without even breaking a sweat. He wished he had a few pills though, then he knew he'd have her eating out the palm of his hand. As he eased his way towards her, he stared into her eyes without blinking. He watched as her chest rose with anticipation. 'Yeah, this bitch here might start hyperventilating. Please don't scream rape,' he thought to himself as he got closer. Licking his lips, he bent his head to her neck to kiss her under her jaw. Phyllis' breath increased as he hit her hot spot. She reached out to rub his dick through his khakis. He pulled back and lifted her on the desk before ripping her blouse open. He didn't have a reason to care they were in a clothing store. She probably had something to change in anyway. He grabbed at the front snapping bra and released her full D-cups. He was surprised that they didn't sag. They'd probably were silicone, but they didn't show any scars nor felt fake as he placed one of the nipples in his mouth.

Phyllis pressed his head closer to her enjoying the sensation. She went back to fondling his shaft through his pants increasing her want to feel the actual flesh. She tugged at his belt and zipper as she stood up straight. At the same time Stacks was easing her dress up until it was around her waist. When his pants fell to his ankles and she saw the size of him she quickly pushed him into the chair in front of her desk. She dropped to her knees and began stroking him like it was a genie lamp.

"Don't play with baby. If you really want it, you better get it now while you can," he made known. She descended on him and began snaking her tongue over the head before raining kisses down the shaft. She left a coat of saliva all over him before putting him into the warm confines of her mouth. He leaned all the way back as she began to bob up and down on him. "Yea do that shit."

"Mmm," Phyllis moaned as Stacks pinched her nipples. She continued giving him vigorous head before suddenly stopping and releasing his dick with a pop. She stood up and shimmied out of her panties. She didn't hesitate to straddle him.

Before he could protest about getting a rubber, she already had half of him inside her. "Oh, it hurts so good. I feel every inch of you," she groaned easing all the way down on him. She began rotating her hips to ease Stacks upward thrust, but he wasn't having that. He raised up and carried her right back to the desk. He put her legs in the crook of his arms and started pounding into her. She tried to hold on to the edge of the desk, but it felt like she was in an earthquake. "Oh yea, fuck that pussy. Shit, it feels good. Do it Tony, do it," she hissed on the verge of cummin.

Stacks stopped and snatched her off the desk. He pulled her dress all the way up her back and slammed into her. He thrust so hard she came of her feet for a brief second.

"Oh My God!" she shouted

Stacks placed his hand over her mouth and continued pounding into her. "This what you wanted now take it," he stated. She responded by pushing back on him meeting each thrust. He felt the tightening of her walls as she started cummin. She had to bite into his hand to keep from screaming. He yelped at the hard bite, but it caused him to release himself. He pulled out and came all over her back and ass. He stumbled back and fell onto the chair trying to catch his breath. He watched as Phyllis rubbed his cum into her skin as if it was lotion. He shook his head when he saw her licking her fingers.

"Yeah. I'll say that'll get you a few weeks off. Boy, I don't know what I was thinking waiting so long to experience a black man. I gotta get you to my house and find out what else you're good at."

"Now *that* would cost you." Stacks stated as he fixed his clothes.

"We might can work something out," she shot back as she walked to a closet that was filled with an assortment of clothes.

"We'll see," he said heading out of the office. He didn't stop to clock out as he left the store. He was going home to freshen up and hit the block and see what was jumping. Hopefully Piko wasn't letting his argument with Iris mess up his judgment skills. He felt that it wouldn't be long before he had to take over their partnership. It was either that or start risking frequent setbacks. He allowed Piko to play the tough man role and bully his way through the game. He didn't know that Stacks was the reason nobody never got at him or fucked his money up. All Piko saw him as was a heavy hustler. He just hoped he never had to prove to him otherwise. It wasn't until lately that cats been testing him more than usual and he had to see what it might be.

Stacks laughed as he thought back to the sexcapade earlier. Just when he was getting clowned on by Piko about not getting any pussy. What he'd have to say now? He wondered where Piko was at or better yet doing.

CHAPTER 8

Monica was an all-around lady's hustler. From boosting to credit card fraud, she dealt in it. She was a white collar criminal and never thought to deal in any other type of crimes. They were too strict on drugs and guns, or anything else that provoked violent.

"Well, you've never been one to bullshit around when you want something. If you feel like it's worth it, do you."

"You know I am."

"Have you called him?"

"You know I did."

"And?"

"Voicemail."

"Shit, why you didn't call him again?"

"That ain't even my style. I'm not going to swear at him. If he's as interested as I am he'll get back to me."

"Are you ready to order yet?" the waitress asked.

"Yes," Monica answered. "Give me the fish platter with hush puppies and fries."

"And you?" she asked turning to Cassie.

"Give me the same thing."

"That'll be coming right up."

"Thank you."

"Anyways. Just when you holla at him see what's up with his boy Piko."

Monica laughed." What is it? The gold tooth? He looks like a nightstick."

"And probably has one too."

"Damn you's a ho."

"Bitch please. And what you trying to tell me? That you wanna see how good Stacks outs clothes on rack?" Cassie questioned daring Monica to tell a lie." That's what I thought."

"You know what. Hold on," she paused as her phone rung. "Hello?"

"Where you at?"

"Who is this?"

"The man you need in your life."

"You must have the wrong number."

"So, this isn't Monica?"

"Yes, but I don't know nothing about needing a man unless his name's Franklin or Grant."

"So you's a gold digger?"

"No, but I don't fuck with no broke niggas."

"I know that's right,' Cassie chirped slapping Monica five.

"They don't call me Stacks for nothing."

"Oh, what's up boo? 'Bout time you called me," Monica said looking at Cassie with a smile on her face. She mouthed Stacks when she asked who it was.

"Yea I know, I've just been busy. But what's good with you tho'?"

"I'm on my lunch break right now, but I get off at five-thirty."

"Where you work at?"

"Bank of America by Friendly Shopping Center."

"I know where you at. You mind if I meet you after work?"

"I don't know, depending on what you have in mind."

"I'ma put it this way. If you want to experience what life is really about, say yes. If you love the low-level world you live in, then say no."

"Oooh, don't you sound confident."

"I am. Plus I don't play games. Didn't you say you're a hustla?"

"Yup."

"Then fuck with a real one and there'll be no limits."

"Well since you put it that way. You better be here before I walk out that door 'cause I ain't waiting."

"I can dig that," he said laughing. "I'll see you then, ok?"

"Okay," she said hanging up.

"What's up?! What pretty boy want?!" Cassie questioned all excitedly wanting to know what the move was. Especially being that it would be her way of getting close to Piko.

"To meet me after work. What has he planned? I don't have the slightest idea, but I'm a damn sure find out."

"That's it?! Come on now, there has to be more than that."

"That's it."

"That's some bullshit. Just don't forget to ask about his boy for me."

"You remember what Bone said on Training Day."

"What?"

"You gotta put in your own work around here homie." Monica smiled.

"Oh word? Well at least introduce us."

"Damn, can I see what's up with this nigga first before you start wanting to go on double dates and shit?"

"Double dates? That's some white girl shit, but if that's what it'll take..."

"Whatever. We gotta get back to work before they start thinking we quit."

"I just might. All that standing be having my feet hurting."

"I know right?" she replied getting up after taking a few more bites of her fish.

After paying for their meals Monica began to ponder on what Stacks had on his mind. She wondered what he meant by 'experiencing life'. Even if he never said what he did she'd still would've wanted to see him. But now he had piqued her interest.

Monica stood at her workstation counting money for one of the bank's customers. "Two, three, four. Twenty, forty, sixty, eighty, five hundred," she said before placing the money in the bank's stamped envelope. "Will there be anything else Mrs. James?"

"No sweetie, that'll be all."

"Well have a happy thanksgiving."

"You too dear,"

Mrs. James replied walking away.

Monica turned slightly to close her drawer before waiting on the next customer. Looking at her watch she saw that she had fifteen minutes before she could clock out. She figured one more customer before she started shutting down.

"Damn, Mrs. James might have a thing for you."

Monica looked up and stared into the face of Stacks. She smiled so hard she thought she might pull a muscle. "Don't say that she's a sweet old lady."

"Yea, she sweet alright. But what's up am I too early?"

"Not really, I have about five minutes before I can close my window."

"You might as well shut down now."

Monica paused for a second then did as he said. As she counted her drawer she was in a bit of shock. She never let anyone tell her what to do. Yet she found herself turning her drawer in. When she came back out, she saw Cassie talking to Stacks.

"My boy is going through something right now, but I'll be sure to deliver your message."

"I'd appreciate it."

"Okay I'm ready," Monica blurted out killing any type of conversation Cassie might try to induce.

"Alrighty then. Cassie it was nice meeting you," Stacks mentioned heading for the door.

"Don't forget."

"I got you."

"'Don't forget' what?" Monica asked once they got outside.

"She asked about my homeboy."

"Oh."

"Let me find out you were jealous for a second there?"

"No," she replied shaking her head to match her words. "I just know how she is."

"But that's your girl ain't it?"

"All day."

"Well, if you can't trust your closest friends, then you don't need to have them around."

"I trust her, but...Anyways this isn't about my friends. What's all that big boy talking you were doing earlier?"

"Oh, I was just bullshittin' hoping to get your attention."

"Uh-uh, no you didn't"

"What? Damn, I have to come with all that to get you to go out with me?"

"I told you I ain't no..."

"Gold digger. Yea yea yea. And I was just fucking with you," he said looking at her attire. She had on a light brown ankle flowing dress with tan swirls in it. Three inch brown Jimmy Choo boots. Her brown mid-length trench coat showed that she knew how to put her clothes together. Her hair flowed down the sides of her face in long spirals that's accentuated her features. Two gold loops in her lobes and a Gucci clutch finished her get up.

"What?" Monica asked wondering why he was looking her up and down.

"Just checking your gear out."

"For what? It ain't like we going to a fancy restaurant or anything. Or are we?"

"Nah just seeing if I recognize any of it from my store," he replied and busted out laughing.

"Haha very funny."

"But nah, you can sometimes tell by how a person dresses who they are."

"Is that so? So, what type of person am I?"

"Tell me if I'm wrong ok. But I can see you have style. You match from head to toe meaning you're self-conscience and a bit OCD. But that might not carry over into your living area. I don't smell any perfume, so you're more than likely a naturalist who takes things into their own hands. All in all, you're a leader that doesn't take nothing lightly."

"Wow, all that from the way I dress? Now that's crazy!"

"I'm just very observant. And a good analyzer."

"You should be a philosopher or some type of scientist."

"On no, that's too much work. I try to keep my labor to a minimum."

"So, I've heard."

"Heard what?" he asked suspiciously. He worked too hard to stay under the radar to have someone he didn't even socialize with to know anything about him. "Wait, why are we still standing here? We're supposed to be getting something to eat that's the real reason I was looking at your clothes."

"Oh okay. What you have in mind?"

"Just follow me?"

"Okay."

Stacks jumped in his car and waited on Monica to do the same before pulling off. He pulled onto Friendly then Wendover and headed to the north side of town.

Monica didn't know where they were going being that all the restaurants on Wendover Ave. were in the opposite direction. She was still at a loss as they got off on the Yanceyville St. exit then turned on Cone Blvd. When she followed him into the parking lot where the old Harris Teeter was, she was definitely confused. She didn't know what his intentions were, but she was now on guard.

"Nice car," she said getting out of her own.

"Yours isn't too bad either," Stacks replied while hitting the alarm button. He was referring to the silver S-type Jag she drove.

"Perks of the job," she smiled.

"Which one?"

"All of them."

Stacks laughed out loud as he guided her to the door of Funderburk's, a black owned restaurant.

"So Stacks, tell me something?"

"What's up?" He answered putting a piece of smothered baked chicken in his mouth."

"What is it that you do besides work at a department store?"

"I can't really say I'm into so much. Like I told you I respect all hustles, so I got my hands in a little bit of everything."

Stacks stared at her for a brief moment not sure if she was trustworthy enough to disclose the *exact* things he was involved in. Not even Piko knew about all of his ventures. That was the thing with Piko, he only had a one track mind. All he knew was the drug game. Stacks was multidimensional getting involved in numerous hustles. That was the reason he told Monica that if she 'fucked with him she could elevate her status' instead of the petty things she was doing around Greensboro. She was supposed to know that the town was too small to really get the type of money she was after. Stacks wasn't ready to expose himself, so he switched subjects.

"Who are you?"

"Huh?" She asked confused.

"Who are you?"

"What you mean by that?"

"Who is Monica? What makes her tick? What's on your mind, your goals? What do you want in life?"

"Nobody's ever asked me that before."

"That's because nobody cared enough to know who they were dealing with."

"And you do?"

"I asked you didn't I?"

"Yea, but you can just be saying that to get what you want."

"And what exactly is it that I want?" Stacks asked on the verge of frustration. He disliked when he was categorized as a player. He was single but he didn't date. Nor did he put any effort into doing so, and this was part of the reason.

"I don't know. How about telling me."

"Haha, I liked how you tried to get the light off of you, but go ahead and tell me what I asked and then we can talk about me."

"Well, I..."

"Nah, start from the beginning."

"Beginning of what?"

"Your life. Tell me your name, birthplace, etc."

"Okay," she breathed wondering where to begin." Monica Trace. I was born in New Bedford Connecticut. Only child. Parents moved down here in the early 90s. Graduated from Smith High School in '04. Got a degree in Technology, minor in Literal Arts. Got a job at Bank of America where I've been for the last five years."

"So, when did you decide to cross over and become a criminal?"

"It's only a crime if you get caught."

"Right," he agreed sipping on his glass of Bel-Aire Rose to wash the chicken down. "But you know what I mean."

"I've always stole little things since I was a kid. It's like a thrill knowing you got away with something illegal. It wasn't until I got older that I started boosting for money."

"And that's something you like doing?"

"Well not like I did when I first started, but since me and Cassie been working at the bank my girl Misty..."

"Hold on, Misty?"

"Yea, Misty. The other girl that you saw with us."

"Oh, okay."

"But as I was saying my girl Misty put us on to how we had access to all we wanted."

"And how long has this been going on"

"About six months now."

"All under your leadership?"

"Yea, why?"

"Because I needed to get you to confess to that on tape," he said looking her straight in the eye. "Hahaha, I'm just bullshitting. Yo, you should've seen the look on our face."

"That shit ain't even funny."

"Yes it was. But nah, I just like to know who I'm dealing with especially if I plan on dealing with them for a while."

"And who's to say I want to deal with you?"

"You're here, aren't you?"

Monica didn't have a quick comeback being that he made a valid point. Her best defense was to take the spotlight off of her. "Well since I've told you about me what about you? Tell me about Stacks starting with your *real* name."

Stacks smiled, then wiped his mouth as he looked Monica in the eyes. He grabbed his glass again before speaking. "Ecclesiastes Knight, but everyone in my family calls me Tony which is my middle name. It's in honor of my uncle. I was born in Boston, Dorchester to be exact. Lived there 'til I was about nine or so before my mother relocated us down south."

"A fellow New Englander."

"You got it. I graduated from Dudley with visions of being a millionaire. I never went to college. I felt that anything that I needed to know I'd pick up along the way. I saw too many people go through four years of extra schooling and end up living at home with their moms. Either that or on the streets begging for change. I couldn't see myself being like that, so I hooked up with my man Piko, who I've known since middle school. He jumped in the game head first and you can say I took up the rear."

"So, you're a drug dealer?"

Stacks suppressed the look of disgust that almost covered his face realizing she didn't know any better. He hated being referred to as a drug dealer. "No, I'm a hustler."

"What's the difference?"

"A true hustla can make something from nothing. Doing anything he chooses. A drug dealer is just that. That's all they know. Plus, I don't sell drugs."

"Then what is it exactly that you do?"

Just as he was about to respond his phone rung.

"Yo."

"Where you at?"

"Out nigga. Why what's up?"

"I just came from Brady's spot trying to get the car he sold me right?"

"Yea, and?"

"He say that you never gave him the down payment. So now I'm sitting here thinking if I should go ask him again to make sure he doesn't have you mixed up with someone else."

Stacks sighed with frustration. He knew that Piko wasn't going to do anything to fix the problem. That was the very reason he called him. "Nah, go home. Fuck the wife. I'll go talk to him. He probably doesn't recognize my name."

"You sure?"

"What I say?"

"Aight bruh, get at me if you need me."

"Yea," Stacks replied hanging up. He was getting tired of these situations popping up.

"What's up?" Monica asked overhearing the conversation from Stacks end.

"I have to make a brief run. I hate we were interrupted, things seemed to be going good."

"Let me go with you then. Unless you ready for the night to end."

"Too dangerous."

"Probably nothing I haven't been around before."

Stacks thought for a second. 'Why not? If she still wants to deal with me after seeing me work, then she might be a keeper. I'm a have to test her one day anyway, why not now?'

"Fuck it. But you're gonna have to leave your car."

"At least let me park it at my house."

"Where's that?"

"Magnolia."

"Aight cool. That's the direction I gotta go in anyway."

"Oh, okay."

———————————————

"So, what exactly is it you have to do?"

"There's someone trying to shit me and my mans out of some product that we paid for in advance."

"Thought you weren't a drug dealer?"

"I'm not."

"So why are you paying people for product?"

"Pull the top of your dress down," Stacks demanded as he drove down Battleground Rd.

"What?!"

"You heard me. You've been asking me about drug dealing all night. Only the alphabet boys ask that many questions about one thing."

"The way you questioned and joked with me this how you coming?"

Stacks pulled over on the side of the road next to an empty patch of woods. He cut the headlights off and the interior ones on. Reaching under his seat he pulled out a nickel plated .357 snub nosed revolver and placed it on his lap.

"Please do as I say Monica, I don't want to hurt you, but I will if you make me."

"Stupid motherfucka," she mumbled as she shrugged out of her coat. "I was just trying to get to know the man I'm dealing with," she stated pulling down the straps on her dress. "That good enough for you?!" she hissed looking at him with anger in her eyes.

Stacks scanned the top of her cleavage in search of any exposed wire or clippings that might be along the edge of her bra. When he saw none, he breathed a sigh of relief. "Yea, I apologize for that, but in my line of work you can never be too careful."

"Yea whatever. I'm just not believing you would think I was the police."

"I had to be sure," he said cutting his eye at her as he pulled back onto the street. "Don't be mad at me, just try to understand where I'm coming from."

"I don't know. It's gonna take a lot to fix this."

"Name it and you got it."

"Just hurry up and handle your business so you can take me home."

"Okay, okay," he replied not knowing what else to say. He decided to just ride in silence.

Stacks pulled into a long tree surrounded driveway and turned to face the street before turning the car off.

"This shouldn't take long," he said reaching in the glove compartment and pulling out some leather riding gloves. He hit a button on his armrest and waited for it to slide back. Inside was another .357.This one a Desert Eagle model. "I'll be right back."

Stacks got out of the car and tucked his two guns in his waistband. He pulled his coat tight around him to conceal them. As he walked up to the lit porch he saw someone sitting in a rocking chair.

"Tito, what's happening? Kareem home?"

"Stacks what up? Yeah, he in there go on in."

Stacks walked into the brick house and paused as he shut the door. He liked this spot. It wasn't nowhere near the city limits so if anyone came out here it was more than likely for business. Stacks walked into the living room and saw Kareem snuggled between two women. They were watching a movie on his 80" screen TV.

Kareem didn't hear Stacks nor sense anyone behind him. One of the girls started getting little frisky and sat up to take her shirt off. That's when she spotted Stacks standing there.

"What's wrong baby?" Kareem asked then turned to see what she was looking at. "Stacks. What it is my man?"

"Nothing much just came by to check on you is all."

"Yea, your boy left about an hour ago."

"I know, he told me. He also told me you not delivering the product like you suppose to."

"What're you talking about? I gave him everything."

"Bruh, I'm not going to stand here and argue you with you. I just want what's mine."

"There has to be a mistake. Call Piko up and ask him what it is he's supposed to be missing."

"Your already know what's missing," Stacks said then pulled out his guns. "You can either give me my shit or we gonna have a serious problem."

"Okay, okay, don't do nothing crazy. I'll get whatever you want just don't shoot me," he said moving towards the side of the entertainment system.

Stacks looked down at the two woman and smiled as the shirtless one tried to cover up. He watched as Kareem pushed a combination of buttons causing his bookshelf to slide back. You could see the plastic wrapped kilos sitting on the shelves. But Kareem didn't reach for any of them as he turned around and started shooting an AR-15.

Stacks quickly ducked down behind the couch letting off a couple shots on his way. He heard the women scream as they ran for cover. As soon as one ran by, he reached out and grabbed her foot. She was so light that when he jerked her back, she fell on her face. He grabbed ahold of her hair and pulled her to him.

"I got your girl 'Reem. Stop shooting or you might hit her," he said wrapping his thick arm around her neck.

"Fuck her. Bitches come a dime a dozen."

"Let's talk 'Reem."

"Oh, now you wanna talk. Y'all niggas been trying to handle me for the longest and I'm tired of it."

"What the fuck you talking about? I've treated you like a brother."

"Save that shit for someone else. I know Piko's your front man. Your puppet."

"Nah, we partners."

"Then you just as guilty for the shit he be doing."

"This is bullshit. You know why I'm here," he said bending his knees ready to make his move. 'Just keep him talking Stacks,' he said to himself. He let off a shot in the middle of Kareem's sentence before jumping to his feet with the girl shielding him. He let off another shot hitting Kareem in the leg. The bullets that came back at him would've been dead center if the girl wasn't in front of him to take the impact. Two more shots hit Kareem in his chest. He let the girl go and she fell to the floor with a hard thud.

Stacks walked towards Kareem and shot him two more times in the face to make sure he was dead. He headed to the hidden closet ready to clean the shelves off when he felt a slight burn on the side of his head. He spun around and unloaded in the direction that the bullets came from. Standing there was Tito. He had forgotten all about and was surprised that he didn't come through sooner. But Tito was the scary type not a shooter. He more than likely had to hype himself up to even get out his chair.

Stacks hurried up and grabbed the coke and money off of the shelves and put them in a duffle bag that was inside the closet. He had to get out of there before someone else came. That's something he *knew* Tito did. Call for help. The whole time thoughts of Monica sitting outside in his car never crossed his mind." Damn, I hope she's aight," he mumbled picking up his pace.

Monica heard the shots coming from the house and started panicking. Her instincts told her to 'get the fuck out of there', but she didn't even know where she was. Nor if Stacks was dead or not. She saw when the guy on the porch got up and went in the house. She began getting nervous as perspiration started to build up under her arms. She hated sweating and hated these types of situations even more. She wondered if they even knew she was in the car. Of course they didn't, because it was too dark out. But if they killed Stacks then they'd eventually come dispose of the car and find her.

"Shiiit, they just gonna have to come get me, but it ain't gonna be easy," she said to herself. She started fiddling with the armrest in hopes of finding the button to release Stack's secret compartment. After about ten minutes of searching, she found it. Opening the compartment she saw the Mac-11 and grabbed ahold of it. It had been a long time since she held a gun, but she never forgot how to use one. She checked the clip before cocking the lever back to out a bullet in the chamber. Placing the gun in her lap she waited.

It wasn't long before Monica saw Stacks came out of the house carrying a duffel bag over his shoulder while waving his gun at anybody that might be in his way of escaping. She sighed with relief as she reached over to turn the key in the ignition with the need to get out of there as soon as possible. Her eyes stayed on Stacks making sure he was coming straight to the car. Just as he reached the car door a female came out of the house with a gun in her hand.

"Stacks!" Monica yelled, opening her door and aiming the Mac at the female. In a sense it looked like she was saving Stacks life, but in all actuality it was more for her own sake. She wasn't trying to die nor was she ready to either. At least not like this.

Stacks heard Monica yell and dropped to the ground. He reached for his other gun to shoot at his pursuers, but heard some rapid fire coming from an unknown place. He didn't look until the shooting stopped. He saw the girl that was hugged up with Kareem laying there dead. He looked over his shoulder to see Monica holding his Mac. He gave her a knowing nod then ran back into the house. He wanted to make sure that there wasn't anyone else lurking around. He was caught off guard twice in one night and wasn't trying to see it a third time. When he didn't find anyone else, he came back outside grabbed the bag and got in the car. Monica was still standing there holding the Mac. "Get in, hurry up."

Monica was in a slight daze, but snapped out of it at the sound of Stack's voice. "What the fuck was that about?!" she asked when they were a good distance from the house.

"Welcome to my world," was all Stacks said.

CHAPTER 9

Stacks whipped his car back into the city limits in silence. Monica didn't speak on the situation that just took place, but it was eating at her to say something. Stacks could sense it. He peered over at her every few seconds.

"You need to put that back before we get pulled," he finally said referring to the Mac-11 resting in her lap on top of the duffle bag.

"I feel safer with it. I don't know what to expect with you."

"Where'd you learn to shoot at?"

"My father's an ex-seal."

"You left that part out when telling me about yourself."

"There's a lot of things I left out just like you did. Maybe it's time we be totally honest with each other, or we can end whatever we thought we could've had."

Stacks glanced at her and began to chuckle.

"What's so funny?"

"My whole life I've been running in these streets and outside of my mother, sister, and niece. I never gave a fuck about a bitch, no offense. I've been stuck on that pimp shit. If it wasn't about money I wasn't interested. Then you pop up and I start thinking something that only came up in passing."

"What's that?"

"I told you the only women in my life is my mother."

"Don't forget your sister and niece," she said sarcastically.

"Yea them too. But after seeing you, especially tonight. I'm really trying to see what's up."

"Don't you think you're reaching a bit?"

"First let me ask this. And if I'm wrong I'll apologize and'll forget this ever happened."

"Talk."

"If you weren't feeling me you would've never asked for my number. Nor, let me take you out on the spur of the moment. Plus you would've bounced soon as you heard them shots being fired."

"Ok, you might be right. I'm kinda digging you but I didn't expect this."

"So, your girl Cassie didn't tell you about me?"

"She told me about your boy Piko, but made you out to be something like his shadow."

"That's the picture I like to paint. I do my best not to drawer attention to myself. I'll tell you what. If you're still interested I'll tell you everything about me as long as you do the same. If not, I'll drop you off and we can go our separate ways, deal?"

Monica stared out the window while thinking over what he just said. Never before did she have to weigh her options when it came to such a matter. It was nothing to get any guy she wanted, but there was something about Stacks that strongly attracted her to him. She didn't care too much about what happened tonight being that they made it out alive. Her life was too orderly. She needed some type of excitement in it. Her adrenaline hadn't pumped like that since the last time she shot a gun. Like Nas said, 'I gave you power'. She didn't really see what she had to lose. "Okay, but if anything starts looking or sounding crazy I'm gone."

"Bet," Stacks agreed before grabbing his phone and dialing a number. "Yo, Chico, I got an immediate delivery."

"You caught me just in time homes. Come through."

"Where we going now?" Monica questioned.

"To the repo man," he said turning down Gate City Blvd then pulling into the garage of a detailing shop.

"Stacks my man. What you out so late for?" Chico asked closing the garage door.

"You know a real hustla never sleeps," he replied as he got out the car and walked towards him.

"Right, right."

Chico was about fifty years old and ran the auto detail shop as a front for his chop shop. He stood at 6'1" a hundred and ninety pounds. His bald head stayed shiny from the frequent trips to the barbershop for a soothing razor shave. Yet this time it wasn't from the oil sheen and shear butter massaged onto his head. It was the hot temperature inside the garage.

"So what can I do for ya?"

"I have to get rid of my baby."

"Business good like that?"

"Not really, but she doesn't need to be seen anymore."

Chico looked in the direction of the Beemer and shook his head. "Who's the lady?"

"My girl."

"What?!Come on homes! Not Stacks the hit and quit it man?"

"If you're asking if she's official, absolutely. That's why I need to get rid of the whip."

"I don't want to know. What you want for her?"

"What you got?"

"What kind of question is that? Follow me," he said leading him out to the back of the shop where he had an assortment of cars in an adjacent building.

"You weren't lying were you?"

"Have I ever? So what'll be? Another Beemer or do you like the new E-Class?"

"It's 2019, but I don't want anything higher than a '16. I'm through with the coupes and sedans tho. I need to ride high, I got a girl to show off."

"Ahhh, I know exactly what you need," he said walking towards a concealed SUV and pulled the cover back." I just got this baby three days ago. She's a 2018 though."

"What's the intel on her?" Stacks asked staring at the champagne colored Bentley Bentayga.

"Fully equipped. Cream leather interior. Navigational system, digital console. Speakers all from the Beats collection so you know that shit knocking. I had to be thinking about you when I got her."

"Yea? How's that?"

Chico just smiled, grabbed a set of keys off the rack and went to the SUV. "Come here migo," he waved Stacks to him then jumped in the driver's seat. He turned the key in the ignition and smiled as she purred to life. "Sounds good huh? Open the back door."

Stacks did as he said then felt the seat slowly open up and push out to reveal a hidden compartment the length of the seat. "My mans. But couldn't someone just rip the seats off and get to the stash?"

"Why do you try to insult my intelligence? The console is covered with a steel top. Without the proper computerized sequence it won't open up."

"Bet, I'm a need tint on her too."

"Not a problem. Anything else?"

"How much?"

"For you, thirty-five. That comes with tags and registration. You know, the works."

"Can you handle that right now?"

"I don't see why not. You'll have to come back for the tint tho."

"That's cool."

"You want it in the same name as before?"

"Nah, I got a different one. Let me grab something right quick and I'll meet you in your office."

"Aight."

Stacks headed back to his car and opened the passenger side door. "It's ok, it's only me," he smiled when he saw Monica jump. "I just need to get tha bag right there."

Monica looked in the direction he was pointing and handed him the bag.

Stacks counted out thirty-five stacks from the money he got off of Kareem. When he finished he handed the bag back to Monica. "Put all the guns in there and whatever is in the console," he instructed before walking to the back of the car. Opening the trunk he unloaded two boxes and placed them on the ground. He then grabbed a duffle bag that was folded up in there.

Walking back to Monica he handed her the bag. "Put the money and coke in here along with what's in the glove compartment or in eyesight."

"Where're you going?"

"I'll be right back," he said grabbing the money and headed to the office.

"Goddamn homes you don't be bullshittin' do you?" Chico stated as Stacks walked into the office and tossed the money on the table.

"I don't have time to. It's all there, count it if you want."

"Hombre, I've been dealing with you for too many years. If I don't trust you by now I never will."

"I know that Chico, but I'm always serious when it comes to business," Stacks said taking a pen off Chico's desk and writing down the necessary information.

Chico looked at the name and address as he dialed a number. After a few exchanged words he hung up and turned to Stacks. "I just talked to Sylvia, she'll take care of everything first thing in the morning. You can go by there after twelve and get all you need. Paula will take care of the rest."

"Thanks again bruh."

"No problem. As much business you bring me how can I complain?" he mentioned as he handed him the keys to the SUV.

Stacks took the keys then headed to get his new whip. He drove from the back of the garage to the front and stopped behind his old car. He got out and put the boxes in the back seat. "Monica let's go."

Monica got out of the car and headed to the SUV toting the two bags.

"Put them in the back and get in," he said getting back behind the wheel. "Yo, Chico man, I'll be seein' you homie."

"Aye, aye, where the fuck all those bullet holes come from? Never mind, never mind, I don't want to know. Just be careful Primo."

"I'll try to."

"Aight," he said hitting the top of the hood as Stacks pulled out of the garage. He looked at the receding headlights before letting down the garage door thinking how much he admired Stacks. He knew that Stacks was one of the few honest men he did business with. People of his caliber were able to survive and prosper in their world of crime. But Stacks biggest flaw was that he got his hands dirty when he shouldn't have to.

Stacks pulled away from Lake Jeanette after tossing the bag of guns in it. He rode down Cone Blvd. turning on connecting streets until he got to Spring Garden and crossed over W. Market St. Turning on a dirt road he continued driving with just the headlights guiding him until he got to a cul-de-sac where a small house sat.

"Mine," he said opening the car door to get out. "Help me with one of those boxes."

When they walked into the house Stacks stopped to lock the front door before proceeding to the dining room where he placed the boxes along with the duffle bags on the table. He looked at Monica for a second. "What you wear about a size eight?'

"Something like that"

"I'm not taking you back home tonight so you gonna need somethin' to put on tomorrow. Don't worry, this a two bedroom home so you won't think I'll try some slick shit. Not yet anyway," he said walking to the phone on his wall and dialed Piko's number.

"Yo."

"We need to talk."

"Where you at?"

"Home."

"I'm..."

"Nah, I'll get with you tomorrow. I'm just letting you know."

"You get the car?"

"That's what I need to talk to you about, but it can wait."

"Aight, one."

"One," he said hanging up then turned to Monica. "You hungry?"

"Nah."

"I'm starving," he said going towards the kitchen. When he got to the refrigerator he pulled out some cold cuts, salad dressing, pickles, and mustard. "So where do you want to start?"

"Wherever you feel like you need to."

"Okay, I already told you how I came into the drug game, but being the type of person that I am I know how to take advantage of every given situation. Every opportunity that presented itself to me I capitalized on it. I went from hand to hand dealing to becoming a low level distributor. Which is like saying I'm the man next to the man next to the man if that makes sense," He paused hoping she understood what he was saying. "This brought about the expansion of my circle. I met different types of hustlas of every field and found a way to form some type of partnership slash conglomerate. Guns, cars, fencers, hackers, even boosters." He mentioned that last part to get her attention. He finished making his sandwich and put everything back up. He washed the butter knife and put it in the dish rack. Putting a couple of pieces of ice in a cup he grabbed a bottle of sprite out of the pantry. Walking to the dining room he sat down at the table and waited for Monica to join him.

"So why do you put yourself in situations like tonight?"

"Because I'm loyal. Piko's my brother my heart, but I know without me he wouldn't make it. He doesn't have it in him to put in the necessary work that this shit requires, and I believe he knows it. That's why he calls me anytime somethin' goes wrong."

"Then why not let him handle his own shit?"

"I just told you, he not built for it. I think he thrives off the shit. I don't know if he knows I've been cleaning up after him. Probably thinks I'm just a hell of a negotiator."

"Then quit leading him on."

"You don't understand. I like being behind the scenes moving in silence. I might get my hands dirty but none of it leads back to me."

"But if something was to go wrong then what? Say you get killed, everything you did to keep things together and yourself out of the limelight would be for nothing. And who's to say he doesn't know and is just using you?"

"It's crossed my mind a few times and that's what I have to talk to him about. But that's my story what's yours," he said trying to hide the ill feeling that crept up inside of him from thinking that Piko might actually be playing him. He didn't tell her everything. Like his true position and worth. Nor how much authority his family held up and down the coast.

"Like I said, my pops was a Navy SEAL, so I know everything there is about weaponry and survival tactics," she said then ran down all of her misdeeds even about the first person she shot. It was behind an altercation. A business deal gone wrong.

"You know you got blood on your shirt," she added once she finished her story.

"I'm not worried about it," he said then grabbed one of the duffle bags. Pulling out the contents there was ten brick and fifty grand. There would've been more but he gave sixty-five to Chico for hooking him up with that spur of the moment ride.

"What?" Monica asked after he damn near stared a hole on her head.

"Are you wit me or not?"

"Have I left yet?"

"No, but I need to know that you're wit me. And I mean all the way. Not fifty, seventy-five. Not even ninety-nine point nine percent, but one hundred percent wit me."

"Damn, do I have to answer that right now?" she asked thinking how she just met this guy and was already being forced into an awkward situation.

"No, but I'll be expecting one before you walk out this house," he stated as he stood up. He put the coke back in the bag then went and placed it in the closet by the door. He left the money on the table on front of Monica.

"Monica."

"Yea?'

"Grab those clothes and come on," he said and waited for her in the arch of the dining room entrance.

When she came around the corner he proceeded to the back of the house where the guest room was at. It was only a two bedroom two and a half bath house so you really couldn't tell the difference being that both bedrooms were the same. There was a king size bed in both rooms. A fifty-five inch screen TV with mirrored dressers. The only people who'd been here was Piko, his mother, and sister.

"There should be towels and clothes in the bathroom," he said turning on the light.

"Oh my God," she gasped dropping the clothes.

"What?" he questioned spinning around thinking she saw an intruder which wouldn't have mattered since he was unarmed.

"Your head. It's bleeding."

Stacks patted the side of his head where he knew she was talking about. He knew it was there but being it wasn't life threatening had forgotten about it until now. "It's nothing,"

"No, you have to take care of that before it gets infected."

Stacks smiled at her for showing she cared. Well at least acted as if. "Look, take a shower. I'm a do the same. Wash my wound and if you want you can dress it afterwards aight? Oh, and if you need something to put on there should be a pair of joggers and a t-shirt in one of these drawers."

"You seem to have a lot of clothes for women," she said questioningly.

"Nah, they not women's clothes they mine. Shit I'm not that much taller than you so you oughta be able to fit 'em," he said then walked to his room across the hall.

Stacks went straight to sleep after Monica put some antibiotic cream on his wound along with a gauze patch to cover it. On the other hand, Monica laid wide awake staring at the ceiling. She couldn't sleep. It wasn't from being uncomfortable, but from all the thoughts that were running through her head. She tossed and turned for the betterment of the night.

"What time is it anyway?" she asked herself before glancing at the illuminated clock on the nightstand. The red lights read eleven thirty-five. She wondered why he was laying down so early, but remembered that they both had to be at work in the morning. Then the thought of what happened came tumbling back to the front of her mind. How often did he do this or had done it? It had to be a few times being that he slept so soundly despite what occurred. She laid there for five more minutes before she gave up. Slinging off the covers she made her way over to Stacks' room.

His door was wide open. He liked it that way because he didn't want to feel like he was closed in in his own home. She tapped lightly on the door as he lay there softly snoring. When he didn't respond she walked in and stood beside his bed. Staring down at him she saw how he slept on his stomach with the covers up to his waist. The light from the window shined on the tattoo that covered his back. It was of a man laying on stacks of money smoking a cigar. The design blended in with a few scars that looked like knife and bullet wounds. She reached out to touch them but was stopped short when her wrist was caught in midair. He pulled her on top of him as he rolled onto his back.

"It's not polite to wander through a person's home," looking into her face.

"I couldn't sleep," she whispered pushing a strand of hair behind her ear.

"So, you decided to disturb mine?"

"I thought you were sleep. I heard you snoring," she smiled.

Stacks liked the way she felt against him. She didn't inhibit herself by putting her bra back on allowing her soft breasts to press against him through the t-shirt she wore. He figured she didn't bother with any panties either especially being that she didn't pick any out from the box of clothes.

"I'm a light sleeper."

"I see," she said looking into his eyes. She didn't know if it was her or the way that the moonlight hit them, but they seemed to change colors. "What you doing?" she asked as Stacks' hands began to drift below her waist.

"What you've been wanting me to."

"And what's that?"

"Just tell me when to stop," he said pulling her face towards hum.

When their lips met, she didn't put up any resistance. He eased his tongue and traced her lips tasting the minty toothpaste she brushed with earlier. Stacks felt himself getting hard from the small contact. He moaned as he eased his hand under the pants seam and gripped flesh confirming his earlier theory. She returned a moan of her own as she pressed down on his erection.

Reaching under the cover Monica felt the silky flesh and gasped. It wasn't from the size of him that caused it but the fact that he was naked. "You're not wearing anything."

"Yea, I like to let my body breathe," he replied then started sliding the pants off of her. She helped by lifting her hips up a bit allowing them to come off with ease. The shirt was next freeing her D-cups. He slid his thumb over the left nipple causing it to spring to attention. Kicking the covers off he flipped her over onto her back then he reached over to the nightstand to cut the lamp on.

"Why'd you cut the light on?"

"So, I can see all of you," he answered before kissing her with want and aggression.

He bit down on her lip until he tasted blood. He expected her to jump or try to push him off, but instead she let out a lustful moan. 'Oh shit, she likes that rough shit,' he thought to himself. He traced her neck down to the collarbone where he sucked on the hallow area. Moving down her right side he teased the area around her nipple causing goose bumps to form before placing it in his mouth. She arched her back as if to tell him to suck harder. He didn't linger there too long before occupying the left one. Monica dug her nails into Stacks' shoulders as he administered his pleasure. He let loose of her nipple and traced a trail down the middle of her stomach until he reached the top of her pubic hairs. As he eased lower, he inhaled deeply to see if there was any odd odor before he went any further. All that invaded his nose was the scent of Shea Butter soap and her bodily fluids.

He spread her legs open then leaned back to look at the shape her lips made. He placed his fingers on each side to open them up before sticking his tongue and slightly swiped up the middle. That caused Monica to give a small jerk. Stacks smiled before placing her legs over his shoulders and his mouth on her mound. He looked up to see Monica biting on her lower lip while squeezing her breasts. His tongue snaked out and slid in her slight while his thumb put pressure on her clit. She thrust her hips at him on the verge of going wild for it had been a long time since anyone had touched her. The bucking didn't deter Stacks one bit as he tightened his grip on her thighs. The scream from her orgasm echoed through the house as she convulsed with pleasure until it subsided, and she settled down enough to catch her breath.

Stacks raised up on his knees ready to slide into her but was caught off guard when Monica used her legs to flip him over onto his back. She sat on top of him looking into his eyes and became mesmerized as she watched them change colors letting her know that what she saw earlier wasn't an illusion.

"My turn," she said flipping her hair over her shoulder before bending down to kiss him. She administered the same pressure and pain he did to her as she bit his lip. She continued to take little nips at him even when she got to his chest which she sucked and bit into causing him to squirm a little bit. No one ever understood his aggressive ways. His rough sex. That was one of the reasons women didn't last long with him. They felt he was too rough. But Monica was matching his aggression as she teased her way down to his midsection. When she got to his erection, she didn't hesitate to continue her nibbling, but a bit softer knowing she was in a very sensitive area. When she ran her tongue down the crease of his dick he let out a loud groan. She pecked all over him until he stood at full attention. She gripped him in her hand and pulled until a bubble of precum formed at the tip. She caught it with the tip of her tongue before taking him into her mouth. She bobbed on half of him making sure she used plenty of spit as she put more and more in her mouth. "Mmm, mmm, mmm," she moaned each time she descended. She began playing with his scrotum as she continued to move up and down on him.

Stacks' toes started curling as Monica's mouth tightened on him. Her head game was top notch. Way better than Jay's. He figured every city had their own Superhead. He ran his fingers through her hair before balling it up in his hand to help guide her movements as well as to make sure she kept going.

She let go of him and began sucking on his nuts as she started jacking him off. As soon as his sack tightened up, she put her mouth back over the head to catch the shot that had built up over the last thirty minutes. Stacks started coughing as the sensation ripped through his chest.

Monica thought something was wrong with him as he began coughing and jerking. "You, you okay?" she asked nervously.

"Yea, yea, I'm good. Come here," he replied pulling her up towards him. He kissed her in the mouth mixing both of their sex fluids.

Monica eased up a bit after feeling that he was still hard underneath her. When she gripped him and started to put him inside her, he tightly grabbed her waist. "Whaaat?" she whispered.

Stacks didn't say anything just reached into the drawer where he grabbed a condom. He hurriedly opened the wrapper and slid it on while Monica hovered over him. Soon as it was in place, she eased down on him real slow. He grabbed her butt to spread her open and thrust upwards.

"Ooooh," Monica breathed before moving up and down on him. She was soaking wet as she glided smoothly on top of him. Stacks still gripped her butt as he spread her further open and guided her at his own pace. She got into rhythm as she dug her nails into his chest and threw her head back. She kept riding him coming down harder and harder as her orgasm began to build. "Uh, sss, uh, sss, uh, yea, yea, yea. Shit!" she yelled as she came a second time.

Stacks rode out her convulsions. He bit his own lip to keep from succumbing to the feeling. As soon as she stopped shaking, he flipped her back over and started pounding into her while still gripping her butt. He didn't want her to trying to get away from him as he administered his lust filled attack. The thing being was that she didn't want to get away as she wrapped her legs tightly around his back.

"Get this pussy nigga," she said getting more turned on than she had ever been. "Don't be scared, get it! You wanted it, get it!" she grunted.

Stacks got extra hard from what she was saying. She was bringing out a different animal as he pinned her legs all the way back and grabbed her shoulders. "I'm a get it."

"Ah, ah, ah, that's it right there. Right there daddy, g "Ah, ah, ah, that's it right there. Right there daddy, give it to me daddy," she moaned coaxing him on.

Stacks couldn't take the tight squeeze her muscles were placing on him. That along with the way she was talking drove him over the edge.   "Aarrgh," he growled biting down into her shoulder. "Fuck," he said as he rolled over to catch his breath.

Monica put her head on his shoulder and started rubbing on his chest. "Thank you."

"Huh?' he asked not really hearing her. He was just trying to get heartbeat back to normal.

"I said thank you."

"For what?"

"The release."

"What's that supposed to mean?"

"I've never been with a man I didn't have to hold back on."

"You mean that rough shit and talking dirty?"

"Mhm," she nodded in agreement.

"That's how I feel. One of the reasons I don't have a girl now."

"Well, maybe us meeting was meant to be."

"Maybe. We had a crazy event but, it's a possibility. But I hope you don't think just because we had good sex that that's a sign, 'cause I can get that anywhere."

"Not anymore."

"What you mean?"

"You got me now."

"Is that right?"

"That's what I said isn't it?"

"After everything that happened are you saying you wit me?"

"There's a lot of things I could be doing in life, but it'll more than likely be boring, and I can't stand being bored. So yeah, I'm wit you."

"A hundred percent?" Stacks asked to make sure she understood that he meant what he said about not wanting any partial dedication.

"One hundred percent," she replied looking him dead in his eyes.

Stacks pulled her face towards him for a kiss. The thought of finally finding a rider seemed surreal. It turned him on.

"Looks like somebody agrees with us," she said looking down at his erection.

"Yup," he agreed before rolling over on top of her to go at it again.

CHAPTER 10

They woke up to the buzzing from the alarm th quickly hit the snooze button on. He was not ready to day. Monica was curled up beside him like a baby lo God's gift to man. He kissed the top of her forehead befo out of the bed and heading to the bathroom to take a s

When he came back out of the bathroom Moni there. He walked into the other room and when he did hear her there either he began to panic. He felt he spoke about having a rider and though about how she was a m artist.

He ran down the hall wondering if she bounced on his drugs and money. When he passed the kitchen doo caught a glimpse of someone bent over in the ref Monica stood up with her phone to her ear and a carton juice in her hand.

"Hey baby."

"Who you talking to?"

"I was calling my manager to let him know I'll be r little late," she smiled.

"Oh. And what you smiling at?" He was relieved didn't do what he initially thought.

"You. The way you looked you thought I had bou you huh?"

"Honestly, yea."

"Well, you gonna learn that I'm a woman of my word. I said you got me, so you got me baby," she reassured him while walking towards him and giving him a kiss.

Stacks smiled at her before walking back to his room to get dressed.

Coming back out in his work attire he made his way to the dining room where Monica was sitting at the table eating a bowl of cereal. He wanted to laugh at how she looked like a kid as she placed a spoonful in her mouth. "You 'bout ready?"

"Yea, let me finish this first."

Stacks walked to the table and pushed a couple of the stacks of money he left there last night towards her. "I want you to do me a favor."

"What's that?"

"I want you to open a bank account in your name," he said pushing some more money towards her.

"I already got one," she replied putting her last spoonful of cereal in her mouth before tilting the bowl up to drink the milk.

"That's thirty-five Gs right there. Add five to your account the take ten and buy some CDs and Bonds. Invest five more in mutual funds, and stash the rest."

"You can't deposit more than nine without raising a red flag unless you have some type of business account."

"So, you're telling me that you've been working at this bank for two and a half years and don't know how to get around the system?"

"I didn't say that, but you're asking me to do a lot at one time."

"Who said anything about doing it all at once? Take your time, just as long as you get it done. And since you mentioned it, maybe we oughta come up with a dummy corporation."

"Whoa, whoa, don't you think we're moving a little fast here?"

"Experience what life is about or stay low key?" he repeated the statement he made when he first called her.

"But you want me to come up with a way to wash your money?"

"Nah, *our* money. You said, 'You're wit me all the way', so everything that gets done by us is fifty-fifty."

"Well, I might need to pull in my girls for this."

"That's fine, but let 'em know this is serious business. Also, that petty shit ya'll be doin' is over."

"Huh?"

"If you're trying to get money then you're gonna have to listen to me. You don't have to question me because I won't steer you wrong. I haven't lasted this long by being careless."

"So, what is it that you'll be wanting us to do?"

"When the time comes, you'll now, but until then handle what I asked you to do okay?"

"Okay," she said going over to the sink and placing the bowl in it. She walked back over to the table and put the money in her pocketbook. "I'm ready to go if you are."

Stacks looked over at the sink and shook his head. "I'm a have to teach some housekeeping," he said picking up the other stacks of money. He went to the hall closet to grab the duffle bag with the bricks in it. He placed the money inside, got his keys off the hook by the door and stepped outside.

When they got in the SUV, he opened the duffle bag and started placing the accessories where he saw fit. Once he was finished, he put his Makaveli cd in and cued up a song. As he backed out of his driveway the intro to the song came on. "I'll kill all you mothafuckas. Die mothafucka die," the female yelled before the beat came on. "All I need in this life of sin, is me and my girlfriend/ down to ride to the bloody end, just me and my girlfriend."

Monica shook her head knowing what Stacks was getting at by playing that particular song. They didn't say anything as they headed towards her house.

Stacks stood behind the register waiting on customers, but his mind wasn't even on his job. It was on creating different type of schemes involving Monica and her girls. His mind was like a money machine. If it didn't consist of cash, there was no need to involve Stacks. He was also thinking about how he was going to deal with Piko. Maybe he'd end all of his dealings with the drug game. He knew that something had to give, because all the situations that Piko had him getting into was starting to get out of hand.

CHAPTER 11

Piko laid on the masseuse's table enjoying the feel of her small delicate hands kneading his back. His thoughts drifted towards the situation at hand. Two days had gone by and he still hadn't heard from Stacks. He really didn't know what he wanted to speak to him about even though he did mention Kareem's name. Shit, he already had his take, he was just giving Stacks the heads up to go get his. He knew he was probably over doing it when he called Stacks about the predicament he didn't want to handle himself. He figured he'd find a way to take care of it. He always did.

Piko knew it wasn't right to take advantage of Stacks loyalty. They'd been friends since middle school. Whichever direction one went the other followed. When Stacks' brother Devante put him in the game, he brought Piko along with him. Piko knew that he was selfish, but he couldn't help it. He grew up in poverty. Living from Section 8 apartment to Section 8 apartment. At times his mother didn't even have a place for them to live. They'd have to sleep on park benches and wear holey clothes. In the neighborhood

Not having nothing and seeing how easily things could be stripped away from you he vowed never to be in that predicament again. With that mentality he started keeping anything he got his hands on to himself. It didn't matter how close they were or how wrong it seemed he refused to do without ever again. The sad part is that if it wasn't for Stacks, he'd more than likely be in a similar situation. He remembered when they became close friends.

They were twelve or thirteen running around with two other bad ass little kids. At times they'd go hang with these guys that were ten years their senior. That's who got them to start smoking weed. The thing was that they liked Stacks more than any of them in their crew. Piko didn't care being he was second favorite amongst them. The other two were accepted because of Piko being that Stacks wasn't always around. One of them, Mark, didn't really like Stacks, who went by Tony at the time, because of all the attention he got from females. Mark felt like he should be getting the attention, but he kept that and his dislike to himself. He was too shook to approach Stacks directly, so he'd make things up that got Piko mad and caused them to fight. They had gotten into numerous altercations off that alone. Other times Stacks would get fed up with Piko's bullshit and spark a fight of his own. It wasn't until one day Stacks ducked one of Piko's wild swings and caught him on the chin knocking him to his knees that they chose to stop fighting each other. When they were by themselves Stacks gave him a serious pep talk.

"Yo bruh, this here's some bullshit. We fightin' damn near every week for nothin'. Them niggas mad 'cause we tight. That's why they always whispering in your ear when I'm not here because they know you gonna go every time. But think about it, I don't even fuck with them except when you around so when was I supposed to say anything? Ain't neither one of them got shit. They hate me because they ain't me. They've been trying to figure me out since I've moved here, but they never will."

"Fuck 'em. Like you said they've been hatin' how close we are. You say let's get money then let's get money."

Piko laughed at the thought and hated that he was putting Stacks through so much bullshit. He was still his ace though and glad that nothing had happened to him over the years. He knew Stacks was too smart to get caught up and God forbid the person who thought that they could outsmart him. At the same time, he was still trying to keep Iris happy and out of his hair. Thanksgiving was in a few days, and he was wondering if he should spend it with both of their families or take her out of town. He wanted things to get back on track with them and thought about what Stacks said about getting her pregnant. That way she'd be obligated to stick around. He felt he needed to stop cheating on her anyway.

Piko looked up once the masseuse finished working his back. "You finished?"

"You want other service?" she asked with a smile.

"Fuck it, might as well," he said then laid on his back letting his towel to fall off of him. He figured he could wait another day before giving up his cheating ways.

CHAPTER 12

Iris laid curled up on her couch with a blanket covering her body as she watched The Real Housewives of Atlanta. She felt like a *Desperate* Housewife. She was in need of some serious attention. The every now and then sex that Piko gave her wasn't working. In the beginning they would go at it like rabbits. It didn't matter the place or time whenever the urge occurred it went down. They've been together for over thirteen years. He was her first and only love, but now that love seemed to be diminishing. She never thought about cheating before, but Piko had her heavily thinking about it. It was all his fault. She did everything that she was supposed to do to satisfy him. Cooked, cleaned, dressed up, and did any type of sexual act he requested of her. If that wasn't love, she didn't know what to call it. Now she was down to playing with herself and passing the time eating ice cream. Rocky Road to be exact. The ION channel had become her favorite to catch all the 'How to get away with murder' episodes. She only turned it to the sports channel to fantasize about the bug muscular men.

Iris' temporary down time was interrupted by a knock at the door. She got up placing her feet into her Pink furry slippers and shuffled to the door. She looked through the peep hole and saw that it was Stacks.

"Damn," she whispered. She never let him see her at her worse. She tried to straighten herself up before opening the door. "Hey Stacks," she said greeting him with a brotherly hug.

"How you?"

"I'm good. How 'bout yourself?" she asked closing the door behind him once he crossed over the threshold.

"Livin'. But you know life is hard."

"Tell me 'bout it."

"Where's Piko?"

"I don't know, not here. He left about an hour ago. Said he had some business to take care of."

"Yo, I specifically told tha nigga I was comin' through and not to go nowhere. See this the shit I be talkin' 'bout."

"Well, why don't you just chill he should be back in a little while."

"The thing is Iris, all this side shit is how you get caught up. The only way to keep shit together is if you stay focused and follow protocol."

"But you know how Piko is. He does things spur of the moment."

"And that's the problem. I laid shit out so we could stay on top of things and under the radar. He doesn't seem to move with that in mind. I know he's smarter than he acts, and I think that's what pisses me off."

"You need to relax, this ain't like you to get all worked up."

"That goes to show how frustrated I am. But you wouldn't understand because you don't know what's goin' on."

"You right, I don't know. You want something to eat or drink, I got some fried chicken in the fridge I can heat up for you?"

"Nah I'm good. I'll just wait on Piko," he said sitting on the couch.

"Alright, if you say so," she replied coming up behind him.

Stacks always treated Iris like a sister and showed her the upmost respect at all times. She in turn did the same. She knew that he was tensed and to the point of losing his cool. One thing you never saw Stacks do. These were the things Piko drove you to. He didn't understand what he was doing, causing, or creating with his actions. As soon as Stacks sat down, she began massaging his shoulders.

"Just relax, it ain't even like that," she assured when he tried to raise up. She knew he was probably thinking she was trying to come on to him. But she honestly was just being the sisterly friend she had always been. "You're real tense right now and that's not good. Damn Piko be getting to everybody huh?" she asked jokingly.

"I know, I know. It's just I have a lot on my mind and Piko's supposed to be my partner, but we haven't been seeing eye to eye lately."

"Well, talk to him. Make him understand."

"That's why I'm here."

"Well, you can talk to me until he shows up."

"This ain't your business."

"You don't have to talk about business. That's what's wrong with men today, acting as if women can't be talked to."

"You know I don't feel that way."

"No, but at times you think I'm too naïve to know what's going on or to ask my opinion on certain things. Well, at least that's how Piko feels."

"I'm not Piko."

They continued on like that, discussing certain situations. From everyday life events to politics to simple things such as people's actions and why they do what they do. They were laughing at a David Chapelle Netflix special when Piko walked in.

Piko heard the laughter as he walked into his home. He immediately recognized the voices and wondered what was so funny. As he rounded the corner, he saw Iris sitting next to Stacks. It was a little too close for comfort for him as he watched her lean into while bursting out in laughter. He wondered what had been going on in his absence, but out it out of his mind. He knew Stacks had probably been waiting awhile for him being that he had called beforehand to let him know that he was coming through. He had stepped out to make a few deliveries and set up some deals. He felt that Stacks was up to something he just didn't know what. The streets were talking, but they weren't saying enough. They might mention Stacks' name, but it wasn't nothing major. People figured that without Piko there'd be no Stacks and he thrived off of that. But Stacks was too smart for his own good. He always thought four moves ahead of the next man. To keep up with him you'd have to get up on a Sunday just to get a whiff of what he was planning that Friday. So, to figure him out was damn near impossible and that infuriated Piko. He hated being left clueless about his business dealings and he was determined to get some answers before he did anything else.

"Yo, what's funny?" he asked stepping into the living room.

Iris and Stacks were caught off guard as they turned to see who was speaking to them even though it could only be one person.

"Oh, what up P, we were just watching Mike Epps," Stacks said.

"Oh yeah?"

"Yeah. And it took you long enough too. I've been waiting for damn near two hours for your ass to show up."

"I had some B.I. to handle."

"You should've told me that when I called."

"Well, I didn't know I had to tell you my every move. You do your thing, I'm just doin' mine."

"What the fuck you talkin' bout fam?" Stacks inquired rising up off the couch.

"I ain't seen you in a minute, so obviously you got somethin' else goin' on. Therefore, I'm getting involved in other shit too."

"I ain't trying to argue wit you bruh. I came over here to talk to you about somethin' more important than what either one of us are doing on the side, because it involves both of us."

"Well talk then."

Stacks looked over at Iris questioningly.

"Ok, ok, I'll leave you two alone. I'll be in the bedroom if you need me," she mentioned as she got up to leave.

"So, what's up?" Piko asked once Iris was out of earshot.

"Look it here bruh, I'm not diggin' this little attitude of yours. I came here to discuss business not see whose nuts hang the lowest."

"Whatever, just get to the point."

"Fine. The dope game ain't movin' like it's suppose to."

"What you mean?"

"I've been doin' too much unnecessary leg work lately that I shouldn't be doin'."

"Like?"

Stacks was trying to figure out a way to break everything down to Piko without sounding conceited. "I shouldn't have to be meetin' nobody to straighten shit out. Niggas know what the deal is. If they ain't tryin' to come correct when you around then you need to step your shit up."

"What you sayin', I'm soft or somethin'? I gets mine every time, dudes don't want to come off *your* shit. That's why I be callin' 'cause niggas be tryin' to handle *you* not me."

"I'm not here to argue bruh. Like I said this shit ain't how it's supposed to be so this the deal. If you feel like you can handle it, we gonna split this thing up into two zones."

"Zones? What you mean zones?"

"You supply a certain area and I'll supply the other."

"We're basically doin' that now, so what'll be the difference?"

"The difference will be that I won't have nothing to do with your zone and you won't have nothing to do with mine."

"So, we not partners no more?" Piko asked starting to feel the anger rise in his chest.

"I ain't say that. But this how it's going to be. Every third week we put our money together. Dependin' on what you put in is what you'll get back. That way we'll be seein' exactly what we're makin'. You won't have to wonder if I'm getting over on you or not," he mentioned just to rattle his thoughts. He wasn't sure if he was thinking that way or not, but just in case he wanted to put that out there. "And we won't have to wait on each other to pick up. It'll be our own responsibility to have the money to reup."

"Piko looked at Stacks wondering what his angle was. Every time he thought he had him figured out he'd throw him for a loop. "So what you have in mind with this zonin' shit?"

"Let me show you," Stacks said looking through one of the kitchen drawers for a pen and paper. Once he found some, he began drawing a makeshift map of Greensboro. He boxed off the two zones he mentioned.

"So, which one will I be controllin'?" Piko asked looking down at the paper.

"Bruh, you know me. I ain't greedy. I can get dough anywhere. You know that. So whichever one you want I'm good with it."

"Nah, nah, you not gonna pull that shit on me. Fuck around and pick one and you gonna swear I was tryin' to get over on you. So, you go ahead and choose."

"Aight I'll pick this one," he said pointing to what he marked as zone one.

"Oh, hells nah. You know that's where I got most of my workers at."

"Then why ain't you pick like I said. It doesn't even matter to me bruh," Stacks said. "And don't try to switch up later on either. You got your zone I got mine ya dig?"

"Yea, I got you."

"Just make sure you remember where the lines cross, because if we don't follow the system shit's gonna get fucked up. Being that my zone is smaller than yours there shouldn't be any of your workers in there ya dig?"

"I don't like this bruh. It's like you tryin' to split from me. I'm use to doing everything together."

"Cut that Babyface shit out. We still together. You my brother dog, ain't nothin' gonna change that, but I'm preparing you for the real. You have to learn to do things on your own, 'cause one day I might not be around. Then what you gonna do?"

he asked seriously. "You can't even answer me, can you? That's the shit I use to tell you when we started getting' deep in the game. You can't put all your eggs in one basket. You can't make a career out of thus shit. It's a get in get out hustle. That's why I don't dwell on shit like you do. You say you got other things going on, handle that bruh. Just make sure it's worth it. Don't let this hustle be your bread and butter or you'll be FED bound."

"Aight Sun Tzu," Piko laughed. "I got you. I'm a stack this paper and invest in a few businesses."

"Now that's something we definitely can do together as long as you got your head on straight, but then again that's what you got Iris for. She has a business degree you should take advantage of that. Women *are* more than a piece of ass my nig."

"Nigga you just mad that I...."

Stacks quickly shook his head and nodded towards the bedroom where he felt more than likely Iris was by the door eavesdropping.

"Yea, you know what I'm saying. So, we still got the same connect?"

"Of course. But we not fuckin' wit Kareem anymore."

"Why not?"

"He's retired," Stacks answered looking deep into Piko's eyes.

"Huh?"

"He retired, so we gonna use a different pick up man."

"Like who?"

"You picked the last one so this on me. I'll let you know tho."

"What you running a secret society now?"

"Nah, I just don't who it's gonna be yet, but you'll know as soon as do aight?"

"Whatever yo, let's just get the ball rollin'. I should be ready in a couple days."

"Be easy. Give me until next week to put everything together then I'll get at you."

"What?! A whole week? Come on dog. You doin' too much now. I got custis to take care of."

"You wanna do this? Go 'head. Be my guest. But if you not tryin' to draw heat you need to wait like I said. Have I ever led you wrong? Without order there's only gonna be chaos."

"No you haven't, but you never talked about doin' shit like this before either."

"Are you with me or not?"

"Do I have a choice?"

"Everyone has a choice bruh. You don't have to agree to any of this. You can do your own thing and I do mine, but I'd rather get money together."

"Right. You lucky you my boy."

"And if I wasn't?" Stacks asked really wanting to know.

"I'd beat your ass," he replied smiling.

"Maann, I've been beating your ass since we were little jits. Ain't nothing change but the age homie."

"Them lucky blows won't work these days I'll knock your ass out now."

"Hey, hey, hey. Ya'll cut that crazy talk out. Won't be no fighting going on in this house," Iris said coming out of the bedroom confirming what Stacks had been suggesting earlier. She wanted to know what was so important that they needed her to step out of the room.

"Baby we good, just talkin' a little shit like we always do." Piko stated.

"Ay, man I'm a get at you when everything's in order aight?"

Stacks said reaching his hand out to give Piko dap. He turned towards Iris and gave her a light peck on the cheek before heading to the door.

"Just make sure you get at me," Piko threw at his back as it walked through the door. He didn't let on to how the whole conversation didn't seem right. He figured he'd hold that in until the time was right. He didn't want to not trust him, but the best way to survive in this game was to trust nobody no matter how close you were. People switched up every day. He'd just stay on point from here on out. "Any more of that fried chicken left?" he asked Iris channeling his thoughts towards his stomach.

Stacks was a master of manipulation. He knew Piko's reaction to just about everything and weighed them out accordingly. He knew the zones he drew out were disproportionate. He made sure of that. He also knew that one area in particularly was Piko's bread and butter. So, when he drew the zones out he made sure to place that area in it and make it bigger than the other one. He expected Piko to play like he was being forced to take the bigger zone. Stacks didn't care because even though Piko got money, he didn't know the geographical makeup of the money spots. That's why Stacks would always stay ahead of everyone else. He did his homework in whatever he chose to do. The zone he was to run might've been small in size, but it brought in more money than the wanted to be a multi-millionaire by thirty. He told Piko to give him until next week, but that wasn't to get up any money. He had just made a quick hundred and fifty grand a few days ago after selling the bricks he got off Kareem to some out of town cats for fifteen a piece. No, he needed time to figure out who he was going to get to replace Kareem. He figure that that's where Monica would come in at. That wasn't a problem though. Right now, he wasn't worried about nothing. He said his piece to Piko and gave him until next week to handle everything. His concern now was getting to South Carolina for Thanksgiving.

CHAPTER 13

"What we got?" Detective Lawrence asked walking under the crime scene tape. He was a brown skinned man with a low wavy hair that stood at five nine one hundred eighty pounds. His build was solid from extensive weight training. He was at the top in his line of work when it came to solving homicides. He stood on the porch where the multiple murders took place awaiting for his fellow officers to give him an answer.

"Four bodies. Three inside, one out," Detective Sparks said taking a bite of a six inch Philly cheesesteak. "Excuse me but they caught me on my lunch break," he explained.

"Go ahead. What else is there?"

"There seemed to be a lot of shots fired as you can see from the multiple shell casings. Come inside, I'll walk you through it."

They walked into the logged makeshift house and into the living room area.

"That guy there," Sparks pointed at the body splayed out by the wall. "Seems like he was running to protect himself."

"Why do you say that?"

"That closet isn't just a simple bookshelf. It had coke residue as well as a cache of guns. He was either got hit trying to reach this area or while trading shots with one or two people. You have bullet holes in both adjacent walls as well as the couch making me believe someone was using it as a shield of some sort."

"Who is he?" Detective Lawrence asked in reference to the body in front of the bookshelf.

"One Kareem Muhammad. Use to be Kareem Jones before converting to Islam while in prison."

"Number one trafficker in the Triad."

"Yea, guess he didn't fully convert himself. With that being said, this could be one of two things. Either this was a robbery, or a transaction gone bad."

"And I guess this is his partner over here?"

"Tito Santos. He was probably trying to sneak up on the action and got hit by a stray. Everyone knows he's just a lookout man not a shooter."

"What about the one outside?"

"We don't know about her. More than likely a victim of casualty."

"Any prints?"

"Forensics is running them. But I doubt there'll be more than the accounted for. I believe whoever came in here came prepared to do whatever they needed to."

"So, all of this was done by one person?"

"Hells no. we found different shell casings in the driveway to far from any of the bodies to be from their weapons."

"And nobody heard this?"

"Come on Steve. We damn near in the middle of nowhere. The next house is close to a mile away so who would hear anything?"

"Then who reported it?"

"The mailman."

"So, we got four people dead with no leads?"

"Looks that way."

"There has to be something."

"That's why they called you in. You're like the Sherlock Holmes of the division," Detective Sparks joked as he wolfed down the last bit of his sandwich.

"You need to slow down on the take-out food. Fuck around someone get behind you and you pass out,: Lawrence kidded back. Sparks was knick-named Fat Albert because of his huge girth.

"Fuck you," he laughed even though he knew what he said was true.

Lawrence walked back into the house and over to the open closet. He began to scan the area for any clues. The area seemed to have been trampled upon by the CSI. He saw the blood on the carpet and knelt down. The blood that was next to Kareem's body wasn't as close to the closet as the other speckles. He noticed how it left a light trail towards the door. Standing up he grabbed the closest forensic worker near him. "Have samples of these bloodstains been taken?" he asked pointing at the two different areas he was referring to.

"Yes sir, it's already been taken care of."

Lawrence continued his inspection throughout the house in hopes of seeing something that that gave him a lead. Something that was overlooked. That's all he needed. A small clue.

Heading outside he saw that most of the casings were collected. Another glance around brought him no help. He kicked the dirt at his feet in frustration when something caught his eye. Squatting down he saw it was a gold loop earring. He wondered where it came from because neither one of the dead women were wearing any jewelry. He took out his pen and scooped it up. Summoning a guy to bring him an evidence bag he let his thoughts start churning. This bit of evidence meant that there was another female involved or at least happened to be on the scene. If he found her he could begin to solve this case. He was the best at what he did, but he also knew that this was going to be one of his most challenging cases yet.

CHAPTER 14

Monica never knew what people meant by getting a taste of that "Thug Love", but now she knew firsthand why it was talked about so much. She was sprung and didn't even know how or when it happened. She didn't care because she was feeling good. Yeah she had her share of street dudes, but Stacks was in a class all by himself. She tried not to be nagging knowing that that was an easy way to run someone off. Nor did she try to be all up under him. She gave him his space and let him do his thing. She didn't trip whenever he went out of town even though she would find herself missing him and yearning for his attention. Even though she always turned him down at least he did invite her to go with him. He wanted her to join him for Thanksgiving with his family, but it was too short a notice being that her own family had plans. She wondered what he had in mind when he mentioned about having her dealing in bigger business. Whatever it was she knew he was serious when he slid her that thirty-five grand. So, she didn't have an issue waiting to see what he had planned

Monica's phone rang snapping her out of her daydream.

"Yo."

"What's up bitch?" Misty's voice came through on the line.

"You ho. What's up?"

"Bored as hell. I'm tired of eatin' turkey and stuffin'."

"I know that's right."

"So, what's up, ain't nothin' jumpin'? We ain't did shit minute. I need some new clothes and doe. Christmas around the concern too."

"Just relax. I told you we not fuckin' with our own backyard no more."

"So, where we goin'?"

"Don't know yet. I have to talk to my man about it."

'Your man?! When the fuck that happen? And why am I just findin' out?"

"I can't believe it myself, but dude put me through some shit that I can't let go of."

"I thought you said dick was secondary?"

"Yea, but this dick is phenomenal. Still that ain't it. This nigga's about his *business.*"

"Quit teasing me. What's his name and what he look like?"

"You already know who he is."

"Don't tell me it's that square ass Stacks?"

"Guurrl. That shit is a front. He's far from a square."

"So what, squares got good dick too. It don't stop them from bein' a square."

"I ain't gonna go in to all that. Just watch how this money start rolling in."

"Well, if that's the case you need to hurry up and talk to that nigga," Misty laughed.

"Yea,yea, I got you. But I might need you to do some other stuff too."

"Like what?"

"I'm not sure yet, but soon as everything is setup I'll let you know."

"Ok just let me know, you know I'm with whatever. Let me go before my family start trippin' again."

"Ok."

When Misty hung up she made another call to an anonymous person.

"Yeah."

"Everything's looking good. Give me like a week or so and we're in there."

"Good. Just be sure to keep me posted."

"Not a problem," she said before hanging up. She leaned back in her chair at her dining room table and popped a piece of turkey into her mouth. "It won't be long,' she thought to herself then let out a low chuckle.

CHAPTER 15

'You's a bad motherfucker,' Stacks thought to himself. He wasn't being arrogant, he just had a high sense of self-confidence. This world didn't take care of those who had a big ego and forgot where they came from. That was the motto Stacks went by. He took advantage of every situation presented not letting opportunities to pass him by. That's why he didn't mind going down to South Carolina for Thanksgiving. He used the time to get up with his gun connect.

As he made his way up I-85 he thought about Monica and how she'd fit into his business schemes. If she handled her business like he told her to everything would be straight. He started smiling as he thought about how she came onto him while he slept. "Fucking freak," he mumbled.

"Huh?"

"Nothin' lil mama," he said forgetting that he was riding with his niece. He liked having her around. She brought him a sense of peace. Something to keep him grounded and remember that there were still some innocent people in the world. He glanced at her as she played with her Nintendo switch game wishing he had a child of his own. 'All in due time,' he thought as he pushed a few buttons on his radio that was connected to his cellphone and waited as it rang.

"Hello."

"How you doin' Ms. Lady?"

"Oh, hey baby. How you?"

"On my way back. You got everything ready?"

"I got most of it done. I just haven't figured the type of business to run."

"There has to be somethin',"he said playfully pushing Destiny in the head.

"Stop!" she whined.

"What you gonna do huh? You don't want me messin' with you?"

"Who you talikin' to?" Monica asked not understanding what was going on.

"My baby."

"Your baby?!" she asked starting to get upset.

"Yea, my baby," he repeated knowing what she was probably thinking.

"I know damn well…"

"Quit it Uncle Tony."

"What's that?"

"Why you be playing?" Monica asked embarrassingly.

"What you talkin' bout? Oh, let me find out you thought I had another broad in my car?"

"I, I was just.."

"You gotta learn to trust me babe. Without trust there's nothin'"

"I know, I'm sorry."

"No need to apologize. I understand. Dudes messed up how you think about men, but I don't want you comparing me to them. When I asked you to be down with me, I meant that. That's why I sat down and listened to you," he said then turned to Destiny. "Destiny, say hey to Monica."

"Hey Monica."

"Hello Destiny."

"This is my heart and closest to a daughter I got. But look, get with your girls and put something together. I'm thinking construction or entertainment. Find a good business lawyer that's on his shit. I got some ideas, but its gonna take some research. Greensboro ain't jumping like could be for some reason. I'm trying to bring money to the city and keep people from fleeing to other cities for what they want or need."

"You know something? You're a very smart man and I like that. I'm a talk to my girls and should have the ball rolling by the beginning of the year. The holidays are in effect, so most people are with their families not thinking about business. At least not start up ones."

"Right, right. Well in the meantime we got some personal business that needs to be taken care of."

"Like what?"

"I got virgin ears around, but you already know."

Monica let out a short laugh. "Well, it's here for you. You just have to come and get it."

Stacks glanced at his watch and seen he had about an hour before he arrived back in Greensboro. That's why he didn't mind having Destiny ride with him. it had been five hours and she hadn't complained once. "I got about another two hours before I'm back in the city," he said. He had the habit of never giving a person his exact time of arrival no matter who it was. He felt it gave him a jump on anyone who was thinking to do something ill to him.

"Just let me know when you get here."

"Okay, bye."

"Bye."

"Uncle, I have to use the bathroom," Destiny spoke up. He'd been expecting her to say that as he switched lanes to get off on the next exit.

"I got you baby girl. I'm a get you something to eat too aight?"

"Okay," Destiny agreed. She was only nine but wise beyond her years. She loved being out with her uncle because he'd get her anything she wanted. All she had to do was point and it was hers.

Stacks exited the highway and rode until he found a Wendy's. Parking right in front of the restaurant he cut the car off and started to get out, but not before grabbing Destiny's little purse. She said it made her feel like a lady and walked with her nose in the air whenever she carried it.

"Baby girl, you forgot you purse."

They walked into the restaurant and headed to the bathroom. Stacks kept his eye on everyone he passed. He felt that you couldn't be too careful.

"Uncle, you can't come in here," Destiny said stopping in front of the lady's room.

"Why not?" he jokingly replied.

"Because you're a boy silly."

"You're absolutely right. Well, I'll just wait here for you."

While Stacks held a spot in line Destiny came out the restroom and skipped over to him.

"Here Uncle Tony," she said handing him a piece of paper. "Some lady in the bathroom told me to give this to you."

"What lady?" he asked suspiciously looking around.

"I don't know. I don't see her."

After they ordered Stacks took the bags and handed them to Destiny. That's when he opened the piece of paper.

"Everything's a go. I'll be in touch with any developing information."

Stacks shook his head as he balled up the paper and threw it in the trash. He thought he was on top of his game, but his man Justus always surprised him. He stayed moving like he was part of black ops. He contacts from state to state that could gather any type of information that you needed for a price. Stacks had wanted to know everything there was to know about Monica and her crew. It was a must being that he was deciding to get involved with them. No matter how he felt you could never be too careful. He just hoped that they checked out, because he already had put things in motion and didn't need any interruptions.

"Hey, hey, don't be trying to eat up my fries," he kidded Destiny as he got in the car and started the engine. He thought about how easily Justus got in contact with him and knew that he needed to work on his vulnerability.

CHAPTER 16

Piko sat in the packed Wal-Mart parking lot waiting on the new contact Stacks said he was sending his way. He kept looking at his Marc Jacob watch wondering what was taking so long. He was looking too suspicious just sitting there blowing smoke out the window. He knew it wouldn't be long before one of those toy cops came questioning him. He jumped at the sound of his cellphone going off.

"Yo."

"Where you at?"

"Who's this?" he asked hearing the sassy voice of a female.

"Tsk. Aren't you expectin' somebody?" she asked sounding annoyed.

"I ain't got time to play games, who is this?" he demanded feeling himself getting frustrated.

"Ya boy sent me. So where you at?"

Piko thought for a second before answering. "Third row, right by the light pole. I'm in a forest green Cherokee."

"I see you."

Piko heard the phone disconnect and wondered who Stacks had sent his way. He hoped it wasn't some crackhead. A tap on his window brought him to the attention of a Stacy Dash look alike staring at him. He quickly popped the lock and opened the door. He saw her thick thighs stretching her jeans as she got in. Her bubble North Face coat hugged her upper body. The crinkly curls in her hair came to her shoulder, the bottom highlights brought out her caramel complexion along with the clear lip gloss. 'Damn, why Stacks send this broad knowing I'm tryin' to stay faithful,' he thought to himself.

"Yo, are you gonna just sit there staring at me or are you gonna handle your business?"

"Oh. Yea, yea, yea," he stuttered embarrassingly from being caught gawking at her. He flashed his gold teeth as he reached in the backseat for the duffel bag full of money. "So, what's your name?"

"Misty," she said grabbing the bag and looking inside.

"Misty huh? How long you've been knowing my man Stacks?"

"Not long. He fuck wit my girl Monica. You know her right?"

"Nah, never heard of her. Just like I never hears of you," he stated in a distrustful tone.

"You not supposed to. This is something that they came up wit, but I don't mind. It's easy money."

"Is that right? So, what's really good wit you besides becomin' our new deliverer?"

"Nothin' really. Why what's up?"

"I'm just askin'. Just a little convo, but you somehow got me off my game," he admitted with a slight chuckle.

Misty grinned knowing exactly what he meant. Her looks always threw most guys off leaving them at a loss for words. She knew the opportunity she had right in front of her and wasn't trying to blow it. When Monica had told her that Stacks had some other work for them to do she thought it was some bullshit. She was surprised to be talking, let alone sitting, with someone at the top of the food chain. Everybody knew who Piko was. If you didn't at least hear his name you had to be deaf or a true square. She would have to thank Monica for this moment.

"How's that? You don't know me to be messed up by me."

"You right, but ain't too many females come off wit your looks and vibe."

"Thanks. Well, I got to go," she said opening the car door. 'Please ask for my number,' she pleaded in her head.

"Damn, baby girl. You just gonna breeze through like that? Straight business huh?"

"What you mean?" she asked halfway out of the jeep.

"I'm sayin', is this the only time we gonna speak. Like can I get your contacts?"

"I don't be giving out my number like that, but you can give me yours," Misty said pulling out her cellphone to program his number in.

"Yo, make sure you use that mothafucka too."

"I will," she smiled then closed the door.

Piko watched as Misty walked away looking like a model. He knew he was at a lost. He'd never be able to be faithful to Iris with all the temptation thrown his way. Plus, the ways she'd been acting lately he could care less. She was still his heart, but with a girl like Misty in the mix he wondered if it would be torn in two. "Fuck you Stacks," he mumbled. Yea, he blamed his boy for waving this fine specimen in his face knowing women were his weakness.

CHAPTER 17

Stacks figured since Christmas was around the corner that everything he was putting together should go into effect around this time. He left the drug game alone except to collect a twenty-five percent cut on all profits. He put his man Kinko over his zone and Misty handle the transactions. He respected his connect enough not to introduce any new faces, so he had him send a decoy. They thought alike because neither one of them wanted to get their hands dirty. His thoughts were on bigger and better things.

After hitting Phyliss off again and convincing Monica to ride with him, he hit I-95 in a low profile Crown Vic that Misty rented for him. He told her that they were headed to Boston to meet his brother Devanté, which was part of the truth. He assured her that there'd be no need clothes for they'd go shopping when they got there.

They hit the highway with her doing most of the driving. 'You got to earn your keep,' he explained to her. He took over once they got to Connecticut. When he reached the Boston exit he became fully alert. Grabbing his iPhone off the dashboard hit asked Siri to call his brother. He didn't bother looking at the tie as the grouchy voice bellowed over the line.

"Yooo."

"I'm home bruh."

"Where you at?"

"Just hit the city limits on Massachusetts Ave. I'm a get a room and hit you first thing in the mornin'."

"You should've thought about that before you decided to wake me up in the middle of the night. Time zones don't change just 'cause you rode up north."

"Quit cryin' nigga. Ain't like you were in the middle of fuckin' or no shit like that. Like I said I'll get wit you in the mornin'."

"Yea, yea, do that," Devanté said hanging up.

"Get what you want babes, but don't try to break a nigga," Stacks said as they strolled through the downtown stores. He had introduced her to his family and showed her around the city of his birth. He took her to the Franklin Park Zoo and the Aquarium. The whole time he kept making passes at her. He couldn't help it. The red shirt dress she wore was hugging her every curve and driving him crazy. When she asked to walk through Franklin Park he took advantage.

Walking across the well kept grass he steered them into a wooded area.

"Where're we going?"

"Sightseeing," he replied as the got to a tree big enough to block them from anyone that might stumble upon them.

"What are you doing?" she asked as he started kissing on her neck at the same time running his hand up her thigh.

"Spontaneity keeps relationships goin'. I'm not your average dude so don't expect average things," he said easing her dress up.

"We might get caught," she said nervously, but at the same time getting excited.

"Just roll wit me," he whispered in her ear as he began opening his fly. He spun her around and hiked up her dress until it was above her ass. Pushing her thing to the side, he quickly slid into her. The woods.

"Ooooh, sss, baby, hurry up," Monica moaned trying to hug the street as Stacks rammed into her.

"I got this boo, just let me drive this," he groaned with each stroke.

"God Stacks, you're driving me crazy," she said trying not to be too loud as she pushed back on him.

"Yeah, that's it, that's it baby, throw that shit back," he said looking at the jiggle of her ass as he pounded into her. The thrill of fucking in the open drove him over the edge as he pushed all the way up in her and released his little soldiers to find a new home.

"Get off me boy before someone comes through here."

Stacks got his composure together and started fixing his clothes as they exited the woods. He knew that he gave Monica something to think about in the coming future as long as she stuck by him. After getting themselves together, he took her to get a soft pretzel and show her uptown to look at the Christmas decorations.

"Yo bruh, when the fuck you comin' back down? Ma and them miss your ass. Plus, Destiny be askin' about you," Stacks lied knowing that he spoiled her so much that the only uncle she thought about was him.

"I don't know bruh. They still might be on the lookout for me and I ain't tryin' to bring that type of heat around ma and them."

"Right, right. I'll tell you what. I'm a check into it and see what the word is. If everything's in the clear you need to bring your fat ass down the way."

"Nigga I ain't fat, juts eating good," he replied patting his protruding stomach. Devanté stood at 5'11" 280 lbs. The only resemblance he had with his siblings was his light skin.

"So, everything's good?"

"Yea," Devanté answered handing Stacks an envelope. "Everything should be in there."

"I'm out tonight, so I'll handle it before I go."

"As long as it's done it don't matter. Just be careful bruh."

"Always."

"Yo, shorty got any sisters or friends? I swear them southern girls be thick as fuck. Got a nigga ready to take that flight risk," he joked.

"Shit, she ain't even from down there. She for the 'Cut."

"Word?" Devanté looked at Monica again. "Shit, it has to be the food then. I bet she been down there close to ten years."

"Somethin' like that."

"Yea, then she might as well be a southern chick," he stated still looking at Monica.

"Man let me get out of here before you go crazy," Stacks laughed.

"Yea, yea, just let me know when you get back home. Oh yea, here you go," he said handing him a Louis Vuitton bag. "Can't forget the most important thing. Don't need my baby brother getting' all upset and shit."

"You right about that," he replied taking the bag he knew contained around hundred grand. "I'll get wit you bruh."

"Aight baby boy. Hold ya head."

"No doubt."

If the clothes were any other color than black Monica wouldn't have thought twice about putting them on. She understood it was cold outside, so the Isotones, thick parka coat, turtleneck, and Gore-Tex boots were understandable. But they looked like they were about to break in someone's house. As she sat in the driver's seat with the heat blasting, Stacks seemed to be in a zone.

"Baby what are we waiting for?"

"Huh?" he said coming out of his daze.

"What we waiting for?"

"Oh, nothing really," he answered looking at his Bulova before glancing up at the building they were parked in front of. A light went off in a third floor window. That was his cue. "I just got to pick something up before we go," he said opening the door. "Keep the car runnin', I'll be right back."

Monica watched as Stacks closed the door then head down the alley on the side of the building. She had a sense of Deja Vu. It was too similar to their first date, but she couldn't be mad this time for she was totally involved.

Stacks looked at the broken fire escape and knew that this was the only way to get to the target. He never considered himself a hitman, but the extra money never hurt. He felt he was like a silent assassin, because he knew what he was capable of doing yet didn't make it part of his livelihood. He was a natural with his hands, which spurred him to become a Golden Glove. But nobody knew about his blackbelt in Ninjutsu. It wasn't meant for people to know. It was his secret. Well, him and his family who watched him kick and punch through the ranks.

Jumping up to grab the bottom rung of the ladder, he pulled himself up and onto the second landing. He continued climbing until he got to the third floor and to the designated window. Peering inside he that the coast was clear. He didn't take long to pry open the window to the kitchen. Looking at his watch he hoped that enough time passed that the occupants had fallen asleep. He crept through the dark towards the bedroom door. The slight snoring let him know that the target had had enough of an eventful night to put him in a deep slumber. Stepping over the threshold he stopped in front of the couple and peered down at them. Easing the silencer covered .25 out of his waist he placed his hand over the woman's mouth so she wouldn't scream and alert her husband. He bent down and whispered on her ear not to say a word as he cut on the lamp on the nightstand.

Tapping the barrel of the gun against the man's face he waited until he came around.

"Wh-wh," he muttered, but got quiet when he saw Stacks with a gun pointed at his wife.

"Junior doesn't like to be disrespected by people who can't take care who can't take care of their business. You're costin' him too much money."

"I was going to pay him."

131

"You've taken too long. Plus, I don't have the time to listen to pleas," Stacks said before pulling the trigger and blowing the man's wife's brains out. He tucked the gun in his waist and waited.

"Oh my God! She was innocent. She had nothing to do with this," he said starting to get up once he saw the gun was put away. He thought his punishment was seeing his wife die, but he was wrong.

Stacks slid the piano wire out of his pocket and jumped on the bed. He wrapped it around the man's neck before he could rise all the way up. He placed a knee in the middle of his back for leverage as he applied pressured. He pulled so hard that he thought the wire would cut through his throat. It wasn't long before he stopped fighting and let everything go to be with his wife.

Monica saw the quick flash come from the third floor window and already knew what it was. As soon as she saw Stacks bend the corner her foot hit the gas from nervousness jerking the car forward.

"Goddamn girl, you tryin' to leave me yo?" Stacks said jumping in the car.

"Stacks, all I ask is that you don't get me locked up," she said pulling off.

"Locked up?! Man please. We don't do lock up. Plus, you my girl now so I'm obligated to protect you."

"And you sure as hell better," she replied not fully knowing how deep she had just gotten herself into his world.

CHAPTER 18

"What?!" Cassie questioned Monica when she first was told what Misty was doing. "That bitch ain't shit. She knows I'm trying to get wit that nigga. And I told Stacks to turn me on, so why he pick her?" she asked pacing back and forth in her living room. At 5'11" 165 pounds, her light brown frame was more of a match for Piko than Misty,

"I don't know. You shouldn't be stressing it though, it's all business."

"For now. You know Misty. As soon as she sees Piko's bankroll she gonna be throwing her pussy at him."

"Damn girl, you act like he the only nigga in the 'Boro or something. Fuck him, he small time."

"That's easy for you to say since you got a certified money maker. I just don't like having my toes stepped on."

"Well, you need to forget about that right now and focus on this here thing we trying to get going. You gonna head this entertainment business or what?"

"I don't know nothing about running a company."

"But you know about what's hot and what's not. You know what'll sell and what gets people in them clubs. You know what'll sell and what gets people in them clubs. That's your advantage. Stacks trying to get more people to seek out the 'Boro. And you got the gift to what will attract people."

"You talk about dude like he's some type of God or something."

Monica looked at Cassie with great intensity in her eyes. She didn't like Cassie with great intensity in her eyes. She didn't like being questioned. Especially when she knew what she was dealing with and getting herself into. She wouldn't mislead her homegirls no matter who being questioned. Especially when she knew what she was dealing with and getting herself into. She wouldn't mislead her homegirls no matter who was involved. Just because her and Stacks were now an item it didn't cloud her judgement.

"So, you don't trust this?"

"I didn't say that. You my girl, so I'm a ride with you regardless. I'm just saying that you might be putting too much trust in ol' boy."

"If you knew, did, or saw what I have, you would too."

"Then help me understand this infatuation you suddenly got in the last two, three months."

"It's too early for all of that. In due time though. Just be happy you don't have to get your hands dirty."

"Yea, yea, yea. You talk like I'm some bougie bitch. I'm as much from the hood as the next bitch."

"Why are we even on this subject?"

"Because you act like I can't handle that side of life."

"You tripping. Are you trying to get this money or not?"

Cassie looked at Monica for a brief second then shook her head in disbelief. She didn't know what to think. "Yea girl. You right I'm tripping. I'm a start getting on this ASAP. Do you know what the name is gonna be?"

"This is your project, we just funding it."

"Damn, ya'll doing it like that?"

"No, we all doing it like that. This is a team effort. I'm hoping that it all pays off, so we'll be sitting pretty by this summer."

"That's what's up."

"This our year girl let's enjoy it."

"I know that's right," Cassie replied even though she still felt that Misty backstabbed her. She could've told them to come get her. But she wasn't gonna worry. Patience is a virtue and in time the opportunity would present itself for her to step in.

CHAPTER 19

Ever since Stacks left him in charge, Kinko had been doing good. He was able to cop a new Lexus off the lot and buy new furniture for his girl's apartment. He was obligated to Stacks for the opportunity he gave him. He was making his daily rounds just like Stacks use to do, but he was more on the lookout for those not sanctioned to hustle in the area. He had just came from talking to his collection man in the Ray Warren Housing projects when one of the neighborhood chicks stopped him. He stopped his car and opened the door when she approached him to block their view. He began rubbing on her thigh as he agreed to the empty promises she asked of him in exchange for sex. Despite what would to anyone else would be a distraction he was alert. Being that he use to hug the block himself he knew what to and not to look for as well as who was who amongst the dealers. And right now, the person he was eyeing serving, on what they called The Hill, wasn't a familiar face and therefore unauthorized to serve over there.

Kinko rose bronze complected six foot frame up from his car seat. Running his teeth over his platinum and ruby fronts he tucked the P10 in his waistband and tugged his coat closed. The skully on his head covered his cold ears. He excused himself as he closed the car door and made his way towards the guy.

"Yo, what's good homie?" Kinko asked once he got close enough.

"What up?"

"I ain't seen you around here before, where you from homie?"

"What do it matter?" the guy said already feeling the tension in the air. He'd been hearing about how Stacks and Piko had split up their areas. He knew he was testing the waters by doing what he was doing, but he felt the need to stir a few things up and watched how it unfolded. He rubbed the itching scar on his chin that he received close to eight years ago. It only bothered him when he was up to no good like now.

"This a claimed spot yo. If you not payin' dues to post up here then you gotta go."

"Piko sent me."

"What?! This ain't his zone dog. You better head over to English St."

"You need to holla at Piko about that. Or better yet Stacks. Maybe they ain't tell you everything."

"That's bullshit! Nigga I..."

Kinko's words were cut short when the guy pulled out a .40 Cal and pointed it at him.

"Fuck Stacks," he said firing three shots into Kinko before running off to his car that he parked around the corner.

Kinko lay in the gravel by the Hill's store looking at the night's sky. His breathing came out in spasms as people came running out of the store to see what was going on.

"Yo Kinko! What happened man? Somebody call the ambulance."

Kinko grunted, then sat up. He fingered his sweatshirt where the bullets had entered and felt the bulletproof vest underneath.

"I'm good yo," he informed the people crowding around him. They helped him to his feet while asking him a number of concerned questions. He ignored them all as he reached in his

137

pocket for his cellphone. They helped him to his feet while asking him a number of concerned questions. He ignored them all as he reached in his pocket for his cellphone. He dialed the necessary numbers while speed walking to his car.

"You alright baby?" the thick legged chick he was talking to before the confrontation took place asked. She was still in the same spot he left her in.

"Move out my way, I got shit to handle," he said shoving her out the way, then got in his car.

"Fuck you nigga," she threw back.

"What?!"

He yelled jumping back out the car with gun in one hand the phone in the other. "Bitch, say something else and I'll make you swallow your words."

"Yo, yo," Stacks voice came through his phone.

"Stacks?"

"Yea, yea, what's up bruh?"

"We got a problem," he said starting his car up and speeding off.

"What kind of problem?"

"Piko not respectin' the new setup."

"What you mean?"

"I just got shot bruh."

"What?! Get the fuck outta here. Where you at?"

"I'm on Dudley right now."

"How the fuck you ridin' and you just got shot?"

"I had my vest."

"You know who it was?"

"Nah, but when I questioned him about serving, but when I questioned him about serving in our area he said something about not knowin' everything you and Piko had negotiated. Tell me I didn't fuck up dawg? Tell me I didn't just get shot for something you didn't inform me on."

"What I told you is what it is."

"Then what's up? What you want me to do?"

"Just chill, I got it."

"Whatever man. There's no way I can just sit back and chill. I just got shot and would be out of here if I didn't have my vest on."

"Just don't do anything until you hear from me. And keep your eyed open."

"Yea, aight," he said hanging up. He didn't know where he was going, but he had to do something. He knew his gun would be sounding off and soon. Someone would pay for this, the thing was that he didn't know who. All he knew was that Piko better steer clear of him.

CHAPTER 20

"Boy you so crazy," Misty giggled at Piko's slick remark regarding how her cooking was probably coated with some type of potion to keep him from leaving her house.

"Shit, I'm serious. I've heard of some weird things women do to get niggas caught up."

"Like what?"

"All types of Voodoo shit like cat tails and period blood."

"What?! Uh-uh, now that's straight nasty. Plus, I don't need no Voodoo to get a man."

"You got it like that huh?" he asked trying to reel her in.

"Exactly like that," she answered leaning back in the opposite side of the couch form him.

"What you do then to get a nigga?"

"Wouldn't you want to know?" she grinned playing the game right along with him. Play like your intentions were innocent. Once you got them in their comfort zone hit them so hard they don't know how to react.

"I wouldn't have asked if I didn't."

"Smooth ain't you?" she mentioned getting up. She put the throw pillow that she was clutching back on the couch and walked barefooted to her room. She didn't have any hang-ups about her feet, being that she got a pedicure every week. She now had her toes painted blood red with black swirls going through them.

"Where you goin'?"

"Relax, I'll be back," she said over her shoulder. "You think I'ma leave you alone in *my* crib? Boy please," she yelled from the back.

"Shit I ain't know what the fuck you were doin". I can't read your mind."

"Don't get your boxers in a bunch, I'm just fucking with you," she said back into the room wearing sweatpants that were rolled at her waist. She had on a midriff Atlanta Falcon number seven jersey. It showed off her flat stomach and dangling heart shaped belly ring.

"You a Vick fan?" he asked trying to act like what she wore wasn't enticing.

"Yea, that's my dude there."

"Only if he could've one a chip before his world got turned upside down,"

"I know right. I know that there's something on besides National Treasure. They seem to play that shit every other night."

"I know right. I think one of those American Gangsta episodes is on."

"Then turn to it," she said turning off the lights.

Piko didn't say anything when he felt Misty's presence behind him. Nor did he say a word when her hands rubbed over his shoulders to chest. All he did was sigh and leaned back. She was leaning so far over his shoulder that all he had to do was reach back and pull her on top of him. As soon as he did this she let out a squeal of excitement. When she up righted herself her jersey was partially up revealing perfectly bare B-cup breasts. He raised her up until her chest was leveled with his mouth as he took one of her nipples into his mouth.

"Ooh," she sighed pushing her nipple further into his mouth. "That feels good."

Piko stopped what he was doing and pulled her jersey over her head. She helped him take off his Nike sweatshirt. Their naked skin touched each other causing a silent current to pass between them. The simple contact wasn't enough as she unbuckled his belt, and both their pants were discarded. Just like up top she was naked under her pants as well.

"I guess this is how you get a nigga huh?" he joked as he gripped him and started moving her sex across his dick.

"You scared?" she asked staring at him seriously in the eyes as if to even dare him to deny he any type of pleasure.

"Don't know the word," he answered and felt her tight walls engulf him. "Shit," he breathed as she put her hands on her shoulders and started her slow grind. The rolling of her hips caused him to be rendered helpless. He grabbed her around the waist and enjoyed the sensation.

"Just relax baby. I got this, just relax," Misty said moving her body like a snake.

Iris drove home with tears in her eyes. She knew that she shouldn't have followed Piko, but she wasn't buying that faithful talk he'd been doing. She knew all those extra moves he claimed to be making wasn't strictly business. She was well aware of his cheating ways. It started with the random texts and calls late at night whenever he came home. Then came the different perfume smells on his shirt. Scents she knew were cheap and wouldn't dare wear. He became careless. Lipstick on his boxers and all he would say was that it wasn't what she thought. They've been together too long to just throw everything away. She wanted to believe him. Tried so many times to, but he kept easing back into his old ways.

She never actually saw any of the females before tonight. That's why she was able to cope with it. As long as she didn't see it, it was bearable. So, it hurt her to her heart to see his arm around another female.

Slamming her car door shut she stumbled to her apartment. She felt that she needed a drink. Might even smoke a blunt. As she made her way up the flight of stairs she stopped short when she saw someone sitting right next to her apartment door. At first she thought it was a robber, but let out a sigh of relief when she recognized who it was.

Stacks had been waiting on Piko to return home for over two hours. The news that Kinko gave him wasn't sitting too well. This was the final straw. He always knew that blood was thicker than water, but didn't know that money could be thicker than blood. He didn't know exactly what he was going to do when he arrived. He was moving strictly off of adrenaline. When nobody answered the door he sat on the stairs with his calico resting between his legs. He chose this weapon as more for intimidation than to actually use it unless he was left no choice. He'd hate to have to kill his man. What happened was probably a mistake that Piko knew nothing about. When heard the keys and footsteps coming up the stairs towards him he tensed up then relaxed as he saw Iris approach him. Upon seeing him she hesitated after noticing that he was dressed in all black.

"Stacks, what are you doing here?" she asked wiping her eyes not wanting him to see that she'd been crying.

"Looking for Piko. You've seen him?" he asked emotionless.

"He's out handling *business*. That's what he always tells me, but I saw him this time. Fucking bastard," she stated walking passed him and began fumbling with her keys.

Stacks shook his head at Piko's stupidity. He was letting his desires interfere with his everyday living. "You've been cryin'?"

"Of course I have. What else happens when you've been hurt?"

"Come on now, you're stronger than that. Here, let me help you with that," he suggested reaching for her keys that she was still struggling to put in the lock.

Upon opening the door he led her to the couch. He then went into the kitchen and placed his gun on the counter before going through the cabinets. "I'ma fix you some hot chocolate and we can sit and talk about it."

"I'm tired of talking. It's over for him I'm leaving."

"You can't say that. You might be readin' too much into it."

"Don't play with my intelligence Stacks."

"Well, I'll talk to him," he said fixing her cup of cocoa then taking it to her. "Here drink this. Relax and warm up."

He sat beside her and pulled her close to console her. "Cut this shit out. Wipe these tears and let me see that smile I'm use to."

"I can't. He makes me so mad," she said leaning her head on Stacks' shoulder.

"Well talk to me, tell me what's really wrong."

For the next thirty minutes Stacks listened as Iris let out everything Piko had been putting her through since he started making *big* money. The women, the let downs. Stacks recanted that it was his fault being it was him who pushed Piko to step his hustle game up. What he didn't know was how reckless a mouth he had according to what Iris just told him. That's why his name was on the tip of every street person's tongue. Male or female.

Stacks zoned out thinking about everything Iris told him. He didn't notice when Iris out her cup down on the end table. He snapped back to reality when he felt Iris' soft lips on his neck. "Hey, what the fuck you doin'?"

"I'm so lonely Tony," she said calling him by his real name. That's how long she's known him. "I just wasn't to fell special if only for a little while."

"Nah, hells nah," Stacks said pushing her away from him. "I can't do that Iris you my homie's girl."

"He doesn't give a fuck about me, and ever since he's

Been getting his own money he more than likely doesn't give a fuck about you either."

"You don't know what you're talkin' bout."

Iris looked at Stacks with red eyes that came from her crying earlier. "I use to really think that, but I realize I know exactly what I'm talking about."

"Look," he said as he began to stand up. "Just let Piko know he need to get at me ASAP. I gotta go."

"Whatever. Leave then. You no better than him," she said getting up and headed to the kitchen. She pulled a bottle of Vodka out of the cabinet. Not bothering to use a cup she drunk straight from the bottle as Stacks closed the door behind him.

Stacks stood on the other side of the door wondering what just happened. Piko was really a heartless motherfucker if he didn't acknowledge what was going on in his own home. He began to think about the situation at hand and started getting angry, something that he rarely did. He was ready to say, 'Fuck both of them', but understood that he was probably the only real friend that Iris had. "Damn," he mumbled to himself as he walked back inside as she took another swig from the bottle.

"What the fuck you want?" she asked venomously while holding on to the counter.

"Shut up and come here," he said putting his gun back on the counter and pulling her towards him. "I can't have you doing nothin' stupid," he said consolingly.

CHAPTER 21

"Uh-uh, you have to move that over a little more to the left. Yea, just like that," Cassie instructed the interior decorators. She was helping design the inside of a small club that was to be aimed for the grown and sexy. She wasn't trying to have a bunch of young people in here acting rowdy and tearing the place up. Plus, the spot wasn't that big just enough for eighty to a hundred people. "Nah, see ya'll starting to get on my fucking nerves with this bullshit. I don't know who sent ya'll, but I gotta have this shit done before the weekend and ya'll holding me up," she said making her frustration known.

"Damn girl, who you ragging on like that?" a female voice asked coming through the front door.

Cassie turned to see who decided to interrupt her this time. Her face scrunched up when she saw who it was.

"Damn, you act like you hate to see a bitch. Where's the love at?" Misty asked.

"Shit, you tell me. You the one been acting like a stranger."

"You know how that go. I've been making a lot of moves."
"So have I."

"You oughta be since we're all on the same team. It seems like you got the easy job though. I guess that's the benefit of being a hustla's wife's best friend huh?"

"Now you tripping. We all girls or supposed to be," Cassie looked at Misty skeptically. She was trying her best not to give her a mouthful, but she knew she had to keep her composure.

Truthfully she didn't know what she was mad about. It wasn't like Piko was all that just a known name. All she wanted to do was ride his wave all the way to the bank.

"Yea you right. So, what's up?"

"Nothing really. Just trying to get everything together for opening day this weekend."

"You got everything in order?"

"Don't do that. If a person doesn't know what's about to jump off by now then my name isn't Cassie," she made known. She took any mention of her not being at the top of her game as an insult.

"I know that's right."

Cassie looked at Misty's outfit. The Gucci one piece hugged her curves as if they were glued to her body. Her Gucci heels made her ass sit up higher than normal.

"What?" Misty asked wanting to know why Cassie was looking at her like she did something to her. She figured there was a reason why the energy in the room was awkward.

"Nothing," she answered shaking her head.

"Come on, this me. I know when something's up. Now quit holding back and say what's on your mind."

"Okay, since you insist," she said letting her true feelings surface. "Why you go see Piko knowing I wanted to holla at him?"

"Huh?" she said thrown off guard.

"You heard me."

'Yeah I heard you. That's what you got an attitude for? You act like I volunteered to go see him. That shit was Monica's decision."

"You should've told her no and send me instead," she made known. Her emotions were on her sleeve and was sounding like a spoiled brat.

"It ain't even that serious Cassie. All I do is make drops. I don't see nobody or talk to anyone but Piko and some dude named Kinko."

"Well, it's serious to me, because I was trying to see what was up with him. So what's up?" Cassie asked snaking her neck intimidatingly as she put her hand on her hip. She was trying her best to keep her attitude in check.

"What you mean 'What's up?'" she asked already knowing what she meant.

Cassie walked over to the bar counter where her purse was and reached in for a Nutrigrain bar. "You know what I mean. You gonna introduce me or what since ya'll should be kinda close by now," she mentioned opening the wrapper. She paused for a second. "Unless you already got him?" she inquired. Her eyes focused on Misty's facial expression for any telltale signs.

"You tripping for real. I told you it ain't that serious."

"I ain't tripping. And I told you that it *is* that serious," she said biting into the bar.

"I didn't come here to argue with you. I came to see what was up with you since we haven't seen each other in a while," she said turning to leave. She didn't want to let her know how deep she had dug her claws into Piko.

"So you just gonna leave?" Cassie asked raising up as she chewed on the last bit of the Nutrigrain bar.

"It's best that I do before you start acting crazy, and I ain't got time for that."

"So you must've fucked him already huh?"

149

Misty stopped in her tracks. "Look, if I did it ain't none of your business. This is my pussy. So when you grow up and stop bitching about stupid shit like this then holla at ya girl. Until then, I'm a do me, so I suggest you do you," Misty said with attitude.

"Bitching? Bitch please. I will beat your ass and you know it," Cassie said walking towards Misty.

"Hey! Hey! What the fuck is goin' on in here?" Stacks demanded as he came through the door. He heard the bickering as soon as he put his hand on the handle. He listened to see if there was anything of importance being disclosed. From what he did pick up it was just another set of females fighting over his homie. He stepped in-between them and could sense the bad energy in the air.

"Ask her," Cassie said looking towards Misty with piercing eyes.

"Don't ask me shit. I'm good. She the one you need to check."

"I don't need to do shit. Both of ya'll need to get ya'll shit together. Now what the fuck is ya'll arguin' about?"

"She mad that she not the one making drops to Piko."

"What?! Get the fuck outta here. Cassie is she for real?" he asked staring into her face. When she didn't answer him he already knew it to be true. "Man, this is some bullshit. I'm tryin' to put money in your pocket, and you worried about seein' some nigga?! You buggin' for real yo. I'll tell you what," he said walking over to the bar and snatching up one of the napkins. He saw the purse on the counter and rummaged through it for a pen.

"What you doing in my purse?"

"Chill out," he said finding a pen and wrote on the napkin. He walked back towards Cassie and handed her the napkin. "Here that's Piko's number. Call him, fuck him, I don't care what you do, but best believe this. If ya'll can't get ya'll shit together I'll find someone else to get this money with, you understand?" he questioned looking from Cassie to Misty, whose face showed disbelief. "What? You got somethin' to say?"

Misty's face straightened up. "Nah, I'm good."

Cassie grinned at Misty knowing what she was thinking. The club's phone rung breaking up the staring contest. She answered it then handed the phone to Stacks. "It's for you."

Stacks walked over to the bar taking the phone from Cassie. "Yeah?"

"Our mutual friend has some information for you. Is it safe to speak?" a lady's voice asked through the phone. Her voice was of a foreign dialect that sounded Polish or Russian.

"Yes."

"It has come to our attention that you have a bug problem in your home. How long you've had this bug and the species of it is still unknown but should be identified soon."

After receiving the information Stacks slowly looked around him. At that very moment everyone was now a suspect. The decorators. The workers that were stocking the bar and kitchen. Even Cassie and Misty were now on his radar.

"Yes, please keep me in the loop," he said as he hung up in a slight daze. So many thoughts were running through his head. Feeling that after all this time of being extra careful they were now on to him. But what did they really have was the question. And this was the reason he kept the best lawyer in the city on retainer. Tapping into the hustler's philosophy of 'Never let them see you sweat' he quickly shook it off. "Yo, I'm out. Remember what I said," he mentioned as he headed out the door.

Misty was right on his heels with the need to get to Piko before Cassie did. After today she knew that it wouldn't be long before they fell all the way out and Stacks wouldn't be there to stop it from happening.

CHAPTER 22

No matter what Stacks told him, he wasn't trying to let nothing go. He didn't know about the next man, but he didn't take getting shot lightly. Dude was definitely trying to put him to rest. Kinko stood under the staircase in the back of project buildings waiting. Since the lights were busted in the walkway all you could see was the red glow from his cigarette. He heard him before he saw him. Once the dude came into view he pulled out his gun and waited for him to open his apartment door. Easing out of his hiding place he put the gun to the back of his head. "Don't say shit or I'll blow your fuckin' head off," he stated pushing him forward and kicking the door shut.

"Yo!" Stacks barked into the phone. His mind was trying to sift through the many faces he dealt with wondering who could possibly be the rat. It was frustrating him because he couldn't figure it out. He didn't know too many of those he dealt with being that it was usually through someone else. Everyone else he knew for years or were family. He wanted to look at Monica or one of his girls, but he had Justus check them out and they came back clean. So why would he send the message of there being a bug around him?

"Goddamn baby boy. You aight?" Piko asked calmly.

"Hells nah I ain't aight."

"What happened?"

"There's somebody amongst us that shouldn't be."

"Huh? Yo, stop speakin' in riddles and tell me what's up."

"A rat around here."

"Who?"

"If I knew I'd take care of it. Just make sure if you find out who it is you handle it."

"What you tryin' to say?"

"I said what I said. Right now I don't trust a soul."

"Nigga, don't even come at me like that. We've been friends since the sixth grade you know I ain't no rat."

"Didn't say you were. And if you were listenin,' I said, 'If I knew who it was I'd take care of it'.

"Yea, but you got your doubts."

"Wouldn't you?"

"Yea, but you wouldn't be anywhere on my list tho."

"Tell me this then."

"What?"

"My lil homie got shot a couple nights ago and your name came up."

"What you mean my name came up?"

"Dude who shot him was in my zone but didn't have permission to be there."

"Okay, and what?"

"He said you sent him nigga that's what! Bro don't play with me right now."

"I ain't playin'. You know I wouldn't do no shit like that bruh."

"Well you need to find out who's behind this shit 'cause my lil homie not tryin' to hear it."

"You sent that nigga at me?" Kinko asked the guy he'd been waiting on. He kept his gun pointed at him as he turned him around.

Bokeem didn't know what was going on when he was pushed inside his apartment at gun point. He didn't like surprises, not these kind anyway. "What you talkin' bout dawg?"

"That nigga who shot me."

"Shot you?! Man you trippin'. I ain't send nobody to do shit to you."

"I know Piko got you runnin' shit out here. Maybe your nuts done got big and you tryin' to let 'em hang."

"I don't know what you talkin' about," Bokeem said in all honesty. He didn't have a clue to what Kinko was speaking on.

Kinko ignored what Bokeem said. He wasn't really trying to listen to him anyhow. He never liked Bokeem. He use to try to tell both Stacks and Piko that the muscular six-three, two hundred and ten pound Trinidadian was a big pussy. "Man I never liked your bitch ass, or the motherfuckers Piko chose to fuck with."

"What you talkin' bout K man?" Bokeem asked in a whiney voice.

"Shut the fuck up! I ain't ask you to say shit. Ya'll motherfuckers think Stacks and his team soft or something. Without us, niggas would've been got at all of ya'll. Piko too.

Ya'll niggas too scared to bust your gun. I know you got larceny in your heart. Matter fact fuck all tis talkin'," he said before shooting Bokeem in the face three times. He hurried out of the apartment after picking up his shells and wiping everything down he touched. He knew people heard the gunshots, but in the projects the residents would never come out to investigate. He just hoped nobody was being nosey as he hustled across the street towards his car. That's the joy of the projects so many escape routes.

Kinko got in his car and peeled off. He was ready to find him a jump off. Pussy was the only thing that could calm him down after he put in some work. His actions might've started a war and would have to put his workers on point. "Fuck them niggas," he said to himself as he turned on Florida St. Stacks didn't know how strong of a team he had, but he'd soon find out. Either niggas were gonna rock or get rolled over.

CHAPTER 23

"Baby what's? You haven' been yourself these last couple of days," Monica asked tracing her finger across Stack's chest as they laid in bed.

"Just got a lot on my mind," he replied. A few months had passed, and he still didn't know who the infiltrator was.

"Like what?'

"You wouldn't understand."

"That's not fair. You told me to be down with you a hundred percent and I've given you nothing less. So don't start distancing yourself from me now."

"You're right. You have kept your word. It's just that I'm at a standstill right now."

"About what?"

"I don't know who to trust anymore."

Monica raised up on her elbow to look Stacks in the face to see if he was serious. "Look at me."

Stacks turned towards her with his hands still behind his head.

"Are you serious?"

"Yeah."

"So, you don't trust me?"

Stacks thought for a second and remembered the last time he tried to affiliate her with the police. The way that she flipped he never doubted her again. Not only that she had caught a body right along who him. So at the end of the day he had no choice but to trust her. "Did I say that?" he answered avoiding the question.

"No, and you better not either or I'll fuck you up," she said trying to make light of the situation as she laid back down.

"This is serious Mo'. There's a rat in our house and I don't know who it can be."

"How long do you think they've been around?"

"I couldn't have been long, because I've been doing this for a minute now and this is the first time I've heard of anything like this."

"I've heard that the FEDs would wait for years to build a case so when they come and get you they can throw the book at you."

"That's exactly how they do, but like I said I've been doin' this since I was thirteen if that isn't long enough I don't know what is."

"True. So it has to be one of two things or maybe both. You have not just an informant but an undercover. And they have to have been someone that you've recently let in the fold."

Stacks had already thought about that last part and didn't want to bring it up. Not at the moment anyway. He'd hate to think that his decision making was off. Yet he knew if it was anyone of the people he was thinking it was he could blame nobody but himself. He usually felt people out before dealing with them. He wanted to see what type of energy they gave off. That's one thing he hadn't been doing lately. Mainly because he wasn't physically involved on the street side of things anymore. He let everybody else get their hands dirty. All he did was orchestrate things from behind the scenes.

"Why you get quiet?" Monica wondered.

"Because I'm afraid to even think like that."

"Like what?"

"The only people I've recently met is you, Cassie, and Misty."

"Oh," she whispered. It suddenly dawned on her where he was coming from. Why he was going through such a dilemma. He wanted to trust her, but he didn't have any issues until he added her and her girls to his team.

"I'm just hopin' that this one time that my people made a mistake. That they got the wrong info."

"if they've never been wrong don't start wishing they are now. It is what it is. All you need to do is keep moving under the radar like you've been doing. Remember, you still got me and I'm with you 'til the end. My hands are just as dirty as yours are. We just have to make sure we clean them. We got the club going, but we need to think of another business or two to help wash the money you got coming in at a faster rate. All you have to do is prove the source of income and you're good. The accounts are moving how they're supposed to. We'll file for a corporation take add the current business to it and apply for a secured loan then pay it back quickly so that money won't get flagged when you start making five to six figure deposits."

"You're scarin' me."

"What you mean?" Monica smiled really not understanding what his statement meant.

"You're too much. Every time I've dealt with a female they were tryin' to get into my pockets. But you. Off the top you was about your business and never had your hand out."

"That's because I don't depend on anyone to get my bag. I'd be good even if we never met. It just so happens that we did, and you showed me a more efficient way to get money. For that alone

I have nothing but respect for you. Not only that, but you've earned a place in my heart that can't be ignored."

"Damn, what you tryin' to do, make mw fall in love or something?" he joked.

"It's too soon for that, but if it happens I hope you don't try to stop it," she stated seriously.

"Don't start getting' soft on me. Not now anyway,: he said trying to change the subject. He didn't want to admit that it was too late. He had already fell for her.

"I ain't getting soft just voicing how I feel. Am I wrong for that?"

"No you're not wrong at all."

"And you might stress to Piko that he get a job before he gets all of us fucked up."

"I know," he agreed wondering if he even wanted to talk to Piko at the moment. He was trying distance himself from everybody. Even Monica, who quickly ended that idea. She was there for the duration and wasn't having any other way. He just couldn't understand how things got so out of hand when everything was going perfect. But that was what he failed to realize. Nothing in life is perfect. And nothing lasts forever. Except death.

CHAPTER 24

Piko was going crazy. Not crazy for real, but that's how he felt ever since Stacks told him that there were undercovers in their midst. He'd been eyeballing everybody he passed during the times he was out dealing with people. He was already leery, but this info had boosted his paranoia. Not only that, his top worker, Bokeem, was dead.

He remembered not hearing from Bokeem for about two weeks. He didn't think anything of it until it was time to collect his money. When he didn't show up to drop off his take he made some calls. The news of his death had yet to reach him because he'd been out of town with Iris. He felt he had to start doing the husband/wife thing or risk losing her.

He drove over to Bokeem's apartment to see what the issue was and came upon nothing but yellow crime scene tape. Later on he found out tha he'd been shot close range, but nobody knew who had done it. He thought back to what Stacks had told him about the run in Kinko had had and wondered if that's who had done it.

It was too much to bear at one time. He didn't know if Stacks was being sneaky, trying to take his workers to war behind his back or what. Plus, the police were sniffing up their ass. At least that's what Stacks had told him. It could be a lie. Something to throw him off knowing he was petrified of the police. He'd be damn near shit on himself at the mere mention of the cops. His brother use to tease him about it all the time. Saying how instead of a box of condoms he should keep a pack of underwear. He didn't understand how he could be so scared living the life he did.

Detective Lawrence was frustrated. He still didn't have a lead on the murders he was investigating. The department wanted him to file it away in the homicide's cold cases. He had no choice but to follow orders since no information was surfacing. When he heard about the murder he was the first detective on the scene. This was his area and knew if anyone could solve this case it was him. There were plenty of informants around that would easily help him. But as soon as he got the ball rolling he was taken of the case. That's when he knew something wasn't right. Either the suspects involved had deep pockets or things were bigger than he was seeing. He knew one thing, he was going to find out what was going on before things got out of hand.

Piko opened the door to his apartment and came upon complete silence, which wasn't normal. Iris would usually be in the kitchen cooking while listening to music. He didn't bother to call her name as he pulled his gun out of his waist. Stepping across the threshold he waited a few seconds to see if he heard any type of noise. Nobody was in sight. No heavy breathing or whispers. He knew that that didn't mean anything. He *didn't* close the front door as he moved across the room. If need be he planned to haul ass out of there at the sign of any mischief. So the door stayed opened so it wouldn't slow him down. The only reason he was still there was because he'd hate to find out later that something happened to her and he didn't help her.

After going room to room with his gun leading the way and finding nobody there, he relaxed. That's when he went back to the front door shut and locked it.

"Damn I need a drink," he said to himself as he headed to the refrigerator. After popping an Icehouse he closed the refrigerator door and noticed a piece of paper hanging up by a purple letter P magnet. He quickly snatched if off and opened it. Immediately noticing Iris' handwriting he began to read the note:

"The reason that I left this letter instead of waiting to speak to   you face to face is because I wouldn't be able to do what I know needs to be done without you trying to stop me. I can't look you in the face right now without feeling some type of guilt. I begin to wonder what happened to us? What did I do wrong to deserve the infidelity? I gave you my all, mind and body, but that didn't seem to be enough. I tried to ignore the telltale signs of your ways, but you continued to treat me as if I was your pet. Someone who would never leave your side. There was a time that I wouldn't, but being with you is not what I expected it to be. It is not what I need nor want in my life. Jakeem, I will always love, but my love for you will only destroy me if I stayed. I need some time to think things through and figure out how I want to move forward. And please do not try to find me."

Love Always, Iris.

"Fuck!" Piko yelled. He didn't think things could get any worser, but here it was. His girl of fourteen years had walked out on him without a clue to where she went. He knew one thing, if anyone knew where she was it was her mother.

Picking up the phone, he didn't care that she specifically said not to try to find her, as he hit the speed dial button. It rang three times before being answered.

"Hello?"

"Mrs. Floss, this is Jakeem. Have you seen Iris?"

"Oh hi Jakeem. She told me that you might call and to tell you to stay away."

"So you know where she's at then?" he asked ignoring the part of her telling him to stay away.

"What happened dear?"

'I messed up Mrs. Floss."

"And *now* you're regretting it? It took her leaving you to make you see what you *been* doing wrong? Boy I tell you."

"I know Mrs. Floss. I just need to talk to her to make things right."

"It's too soon. She needs some time away to clear her head. And once she does. If you two love each other, like you say you do, then everything will work itself out."

"So you're not going to tell me where she's at?" he inquired feeling his frustration begin to increase.

"I'm sorry. I promised not to. Maybe this is what you needed to get your act together and fast. Because if I know my daughter when she's done she's done."

"Well when and if you speak to her, would you please let her know I need to talk to her?"

"I can do that."

"Thank you," he said then hung up before he couldn't hold back his anger. Of all the females he had throughout the city it was Iris that he cared about the most. "Man fuck all this. I ain't bout to sit in this bitch all miserable," he said out loud as he headed back out the door.

Once he jumped in his Jeep he looked around the interior feeling that it was time to trade it in. 'Shit, Stacks been did it why not him?' he thought to himself.

Starting the car he plugged up his phone in and shuffled through his playlist until he found what he was looking for. He didn't know why he wanted to hear this particular song, but he felt he needed it to get the pain out. As the song played he began to feel the hurt in his chest. "Oooohhhwhhooo. Yea, I can't see em coming down my eyes/so I gotta let the song cry...."

The music continued to play as he headed to his destination.

"Steve, this is over both of our heads. All I was told was that there was a heavy operation going on and to steer my men clear of it."

"That's some bullshit John and you know it. Every time we get close to something the golden boys come parading in crashing the party. I'm born and raised in this city and know everything there is about these streets. And these fuckers from west bubblefuck wanna tell us to fallback? Fuck outta here," Detective Lawrence stated as he ran his hand over his goatee while shaking his head.

"I understand where you're coming from and would love for you to be the one to bust this case wide open, but orders are orders detective."

"I'm a still keep my eyes and ears open. If they slip up I'll be there to do what needs to be done."

"Just don't get involved."

"Yea, I got you," he said while walking out of the captain's office. He was wondering who was part of the operation? How long has it been going on? And most importantly, why was he just finding out? It's possible that his captain wasn't telling him everything and it was indeed bigger than them. That wasn't going to stop him from getting to the bottom of it.

Piko knocked on the door hoping the person who lived there was home. He could hear the sound of music being played, but knew most people did that hoping it would prevent a burglary.

"Who?' the voice asked through the door.

"Piko," he answered then listened for the locks to turn. When the door opened he looked into her questioning eyes as she let him in. "Iris left me. I don't know where else to go."

Misty closed the door as he walked by but didn't turn around until she gotten herself together. She didn't want him to see how happy she was for his misfortune but her new opportunity. Her patience was finally about to pay off and if she played her cards right she'd be able to get some of the pressure off of her back.

"I'm sorry to hear that, but don't stress yourself about it. It's her loss not yours."

"That's how I'm trying to look at it."

"Well, in the meantime let me try and help you get your mind off of it," she suggested while taking his jacket off and hanging it up. She wasn't about to mess this up and once she had her claws in him there was no retraction.

CHAPTER 25

Cassie sat in her office watching the crowd on her 19" tv screen. She usually would be on the dance floor mingling with the partiers. Laughing and enjoying herself. But tonight wasn't that type of night. Her mind was too fixed on Piko. She never had the time to call him after Stacks gave her the number. Every time she slowed down enough to pick up the pho ne something suddenly needed her attention. If she had known that running a club was this strenuous she probably would've turned the offer down. She couldn't lie though, she enjoyed herself from time to time. Having the opportunity to have Charlie Wilson come through and perform was a kicker. It benefited that it was a club for older people who liked that old school R&B. Charlie had them going all night.

Cassie knew that the club was being used to wash their money and was grateful that enough people attended on the daily to cover the dirty money. It was a slow process and suggested to Monica and Stacks to get a more lucrative business. If they didn't, the money stacked behind the basement walls, would start to disintegrate.

She sat her glass of Absolut Black down on her desk and flipped thru her rolodex. Picking up the phone she dialed the number she'd been wanting to call for the longest. As the numbers' clicks made their way through the fiberoptic cords to their destination and connected, her heart began to beat faster.

Each ring brought on a wave of nervousness and started to hang up.

"Hello," Piko said answering the phone on its fourth ring.

"Piko?"

"Who's callin'?"

"This Cassie."

"Oh, what up?"

"I'm at the club chillin."

"How's that comin' along?"

"Oh, it's good. Maybe you oughta come thru some time and check it out. Stop acting like you're anti-social all of a sudden."

"Nah, that shit too slow for me. I'm tryin' to stay young as long as possible. So you just called to talk about the club or..." he left the question lingering for her to answer.

"Truthfully, I've been meaning to call you. I just haven't had the time."

"Call me for what tho?" he asked starting not to trust this sudden phone call. Especially after what Stacks said about there being a snake in the crew.

"You know, to talk."

"About what? And why now?"

"Why now? Because like I said, I've been extremely busy, plus I just now getting your number."

"And again, what is it you want to talk about?"

"This shit is crazy," she chuckled nervously. "I'm use to being able to say anything that's on my mind and here I am tongue tied.:

"You shouldn't be so nervous. It ain't like I'm the boogey man or no shit like that."

Cassie giggled like a high school kid with a crush, but got herself back together. "I'm trying to holla," she said leaning back in her chair while grabbing her glass. She was back in her element.

"Oh, I see you've been plotting on a nigga huh?"

"If by plotting you mean me watching you trying to see what's up? Hells yeah I've been plotting. But if you mean on some shiesty shit, nah that's not even how I get down."

"So, why you ain't been said nothin'?"

"I told Stacks and Monica to introduce us, but for some reason it never happened."

"Damn, that's fucked up. Real fucked up on both of our parts. Especially right now."

"Why's that?"

"Because I'm involved wit somebody and we got an understandin' that I don't want to mess up."

"Is it Misty? You don't even have to answer that I already know it's her," she seethed with anger.

"Yea, it's her. You sound like you ain't too enthused, I thought that was your girl?"

Cassie wanted to blow up, but knew if she was gonna be able to catch Misty off guard she had to act normal. She didn't want to let on to Piko that she despised Misty. "Yea, that's my girl. I'm just a little disappointed and embarrassed."

"For what?"

"Because if I knew I could've avoided all of this," she stated moving her hand back in forth in a sweeping gesture.

"Don't feel bad. Shit you never know what the future might hold," he said reassuringly. He knew And understood the game. Always keep your options open. He didn't want Cassie feeling like her efforts were meaningless. That's one thing he knew for sure he had Stacks beat on. Women. Plus he never knew if or when he might need Cassie's assistance. He figured that if it ever came to he could learn what was going on with Stack's side of things. Yea, he learned a lot from him, but until he learned what was really going on he was going to use everyone to his advantage.

"I'm not too god at the waiting game."

"Patience is a virtue."

"But time waits on no one."

'I feel that, but don't give up on me just yet."

"Look Piko, I don't like playing these types of games. Too messy. Plus, you mess with my girl so leave it at that," she stated then hung up the phone.

Cassie let out a sharp breath, hand still holding the phone. "Misty, Misty ,Misty," she said to herself. All she had to do was tell her what was up instead of sneaking around. "That's not what girls do Misty." But Piko left the door open. Niggas that thought with their dicks were always vulnerable. But now it's not even about him anymore. This has become personal. She didn't know what Misty was up to and that's what had got her going in the first place. Something wasn't right about Misty, but she just couldn't figure out what it was.

"Dumb bitches. Think your boy's a fool," Piko mumbled to himself. Misty already told him what was up between her and Cassie. Cassie thought she was slick trying to downplay it. He was hip to it all. He knew Cassie was close to Monica and therefore would know if Stacks was on some snake shit. All he had to do was wait for the right time to make it seem like it wasn't going to work with Misty. And out of a couple drugs she'd tell him everything he needed to know.

"Who you talking about?" Misty asked coming into the living room. She placed a plate on a fold out table in front of Piko then awaited her answer.

"You don't even wanna know," he replied leaning over the plate of food to smell what she cooked. The T-bone steak was evenly covered with A-1 sauce. Fluffy white rice with a rich brown gravy poured over it. Last but not least, the buttery green beans took up the rest of the space on the plate.

"Iris finally call you?'

"Hmph. I doubt she'll ever call me. I think she really is tired this time. It was good while it lasted. But fuck her. I was just talkin' to your girl Cassie."

Misty's face frowned up at the mention of Cassie's name. Piko saw this, but was expecting it at the same time. It just confirmed his earlier observation. These two didn't like each other for some odd reason. When there was controversy other things were bound to happen as well.

"What she want?"

Piko put a nice piece of steak in his mouth and started chewing slow. He did this to buy time so he could get his thoughts together. He wondered if he should say something to try and help them get pass their differences or leave it where it was. His decision was only important to him. No one else mattered for they wouldn't be the beneficiary of his acts. "She asked about you. Said ya'll had bumped bodies and wanted to apologize."

"Then why didn't she call me?"

'Didn't think you'd talk to her."

"You tell her about us?"

"Yea, why? What, you don't want nobody to know we fucking or something?" he asked curiously.

"That's not it."

"Then what is it?"

"Nothing. How's the food?"

Piko squinted his eyes at Misty, giving her his signature scowl. "What you not tellin' me yo?"

"It's hard to explain."

"Well you need to try."

"We got into it because she's mad she wasn't picked to do the drop-offs to you."

"That's all? What was so hard about that? Ya'll some petty bitches," he stated scooping some rice into his mouth.

"Why you always calling women bitches?"

"Ya'll call each other bitches all the time but let a nigga say it and it's an issue. Plus, that's how I talk. You don't be sayin' nothin' when we fuckin' and I call you a bitch."

"That's different."

"Look lets dead this conversation before it turns to something else," Piko suggested

Misty stormed out of the living room but didn't go far before hearing Piko say something in a low tone but still audible.

"Fuck her. Let her be mad. Shouldn't be talkin' stupid anyways. Fucks wrong wit 'em. I don't need theses bitches, they need me."

'I got your bitch,' Misty mumbled under her breath as she continued into the kitchen.

CHAPTER 26

"Yo, don't even worry about that bruh… Nah, look, just make sure Sylvia has everything ready when I come through aight?.... One," Kinko said ending the conversation. He placed the cellphone in his lap next to his gun and leaned back between the legs of the neighborhood hair braider as he got his cornrows done. He was sitting on the bench in Douglas Park. The girl sat on the table. Even though she was busy braiding his hair she was also scanning the area to make sure no one ran down on them. The thing with Kinko was that he loved the streets and wanted to be in them as much as possible. He liked watching the hustle and bustle that came with it. Customers and servers both with shifty eyes as if they were plotting, but only wanted one thing. to satisfy a temporary high. One from making money the other from what took the place of their money. Kinko might've been Stacks protégé but moved differently. Stacks would come through for only a few minutes just to show his face and leave. He said it wasn't good to stick around all day. It made you an easy target, because people could time your movements. You became a familiar face which leads to a familiar case.

He took heed to a certain extent. Instead of making rounds from spot to spot, he had drop off houses. The money would all go there and a someone would pick it up and deliver it to him by the morning. He'd choose a different location to chill at for the day and conduct business from there. Which he was doing at the moment.

"Who's Sylvia?" the hair braider asked jealously.

"What?! Yo, don't be asking me about nobody. Worry about Brandy. I'm not gonna tell you that shit again," he said with authority. "And hurry up wit my hair. It ain't never took you this long to do my shit."

"I'm trying to lace you up, dang if you wanted straight backs then of course I'd be done."

"Whatever, just hurry the fuck up," he said leaning back until his head felt the warmth between her legs.

DS sat in a white Ford F250 on an off street that gave him a clear view of Douglas Park. He kept his eyes on Kinko as he got his hair done. He had to hold back the tears as he thought about the death of his little brother. He felt that it was his fault he got killed because he was following in his footsteps. Everything was all good when they first started hustling for Piko and Stacks. Things didn't start going left until the zones were put into place. He felt that his brother would still be alive if he had been around, but Piko had him in Charlotte. He was doing his dirty work while he spent time with his girl. "Motherfucka ain't been thinkin' about his girl and now the one time he does my brother ends up dead," he mumbled.

"DS what up we gonna take care of this nigga or what?" one of his partners from Claremont asked. He wasn't too happy knowing anybody came into his hood and laid one of his people down let alone someone from the other side of town. He didn't care if it was Kinko or not, he felt that if you weren't from that hood, you should show it some respect or get dealt with. He really didn't know Kinko like that just that they were somewhat part of the same team, and he got money on the southside. But once he heard that he was behind Bokeem's death all that meant nothing.

"I got Kinko, ya'll just make sure ya'll handle the rest of them niggas," he said talking to the other occupants in the truck. He reached in the side door compartment and grabbed the plastic bag that was there. untying the bag he used his long nail on his pinky finger to scoop some of the substance out of the bag. He jerked his head back after the potent fish scale cocaine shot up his nose. A couple more hits later he was pumped up and ready to go.

After pulling the mask over his face he chambered a bullet in his gun. "This is for Bo so everyone dies," DS stated before opening the door and heading toward the park and Kinko.

As soon as Brandy finished the last braid she pushed Kinko's head forward to let him know she was done.

Kinko sat up and brushed the loose strands of hair off his light jacket. Standing up he placed the gun that was in his lap on the table along with his phone. He reached in his pocket so he could pay Brandy. As soon as he extended his arm he saw her eyes get big.

"Kinko, watch out!" she yelled.

He turned in time to see the four masked men running in his direction with guns raised. He quickly jumped over the table grabbing Brandy on the way as the bullets began to rain on them. He noticed that they weren't strictly for him but everyone out there. He returned fire from his MP10 as he began to back up with Brandy held tight in front of him.

Brandy began to kick and scream after realizing that Kinko wasn't trying to save them but was trying to save himself by using her as a shield. The determination to live gave him a strength that she couldn't break loose from. It wasn't long before she caught a load of bullets that ended her struggles. He let the dead weight go and ran behind a big oak tree.

Kinko knew who they were. Not personally, but who they were as a group. If the situation wasn't so serious he'd laugh at their stupidity. That's what he was telling Stacks about Piko's workers not being built for this lifestyle. Yea, they had the element of surprise, but didn't know how to use it to their advantage. Their first mistake was not spreading out to cover all angles. They just bee-lined straight towards him not paying attention to the other occupants in the park. They were all his workers who stayed strapped.

There were two entrances so being they only came in one way left him with an escape route. The major thing was that they didn't have enough people. He had a man on every side and the two on two basketball game was just a decoy.

When the shots started coming from every side and not from his people DS realized his mistake. Driven by drugs and revenge he failed to use the advice passed down from the men in his family who were OGs in the game. One was to never go to war unprepared. But the main one was to never try to fight anyone in their own backyard. These were the things that ran through his head as he laid on his back staring at the sky through the thick tree branches. The blood that began to block his airway was getting thicker as his life source started to get thinner.

"Yo, yous a stupid motherfucka. Should've stayed on your side of town and continued getting money. Now look at you," Kinko said shaking his head as he stood over DS. "Make sure you tell Bokeem what up. I'll see ya'll later," he joked before shooting DS in the face.

"Yo, yo, ya'll pick up them shells and get the fuck outta here. Twelve gonna be swarmin' in no time."

"Yo, Jamal hit," one of his workers said.

"Is it bad?"

"Looks like a flesh wound."

"You know where to take him then. I'll get wit ya'll tomorrow, love ya'll," he made known and meant it. Today they proved their loyalty and heart. Not just to Stacks, but him as well. As he ran to his car he wondered how Stacks would take the news. He had to understand why he shot Bokeem in the first place. If the streets sensed that you were weak then it'll eat you alive and he wasn't having that no matter what. If that wasn't understood then he didn't know what to say.

CHAPTER 27

Monica sat on the edge of her bathtub leaning forward. Her elbows rested on her knees with hands held her head. Fingers gripped her rare unkept hair. The only upside was that it was the weekend and didn't have to leave the house. Her only concern at the moment was her test result.

For the last couple of days she'd been throwing up and feeling exhausted. Even though she'd never been pregnant herself, she knew what the symptoms were. So after the second day of being sick she bought a pregnancy test and was now waiting to see what First Response had to say.

She looked up at the clock that hung on the wall over her towel rack and saw that enough time had passed. Standing up she pulled her silk teal robe tight around her body to conceal the lone black panties. She pulled her hair back in a ponytail with a red hair tie she saw laying on the sink. Taking a deep breath she slowly looked down at the test. She exhaled slowly as she stared at the two bold pink lines as if they were two walls boxing her in. It took her a few seconds to get her wits together and ungrasp the edge of the sink. A few strides out of the bathroom she was standing in front of her full length mirror. Releasing the hold she had on her robe she slowly opened it to reveal her body.

She lifted her breast to feel their weight. They were heavy but didn't sag like most people with non-surgically enhanced D-cups. She pinched her nipples for no other reason than to see if they were still sensitive. Even though it was too early to tell she stilled turned to the side to see if there were any telltale signs of her pregnancy. There was nothing noticeable. Her body was still flawless.

Monica sighed then looked around her room as if there was some type of clue to find that would help her figure out what to do. She was confused, not knowing if she even wanted a child. Well at least not at this very moment. Or if Stacks was the one to be having any by.

Looking at the top of her dresser there were two rows of scented oils. Frankincense, Egyptian Musk, Drakkar, and One Million to name a few. Stacks bought them from his barber Lex that owned Kurtesy Kuts on Phillips Ave. another guy who he knew from the streets and had turned his life around for the sake of his kids. A platinum chain with a medallion in the shape of a star that had the letter S on it, hung from the edge of the mirror. She knew he did this on purpose. It was his way of marking his territory so no one would get the notion that she didn't have a man. He had his own space in the spare room's closet. His toothbrush, brush, and wave grease was in the bathroom. He really had done everything but move in. She didn't have any room to talk because she basically did the same thing at his place.

A picture of them was taped to the mirror of them at Busch Gardens in Florida. Destiny had went along with them since school was out and they had the time of their life. They stayed for three days and that was the longest they had been without sex. She wasn't stupid though. She knew that any trip out of state was mainly for business purposes. Bringing Destiny along was only to fit the family image.

Monica thought about all of this as she reached for her phone. She wondered how he'd feel about bringing that image to life. "This nigga better not start tripping," she said to herself while pressing his contact number.

"Yea, yea who's this calling Big Dick Tony?"

"Boy you stupid," she smiled despite the butterflies floating in her stomach.

"Yea, but I bet you're smiling like a motherfucka tho."

She couldn't help but to blush and smile harder. "You think you know me huh?"

"Know you enough."

"Is that right?"

"So you telling me I didn't make you smile?"

"Just being around you or hearing your voice makes me smile. But if you must know, yes I'm smiling."

"That's what I thought. So what's up you ok?"

"Yes, I just wanted to hear your voice. And tell you something."

"Anything babe what's up?'

Monica inhaled deeply and braced herself. She figured she'd just say what she had to say and get it over with. What's the worse he'd do but deny it or tell her to get rid of it. "I'm pregnant," she finally said. There was a long pause. Too long. She pulled the phone from her ear and looked at it to make sure he hadn't hung up.

Stacks was at his mother's house counting his stash when Monica called. He was contemplating if five hundred thousand was enough to hold at one place. He knew he'd have to move it soon and have it washed. The call was right on time because he knew if anyone Monica would know a way to wash whatever amount he had. It was his emergency funds for when things went to hell, he'd still be okay. He hoped to never have to need it that's why he was willing to invest it in something legit.

He was in a happy place while speaking to her, but was taken by surprise by the news she just gave him. His arm dropped to his side with the phone in it as he gathered his thoughts. "Goddamn boy," he mumbled to himself while running his hand over his face.

"You sure?" he asked after putting the phone back to his ear.

"Yea, I just took a pregnancy test."

"So what's up?"

"What you mean?"

"What you trying to do? You keepin' it or what?"

"I called you to see what you wanted to do Stacks."

"Well I don't believe in abortions, so if you decide to get rid of it I'm lettin' you know I'm not wit it."

"Just answer this one question."

"What's that?"

"Are you going to be my man and a father to our child or just a baby daddy?"

Stacks gave a short laugh. "I told you when I'm wit someone it's all or nothing. What part of that don't you understand?"

"Yea I remember, but niggas change."

"Glad I'm not a nigga then," he joked

"Well if we going to be a family I want to meet *all* of your family. At least those close to you."

"That's not a problem. In fact, get yourself dressed we can do that now."

"Um, okay," she replied kind of thrown off by his suddenness. She didn't think he'd react so quickly. She was still trying to grasp the fact that he was so acceptive of her being pregnant. Guess he was different.

Stacks hung up and ran his hands over his face again before standing up. "Ma," he called out.

"Yes."

"Where you at?"

"In my room, why?"

Stacks made his way to his mother's room where he found her standing in front of her mirror combing her hair. "You goin' somewhere?"

"And if I was. Last time I checked I was grown."

"Dang, I was just askin'," he stated sitting on her bed and watched her. She still looked good for her age and had no problem capturing a few eyes.

"Boy, what's wrong now? And don't give me that nothing mess, because you wouldn't be in here if there wasn't something bothering you."

"Someone wants to meet you and Eve."

"Who?" she asked quickly turning to look him in the eyes.

"This lady I've been dealing with."

"The one you've been telling me about?"

"Yea, that's the one."

"I don't know why you haven't brought her by already. I don't know what's wrong with ya'll kids these days. Your brother's the same way. Act like everything's a big secret."

"I had to make sure she was the right one ma. I don't want you meeting random chicks so you can harass me about them.

nor do I want anyone getting close to ya'll just to say they did. You know how these broads are."

"Yes I do. But if my memory serves me right you've been dealing with her for what? Eight months now? It don't take that long to trust someone enough to meet their family. Plus, you've never kept a girl around this long *ever*, so she has to be someone special. Bring her and I'll tell you if she's the one or not."

"Oh so you psychic now?"

"No. I just know my babies. And it's called woman's intuition. I tried to tell Eve the same thing now look at her. Don't nobody know where that child's father is at."

"I don't even know who he is," he mentioned letting the lie flow out of his mouth. He knew exactly who he was and why he was no longer around.

"It doesn't matter, but if I ever see him again I'ma give him a piece of my mind and whatever else I have in reach."

"And they say I'm crazy," he laughed.

"Uh uh, don't try to get off the subject. Tell me why you all of a sudden wanna bring her around?'

"She's pregnant."

"Ooooh, I see. Is she going to keep it?"

"You know we don't believe in abortions. And you have to be a strong woman to carry a Knight's baby."

"If you say so. You just be sure to bring her by here so I can see if this *girlfriend* of yours is as special as you claim."

"I'm about to go get her now. I'm a stop by Evaline's first, then come back here."

"Well call and make sure I'm still here first."

"Okay," he said standing up. He kissed his mother on the cheek before heading to the front door. As soon as he stepped outside his phone rung. "Yo, yo."

"Bruh, I'ma give it to you before mothafuckas twist shit up and put the blame on me," Kinko said rapidly.

"Man spit it out I got shit to do."

"I ain't gonna say too much over the airwaves, but I'm at Eastsides come thru right quick."

"This better be serious homie."

"To you, I don't know. But to me it is. So just come thru."

"Aight give me like twenty minutes."

"Aight, I'll be parked out front."

Stacks understood Kinko too well. If he said it was serious it was just that. The only concern of his was not knowing to what degree of seriousness it was. That and what happened that he felt the need to immediately meet up about it.

"Yo, let's make this quick I got shit to do," Stacks said hopping out of his truck. Kinko was sitting at one of the tables in front of the store.

"What I have to say might affect your twenty-five percent," Kinko stated then watched as Stacks' facial expression changed. "I figured that would get your attention."

"I'm listenin'."

"Remember I told you about the night I got shot?"

"Yea, what about it?"

"I know you told me to chill, but I couldn't just take that shit layin' down. So when you set up the way things are, I figured if

Piko didn't have anything to do with it then it had to be that nigga he left in charge."

"What nigga? I thought he was handling everything himself?"

"Dawg, dude tryin' to move like you. He got a squad just like us, but they not built like us."

"So who did he leave in charge?"

Kinko hesitated before answering. "Bokeem."

"You killed that nigga didn't you?" he asked already knowing the answer.

"Like I said, if it wasn't Piko it had to be him."

"Okay, but that happened a few months ago and nobody else talkin' about it so what's up?"

"That's the thing. Yesterday niggas came through masked up and tried to take the team out."

"Where was this?" Stacks ask as he felt himself getting upset. He didn't like unnecessary drama. It messed up the cash flow.

"DP."

You know who it was?"

"I only knew one of 'em was DS."

"Who the fuck is DS?"

"Damn, my nigga you don't know a soul on Piko's team do you?"

"That's why I got you."

"Yea, that's why you got me, and I've been holding it down ever since. But back to what I was sayin'. DS is Bokeem's brother."

"So, you think Piko's behind this?" Stacks asked not ready to believe such an accusation.

"Nah. I'm not sayin' all that. But he might feel we on some other shit and have his people keep it hot."

"So, I need to holla at Piko before this shit gets out of hand?"

"You either do or you don't, but best believe I'm firin' up anyone that comes my way."

"Nah, nah we here to get money not go to war. I'm tryin' to put ya'll in position not dead or in jail. And your ass just got a baby to look after."

"Damn. You right man. I just want you to know we out here doin' this for you. You just make sure you understand that."

"I can dig that. That's why I fucks wit ya'll. Loyalty over everything."

"You still don't get it do you?"

"What you talkin' bout?"

"Man, I'm in the streets daily. They see and hear everything. So mothafuckas already know what it is."

"What da fuck are you sayin'?"

"Man, everyone know that without you Piko's name wouldn't mean shit. And you're the *only* reason they still eatin'."

"And that's cool. We all can get this money so what they not as strong as us. As long as lines don't get crossed I'm good. So let me holla at my nigga and see what's what. If he on some bullshit it's every man for himself."

"That's what's up then," Kinko agreed hoping it did go that route. He get rid of them then that was more money for him and his team.

"I'm a hit you up soon as I find something out," Stacks said giving Kinko a pound before getting up and heading back to his car. He wondered if the day could get any worse. He pulled while reaching for his cellphone.

"Yo," Piko said into the phone after answering on the fourth ring.

"Man, what's good yo?"

"You tell me. The way I hear it, you and your people on some wild wild west shit."

"Then you only hearing half the story."

"I know it was your boy who hit up Bo."

"Just like you told me you didn't have nothin' to do wit Kinko gettin' hit up. But I didn't have anything to do with what happened to Bo. But answer this. What would you do if you felt someone was behind you getting shot hmm?"

"Well I got one better. What do you think I'd do if you got killed and I knew who did it? Do you think I could live with myself knowin' that niggas runnin' round thinkin' shit sweet?"

Stacks though about what he said for a second before replying. He knew Piko was right. Even the softest cat would find a heart when dealing with a loved one. And when you're in the streets it had to get handled the same way. "I feel you."

"This shit wasn't supposed to happen. This wasn't what I expected when you were explaining this shit to me. I knew somethin' was gonna happen like this. I felt it."

"Well it's too late now. Niggas ain't tryin' to go back to the way things were. They've already picked sides."

"So this is what it comes down to?"

"Nah. All you have to do is keep your people in line."

"I'll see what I can do, but you know niggas not gonna try to hear too much. Especially after taken another loss."

"If you want shit to stop, you gonna *have* to make them listen. If niggas didn't have that little bit of respect for me I would've never heard about it until it made the news. I'm trying to get money, I ain't stuntin' that other shit bruh."

"You right. You been told me not to get too deep in these streets, now look at me. Fuck around and I'll have to get back on the block my damn self," Piko joked.

"Nah, never that. I definitely won't allow that. In fact, when you stop throwing your money away and get your hands on a loose fifty come see me. I'll help you start up a company."

"What kind of company?"

"I haven't thought of one yet, but by the time you get that money up I'll figure it out."

"Aight, we gonna see."

"We sure will," he said as they dapped each other up and headed to their cars. "Piko!"

"Yo."

"I love you man. And remember I'll always have your back."

"Thanks. You a real one."

CHAPTER 28

"This is some fuckin' bullshit," Cassie yelled to herself as she flipped her cellphone open. She had just finished talking to their corporate lawyer about starting up a real estate and construction company. The lawyer knew that the parties involved were trying to wash dirty money. That's why they hired him. He was an expert on finding loopholes in the system. The money was right, so he ignored the risks he was taking. He felt he'd been doing it long that he was untouchable.

After all the questions Stacks sent her were answered she made her way out of the office building only to find her car missing. She never paid any attention to the no-parking zone when she first arrived. But now that her car was gone it now had her undivided attention. She thought they only towed cars from business areas in the big cities not in North Carolina, let alone Greensboro.

She dialed Monica's number and waited for her to pick up. Instead the voicemail came on. She hung up and tried Stacks, but ended up with the same results. "Damn, am I the only one available to handle business?"

She started to call Misty, but quickly ruled that out. A thought crossed her mind. A smile appeared on her face as she dialed the next set of numbers.

"Yeah?" Piko asked into the phone.

"Oh hey. This Cassie."

"What's up?"

"Look, these mothafuckas done towed my car and I need a ride over there to get my shit. Can you come and get me? And before you ask, I called everyone before callin' you."

"Everyone but Uber or Lyft."

"So I guess that means no?'

"Nah, I'm just fuckin' witcha. Where you at?"

"Friendly Shopping Center."

"That ain't tellin' me much."

"The Costcall Law firm."

"Aight give me like thirty-five minutes."

"Okay."

"These mothafuckas ain't shit. Talkin' bout I gotta wait til' tomorrow before I can get my car," she said getting back in Piko's car.

"That's how they get their paper. If you want I can go in there and make them give you your shit,' he offered putting on the macho act he was known for.

"Nah, I think I made a big enough scene already I ain't tryin' to get locked up. But thanks anyways."

"Ok. So where you need to go now?"

"Can you drop me off at my house? I stay in Jamestown."

"Oh, you fancy huh? Business must be good, good?"

"A little somethin'. But shit you can't talk. You and Stacks been doin' ya'll thing since what 2-12?"

Piko looked at her nervously. "Who told you that?"

"Boy, who doesn't know. But I did use to see ya'll all the time coming through dressed all fly."

"When was this?"

"You really don't remember me do you?"

"Hells nah. You do look familiar tho."

"Cassie Brown? We were in science class together at Dudley."

'Cassie Brown, Cassie Brown," he mumbled to himself. He looked over at her and it hit him. "Ohhh shit! I remember you now. You use to wear all that weave in your head and was skinny as hell. They use to call you Sticks."

"Please, don't remind me," she smiled trying to mask her embarrassment.

"Damn, why you ain't been said nothin'?"

"Come on now. You talkin' like that would've made a difference. Turn right here," she said pointing him in the direction to go to get to her house. "Park right here."

"Shit you never know. But you know how shit be. I haven't ran into too many people I went to school with tha I still fuck with anyways."

"You know ain't nothin' like them Dudley Panthers."

"Right right," he agreed grinning like a cat that just ate a canary. It felt good being around someone from his younger and somewhat innocent days.

"What's crazy is Monica's my best friend and she went to Smith."

"Oh, hells nah. You know we don't fuck with them Eagles. Ah man, I'm a have to get on my boy about that one."

"You serious about that school rivalry shit huh?"

"Hells yea! I mean not like I was back in the day when we were actually ready to throw hands for steppin' on our school grounds, but I'll sure as hell talk my shit to them," he mentioned making them both laugh.

"You trying to come up for a little bit or does your little girlfriend got you on a leash?"

"Nah, P his own man. Plus, I ain't got nothin' goin' on tonight anyways."

"Then come on," she said getting out of the car. "When you get this tho?" she asked referring to the aqua green Tesla.

"Shit, about a week or two ago. It was time for me to step my game up," he answered hitting the alarm button.

"And that you did playa."

They made their way to her building where Cassie pulled out a plastic entry card. Swiping the card thru the panel the door opened. She had to do the same thing at the elevator. And again to get to her floor which was at the top.

Cassie could feel Piko's eyes staring at her, so she glanced his way. "What's up?" she smiled.

"I still can't believe it's you," he laughed.

"Yea, it's me."

"Mothafuckas use to be scared to talk to you."

"For real? Why tho?"

"'Cause you were from Cali and heard your brother was a Blood or some shit. Niggas started actin' like he was Stacey from The Wood."

"Are you serious?" she asked not wanting to believe her brother's affiliation is what kept guys from showing interest in her.

"Dead ass. Stacks was the only one didn't give a fuck the only thing stopped him from hollerin' was the height difference."

"Yea he was pretty short even back then. But my brother wasn't on no bullshit like that. Don't get me wrong he'd set it off for baby sis, but not because someone tried to talk to me," she said stepping off the elevator as the doors opened to her floor. She stopped at her door to wipe her card again before punching in a code.

"Damn, talk about security," he mentioned referring to all the swiping needed to be done just to get to your apartment.

"That's why I like this place," she responded walking into her condo. "Make yourself at home," she said taking her coat off.

"Hmm."

"Hmm, what?"

"You ain't skinny no more," Piko commented looking at Cassie's tight frame that had filled out over the years. Her ass was firm but plump in her metallic Louboutin jeans. Her c-cups sat firmly in a black dress short sleeved dress shirt. The top two buttons were undone giving a slight hint of cleavage. Her hair was cut in a short asymmetrical bob. Her skin glowed naturally due to the fact that she didn't wear makeup. It was like he was seeing her for the first time.

"I was only fifteen how was I supposed to look?" she inquired rolling her eyes.

"I'm sayin' if I knew you'd turn out like this I wouldn't have given a fuck what they said about your brother."

"They say hindsight is twenty-twenty."

"Fuck hindsight I'm seein' shit clear as day right now, he said getting excited.

"Whatever happened to Iris?"

"We parted ways," his voiced dropped at the mention of his first love.

"What?! Ya'll were together longer than married people," she mentioned taking his jacket and hanging it on her coat rack.

"I guess nothin' lasts forever," Piko said walking deeper into the condo. He began scoping out her living room. It was decorated with an L-shaped black leather couch. The lamps, end tables, and coffee table, which held an African wood sculpture on top of it, all had the matching black color to them. The walls had different black artwork hanging on them. The thick beige rug silenced all noise. If this was his grandma's house she'd have him take his shoes off.

"Aye no shoes on the rug my guy."

"I'm diggin' the little set up. Next time I need a decorator I know who to hit up," he said making his way around the room before stopping in front of Cassie. Looking into her eyes he took a step closer leaving little space between them. "What's up?"

"What?" Cassie whispered anticipating Piko's next move.

Piko put his arm around her back and pulled her close. He bent his head brushing his lips across hers then down her jaw.

"What about Misty?" she asked leaning back.

"You seemed to be worried about everyone except Cassie."

"Aren't you? I mean, I don't want anything to come back and bite me in the ass."

"Are you really or are you just nervous?" he asked not trying to hear all the sentimental talk. He knew Cassie didn't care about Misty or anyone else for that matter. Monica was probably the only exception.

She gave no rebuttal letting him know what he already did. He covered her mouth with his as he slowly unbuttoned the top of her jeans. Sliding the zipper down he eased his hand into her panties and felt the neatly trimmed pubic hairs on top of her pelvis. His long fingers slithered down to the hood of her clit

195

causing her to groan loudly. Her legs spread to give him easier access.

Piko let out a low chuckle as he leaned back to look at Cassie's face. Her eyes were still closed and mouth gaped open not realizing he had stopped.

"What's so funny?" she asked opening her eyes.

"You don't seem too worried about Misty now," he replied working her middle again.

"D-don't make me feel so guilty," she stated moving her hips to intensify his touch.

"If this makes you feel guilty, wait 'til I'm done."

"Where's he at?" she repeated the question she was just asked over the phone. "He should be at home, why?"

"You said you were close to the top, which Piko is, but we have yet to see any results. And you not knowing exactly where he is shows that you're not on top of your job as you proclaim."

"I've been gathering the necessary information, but lately all he seems to talk about is his ex. What good is that? I'm getting close to finding out who their connect is, but you have to give me time."

"It's been long enough. Either give us something or face the consequences."

"Don't worry bout a thing. I got Piko wrapped around my finger he not going anywhere," she stated confidently.

Piko respected Cassie's request to use a condom. He didn't want to, but it was either that or the blue balls. He knelt on her Queen size bed and began rubbing the tip of his dick between the seam of her pussy lips. He knew it was gonna be a tight squeeze and wanted to make sure he was well lubricated.

Easing a couple inches into her she let out a loud groan. He decided to take his time, but Cassie demanded more. Pushing forward until he was all the way inside he stood still to allow her to adjust to his size. Gripping her hips he began to rotate his in a circular motion as he moved in and out of her.

"Ah yessss, Piko, that's it. Nice and slow," she breathed digging her nails into his shoulders.

Piko, despite having on a rubber, could feel the snug fit of Cassie's pussy as he kept his pace up. His stomach muscles tightened with each down stroke. In and out he went. The tingly feeling that shimmered up his shaft was indescribable. He continued with his long strokes with perfect precision. In and out, round and round. His nuts slapping against her butt. Looking down he saw her biting her lip in ecstasy. The movement of her breasts matching each thrust caused him to take one of her nipples into his mouth.

"Ohhh baby. Baby, let me, let me get on top," she said between breaths.

Piko stopped what he was doing to roll onto his back never pulling out of Cassie. The slow rhythm continued as she rotated her hula hoop hips with each descent. He had to grip her ass just to keep up with her moves. She leaned forward and began picking up her pace. Her nails dug into him as she popped up and down on his dick. "Oh shit," he groaned as he felt himself about to cum.

"Cum for me daddy. Do it for me," Cassie screamed as her own orgasm began to surface. "Yea, yea ,yea," she kept yelling as rode harder causing the bedsprings to squeak louder. She lifted up and scraped her nails down his body.

'Damn, this bitch tryin' to scar me,' he thought to himself as the sting of sweat landed on his wounds. His thoughts were drowned out by Cassie's climax.

Misty hung up her phone wondering why Piko wasn't answering. She knew it wasn't too late in the night for him not to answer. Especially when he usually stayed up until at least three in the morning. She sat back on her couch and remembered that this is where they had sex at. It was business at first until it got too good for her then it became personal. Her mind drifted to how she ended up in this predicament in the first place.

She used to go from state to state doing a few illegal hustles. Hustles she got away with for a long time. That was until she landed in North Carolina. She wasn't known as Misty then, but Agent Danyel Smith. She met Monica about five years ago doing what they did best. Boost. They admired each other's moves and soon bonded. Monica later introduced her to Cassie, and they became like the Three Amigos slash Power Puff Girls. She kept her identity to herself so not wanting to become recognized. Which was more than likely to happen being how fast news travelled on the streets.

Some would wonder being a cop, why would she even attempt to do anything illegal. The answer is, because she wasn't always on the right side of the law. She came to NC to clean her act up. When she saw that the city of Greensboro was in dire need of recruits she joined. She made her way through the ranks and eventually becoming a detective. But as the saying goes, 'You can take the man out the hood but not the hood out the man." In her case, woman. She was an avid criminal and needed the money. No matter how understaffed the department was they didn't compensate a soul for joining them. she felt that with a badge she could now literally get away with murder. It worked for a while until she ran into a sting, she knew nothing about, involving one of her customers. She tried to finesse her way out of it, but her words fell on deaf ears. If it wasn't for the fact that her boss had a thing for her she'd be in jail. She was asked to resign or be brought up on charges. Not knowing what else to do she suggested that she go undercover to bust those who were involved in the same thing she had just got caught for. They accepted the offer under strict conditions. She had a certain amount of time to bring someone in or the deal was off.

That's how it began and the reason she put the idea in Monica's ear. It was some grimy shit, but this was her career. Plus, she was use to hurting people and ruining friendships. She didn't really care for either. Things got interesting when Piko and Stacks were mentioned. She was told that if she could bring them in she'd not only get full recognition, but a possible promotion.

The power of the pussy got Piko's life story out of him and all that he knew about Stacks. Which was next to nothing. Outside of how they became best friends, got into the game, there wasn't much else to tell. It let her know two things. That Piko didn't know Stacks like he thought he did and was smarter than he appeared. He had Piko actually believing that he was bigger than him when in fact it was the other way around. For things to work in her favor she was going to have to push him to start asking questions or stay in the blind.

"Girl, you got me lookin' like I got into a fight with a tiger," Piko said running a finger over the welts that had formed from Cassie's scratches.

"I'm sorry," she replied running her own finger over the scratches. "I couldn't help myself. You were just…"

"You don't have to explain yourself."

"Yea, but how you gonna explain it?" she asked really not caring. 'Wait until Misty see it. She gonna know I fucked him, because that's my trademark right there and she knew it.' She thought to herself while hiding her smile.

"Tell me somethin'?"

"What's that?"

Piko thought for a second before speaking. He wanted to make sure his words came out right. "What all Stacks got you doin'?"

"Well, according to Monica, he's trying to create businesses to wash his money through. That way he can make a clear exit out the game before the FEDS come knocking."

"That's understandable, but we've been fuckin' wit this shit for almost ten years. Now all of a sudden he wanna go straight? That shit's crazy. Plus, how many businesses he need to clean his money bro paper ain't that long."

Cassie didn't say a word. She just listened to Piko go on and on. The more he talked the more she began to admire Stacks. He stuck the old saying, 'Never let your right hand know what your left hand is doing.' And Piko sure as hell didn't know what Stacks was doing. She began to wonder if his coming on to her was his way of trying to pick her brain about what she knew. If that was the case, he almost had her. Yet, if him and Stacks were as tight as the streets say they were and he didn't know what his boy was up to. Then he wasn't meant to know. And she wasn't going to be the one to help him fill in the blanks. Everything happens for a reason and Stacks obviously had his.

"Let's not worry too much about Stacks. Just keep handling your business and everything'll be ok."

Piko glanced at Cassie and realized that his initial plan wasn't going to work. He guess she wasn't as vulnerable as he thought. Stacks always told him that when a person was loyal to you they'd go to the end of the world to protect you and what you believed in. Now he was witnessing it firsthand. "Yea, you're right, I gotta tighten up. If my boy's tryin' to get out, so should I."

"Exactly."

CHAPTER 29

Stacks loaded the last box onto the back of the moving van he rented. He just came from Monica's apartment to get her things. His was the final stop before heading to his new home. He was taking a major step in his life with Monica. The only woman he had ever lived was his mother. Yet, he felt he needed to take this next step. It would force him to think for more than himself.

Stacks wanted out the game and he began buy using his construction company to build three houses. One in Jamestown for his mother, who, until she saw the blueprint, refused to move of the house she'd been in for over ten years. The other in Brown Summit that he gave to his sister as a birthday gift. All either had to do was pay the utilities and property taxes. The third home was for him and Monica. A five bedroom seven bath mini mansion that sat on ten acres in Sedalia. It was something like out of the magazine Home & Garden.

This was a new beginning, so it was only right that everything else be new too. Alaskan King size beds. Egyptian style living room set. Ten foot white glassed with gold trimmed dining table. Stainless steel two door smart refrigerator. The matching range style stove held two ovens. Marble countertops. Pearl his and her sinks with gold plated faucets. A jacuzzi sized tub sat adjacent to the two man shower stall. The only thing that had Stacks touch was his mancave.

At first Monica wanted to know why they needed so much space. Stacks gave her two reasons. One, was to account for the necessary money spent and two, was he planned on filling the rooms up. He knew a good three quarters of a mil was spent on making this dream home a reality.

"Ayo, can you grab somethin', and don't and not just stand there?" Stacks asked from the side of the van.

Monica stood on the porch eating a pickle. "It's only a bunch of boxes of clothes and little appliances."

"Well, you can grab the boxes with the little shit in it," he stated trying not to get upset.

"It might upset the baby," she smiled while rubbing her three month forming stomach.

"Yo bruh, she straight carrying you. Keisha would've never thought to try that with me," Kinko joked at Stacks.

Lately Stacks started keeping Kinko close to him. He wanted to keep an eye on him so he wouldn't get in something that would cost him his life. Plus, he was showing him the ropes so they could expand to other cities.

"Yea that baby not stopping her from tryin' to fuck me to death every night."

"Word. They say they get hornier when they pregnant."

""Ya'll need to stop it," she said walking back into the apartment to the sounds of their laughter.

"Bruh, I'm for real about what we talked about," Stacks said turning to Kinko.

"What's that?"

"Expandin'."

"Oh yea. Yea, I'm wit all that. All you gotta do is tell me where and I'll have things jumpin' like it is here."

"It won't be long," he said walking into the house where Monica was putting food in boxes while trying not to eat anything in the process.

"You already done the change of address?" he asked.

"Been did that. This should be your last day receiving mail here," she responded handing him a manilla envelope that had Maine as its origin.

Stacks threw the envelope in a box with other miscellaneous things and sealed it up. "I'll open it once we get settled at our new spot. Probably just a bunch of brochures anyway trying to sell get aways."

"I wouldn't mind getting away," Monica piped up.

"Maybe next year. A trip now might put too much stress on the baby," he stated trying to keep a straight face.

"Aaaaa-haa," Kinko yelled.

"Fuck ya'll," she said but couldn't help but laugh herself.

CHAPTER 30

Piko was ready to put all the bullshit behind him and step his game up. Stacks was making major moves and he was just sitting on the sideline letting it get by him. At the same time, he felt that their bond was starting to fade away. No matter what that would always be his friend. They had too much history to just part ways, but the distance would inevitably grow if they weren't headed in the same direction.

Swallowing his pride Piko picked up the phone and dialed Stacks number. He hoped he hadn't gotten too new and changed his number like everything else. He didn't even know where he moved to. The only time he saw him was when he went by his job. He breathed easy when the phone began to ring.

"Bruh what up?" Stacks answered.

Piko was glad that he was in a good mood. "Maintainin'". What's good wit you??"

"Just tryin' to enjoy life."

"I hear that. Ayo, remember you told me you'd help me start up my own company?"

"Yea, that was like four, five months ago."

"I know. I just had to get my mind right."

"Yea, I'm on my grown man shit bro. All that street savvy shit isn't me anymore. I'm tryin' to be a mogul by thirty so I can sit back on my Hawaiian Sophie shit." He stated in reference to one of his favorite rappers first song.

"I know that's right," Piko laughed along with him.

"So, what's up? You ready to step up and get your grown man on?"

"What you got in mind?" Piko asked feeling like he did when Stacks first introduced him to the drug game.

"It's gonna cost you seventy-five."

"I thought you said fifty?'

"I did. But that was then. Nothing stays the same so you can't always hesitate when opportunity starts knockin'. Now, I can come up with the other twenty-five, but I'm tryin' to make this all you."

"Nah, the doe ain't a problem. I'm just making sure. But what kinda business costs that much to start up anyways?"

"A truckin' company."

"Man, I ain't drivin' no semis."

'I ain't talkin' bout you. You get the rigs and hire some drivers to drive them. All you need is the logistics and bid on some loads."

"Oh, I see what you're sayin'. And there's money in that?" he asked not knowing a thing about truck driving let alone logistics.

"Is there?! you'd be surprised. Just get with Cassie and Monica and they'll get your paperwork done and squared away with the lawyer. Once that's done you'll be off to the races in no time."

"Where do you fit in all of this?"

"Nowhere. You my brother. I want for my brother what I want for myself. So I fit in by helpin' you level up."

"Aight I got you. I'm a handle that first thing tomorrow."

"Bet. Don't hesitate to hit me if anything goes wrong.

Piko hung up and leaned back in his chair. He ran a hand over his face as if the decision he just made was a difficult one. Stacks said it was some grown man shit and he, no matter their differences, trusted Stacks. They were throwing rocks at the penitentiary every time they step foot in the streets. Every day that went by was a day they had to look over their shoulders. The jack boys, the killers, and the police. That was too stressful. Stress that money could never mask. And to top it off they still hadn't found out who the rat was amongst them.

CHAPTER 31

Cassie knew she was a speed demon. She couldn't help it. It was in her. Some thought all she had was a heavy foot, but she knew better. That's why her BMW was equipped with a V-10 engine and twin turbos. She didn't mind paying extra to get what she wanted. One thing she didn't want though was the ticket she was holding in her hand as she made her way to the magistrate office. She tried to get there before it closed thinking wouldn't anyone be in line. How wrong she was. "Shit," she mumbled looking at the five people in front of her.

Once she paid her ticket she made her way out so she could get to work. Despite running the club, he rand Monica were still employed at the bank. Stacks convinced her to stay in the light that there might be some opportunities that present themselves. Out the corner of her eye she caught a glance of a female that looked like Misty walking with an older white guy. Dressed in a brown pant suit matching pumps and toting a briefcase had her resembling a lawyer or detective. Cassie shook her head thinking how that couldn't have been Misty. She wouldn't be caught without some type of designer on. She felt she was tripping and decided she just might have to give up the bank job. All this ripping and running was starting to get to her.

Piko and Stacks had spent all day in the small office building Cassie had acquired for Stacks. They were going over business strategies for Piko's newly formed trucking company. Getting contracts. Doing logistics. They already had rigs and were interviewing drivers. It wasn't until around ten-thirty when they switched topics.

"Bruh. When's the last time you've been to the club?" Piko asked.

"Haven't had the time."

"Damn. I thought you were on some grown man shit, not old man shit."

"Man, you wouldn't believe what I've been through in the last year."

"I can imagine."

"All you're getting is a snapshot. I'm shift manager at Belk right…"

"And I don't understand why you're still there."

"I gotta have balance until everything's secure. Plus, I'm locked in the with the store manager."

"Say word?"

"Word. And she a white lady."

"Damn. Better be careful with that you don't want some fatal attraction shit to jump off."

"I know right? But I'm bout to dead all that soon as my business clears enough for me to quit."

"Out of all the chicks I've been with I've never had a white girl."

"And from what I'm hearin' you won't be getting' one either the way Misty all up under your ass."

"Man, you know me better than that. Ain't nobody locked me down since Iris."

Stacks fell silent at the mention of Piko's ex. He knew it was a hard subject to talk about. He'd never admit it, but he loved Iris more than anything. He just got caught up in the groupie bitches who flocked to guys with money. And Piko didn't mind letting it be known he had it.

"Oh yea, I didn't tell you Monica's pregnant did I?"

"Word? Hells nah you didn't tell me. So you just upped, moved, and became the family man huh?"

"Not really. I just had to do things different. You stay in the same place you're basically puttin' a target on you're back. That's what I be tryin' to tell you. We suppose to be doing this to get out the hood not dwell in it. Them boys out here hungry just like we were when we started and will erase the respect you earned for a come up."

"I can dig it, but I'm good for now. But there'll come a time when I will need a change of scenery. So you're gonna be a daddy huh, that's what's up. You know what you're havin'?"

"Nah, but knowing me after this I'll probably want another," Stacks said standing up and stretching. "So you cool with the business structure?"

"Yeah it sounds good so far."

"You just gonna have to learn how to balance your books so that any money you wash won't be detected if ever you're audited."

"I should catch on. Or I'll just get Cassie to help me out."

"I know the office ain't that big bug you can alter it how you want to. Set up your dispatcher right there," he stated pointing to a space that was in sight of the office. "You have enough space on the lot to hold a few rigs which is really all that matters."

"Yea. I'm ready to get the ball rollin'."

"Just find some workers and you'll be on your way in no time. But look I gotta get goin'" Stacks said looking at the time. "Don't want Mo' thinkin' I done slid off. Pregnant women be thinkin' nobody wants them."

"And there you were tellin' me I need to make a baby."

"Yea, so you'd slow down. Done fucked around and jinxed myself," he chuckled. "But it's all good. I'm a get wit you tomorrow and put everything in motion."

"Aight bruh, be safe."

"You too."

Stacks thought about Piko as he walked out of the building. He was still his man, but he didn't tell him everything he knew or had going on. He didn't want to doubt him, but things weren't the same. Information had been revealed to him that caused his trust level to drop drastically. That also made him begin to distance himself from people. Piko included.

Pulling onto the highway his phone rang. He was hesitant to answer being that he didn't recognize the number. The only thing that stood out was the 407 area code. "Yo?"

" I guess you don't have faith in my work anymore."

"Who's this?"

The speaker ignored the question as he continued talking. "I send you the information you asked for, but you have yet to take care of the problem. That doesn't look good for business. And that makes people nervous. And Tony, you don't want people to be nervous."

"Justus?"

"I guess you had to hear it from me personally to understand huh? And here it was I thought you liked women,"

Justus joked in his thick Hungarian accent. "Seriously, why are you playing with this threat to your organization?"

"I'm not understandin' what you're sayin'"

"Did you not receive the package?"

"What package?"

"A manilla envelope with a Maine address."

"I've been in the process of movin'. Probably in one if the boxes."

"Then you need to find it and handle *your* problem before it becomes *our* problem. We like you Stacks, we all do. Please don't waste the resources available to you," Justus said then hung up.

Stacks switched to the left lane and sped to his house. He didn't even let the garage door close before he was out the SUV and inside his home. They still had a few boxes that they hadn't unpacked yet. He tried to calm down so not to wake Monica up. He went through the various boxes until he came to the right one. Seeing the envelope Justus spoke about his heart began to beat faster. Here was. The answer to the main worries he was having. The link to his paranoia. He picked the envelope up and headed to the kitchen. The weight of the package let him know that it contained a lot of information.

Stacks fixed a sandwich and took a seat at the counter before opening the envelope. The first thing that caught his eye was the small picture attached to the papers. He had to look twice to make sure his eyes weren't deceiving him. His heart skipped a beat thinking he was looking at the future mother of his child, but it was her friend Misty. Either way it didn't make him feel any better as he began to read the documents.

Operation: Hybrid

Agent Danyel Smith: UC name Misty Jones
Age:29
Height:5'2"
Weight:120ibs
Eyes: Hazel
Hair: Black
Race: Black

Agent's assignment is to bring down major credit card and boosting ring, while in the process of infiltrating an organization headed by one Jakeem Fuller a.k.a Piko and his associate Tony Knight a.k.a. Stacks. This operation was launched June 5,2021.

Stacks placed the papers down along with the uneaten portion of his sandwich. His appetite was gone. The mention of his name caused his blood pressure to rise. This was the main reason he didn't trust females past sex. He wondered if Monica knew about this. The mere thought made him question everything. Was this part of her plan? Was she in on it too? Was that even his baby? He couldn't believe he let his guard down. He rarely trusted anyone, family included. Now he knew what Justus meant. This couldn't be taken laying down. Something was going to be done about it and tonight.

CHAPTER 32

Kinko didn't mind looking up to Stacks. Dude was solid all around the board. Even though he had his own responsibilities he still had a lot of living to do. He figured that he had much more to learn even though he experienced more than the average nineteen year old has. He did know that he wasn't ready to be like Stacks and jump from one hustle to the next. The streets were too far embedded in him to make that type of transition. At least not right now. The hood was his office, and his gun was his conference phone. He loved the street life and it'd be awhile before he retired.

It was nothing to roll deep to the club with his crew. Plus, ever since he got shot, he kept his people around him. It didn't matter where they went he wasn't going to get caught slipping again.

They walked into The Treasure Club looking and feeling like a million bucks. Kinko having smoked some moonrocks was high, but able to maintain. The fitted cap was pulled low over his stocking capped covered hair. His black Xerxes shades hid his bloodshot red eyes as he strolled through the crowd and headed to his favorite table. He wasn't dressed in the most expensive brand of clothing, yet was still fly.

He wasn't no dummy. He knew the game was to stack, save, and invest. That's what he did week to week. Extra money got blown at the mall or the club. He ordered two bottles of Patrón to start with. Pulling out a stack of money he summoned some of the dancer who already knew that it was about to be a good night for them when Kinko and crew were in the building.

Stacks took a swig from the bottle of D'usse. He sucked in air as the spirits entered his system and tried to take his breath away. His one hand tightly gripped the neck of the bottle. In the other was his rubber grip Ruger 9. He leaned forward in his chair as he sat beside the bed watching the rise and fall of Monica's chest as she slept without a care in the world. The pregnancy gave her a glow that could never be mimicked. He took in her beautiful face that was partially covered with a wisp of hair. He started to move it out the way to get one last look at her, but left it alone. Tears began to well up in his eyes as he thought about what he had to do. This was the first time that he was really happy. He was ready to embrace the family life, but now it seemed it would remain a dream. As a tear ran down his cheek it paused at the corner of his mouth. He stuck his tongue out to taste the salty liquid before putting the bottle down. He reached out to cut the lamp on so that he could see her face clearly.

Monica's eyes flickered open only to be looking down the hole of Stacks' gun.

Kinko's demeanor changed when he saw some of Piko's crew enter the club. Even though Stacks and Piko put an end to their little spat, he still didn't like them and knew it wouldn't take much to set him off. "Ayo, look at them clowns over there thinkin' they hot shit."

"Who that?" his boy Jevon asked.

"You already know."

"Oh, word. Ain't that Chevel?"

"Yup. He took over Bokeem's position."

"I can't front tho. Dude do be about his business."

"I don't give a fuck what he about. Ain't none of 'em got shit on us," Kinko stated ready to turn his anger towards Jevon. "What, you rockin' wit them niggas or somethin'?"

"Nah, but the streets talk and that's what it's sayin'."

"Oh, so you a groupie now? Gossiping like these hoes out here? Fuck outta here. I don't give a fuck about them niggas."

"Man, calm down. It ain't even that serious."

"The hell it ain't."

"What's up K, you know I'm strapped. I owe them niggas anyway," Jamel said rubbing his bullet wound through his shirt.

"Nah, be easy. We ain't even on that type of time tonight. But I'm a show you how to son a nigga," he said getting one of the bottle ladies attention. He whispered in her ear and pointed in Chevel's direction.

"What you tell her to do?" Talon asked with a grin knowing Kinko could be real petty at times. It was funny to them but not to whoever he had his sight set on. And being

"Just watch my nigga, you bout to see," Kinko replied smiling as he sat back to see Chevel and his crew's reaction.

Two minutes passed before a topless dancer made her way to Chevel's table with a bottle of Patrón in her hand.

"When I tell ya'll to, raise your glasses up at them niggas," Kinko said.

The dancer stood in front of Chevel and put the bottle down before straddling his lap. She began her routine grind before saying what she was asked to.

Kinko watched the scene play out as Chevel began to say something back. "Get ready," he said as he watched Chevel's face frown in confusion before looking in their direction. "Now."

"Boy, you crazy as hell," Talon laughed.

"Nah, I'm a boss."

"Yo, they better not come over here talkin' reckless," Jevon made known as he saw Chevel stand up and head over their way.

"Oh, so you on our side again?" Kinko sarcastically asked.

"Man, don't do that."

"I just did. And you better know whose side your on because I'm bout to shut this bitch down," he stated getting up t meet Chevel and his boys.

"Yo, what's that shit about?" Chevel asked menacingly.

"What, I can't show my respect?" Kinko responded not the least bit intimidated.

"Nah, you tryin' to be funny."

"Nah, I'm just showin' love my guy."

"You talkin' like you a boss or some shit. Out here playing with Monopoly money. We the bread and butter out here."

"Is that right?"

"Yea, you know it. So you might wanna save your money just in case you run out of gas on your way home."

"Man this play money," he said going into his pocket. "In fact here, hold that, *money*," he added throwing the knot in Chevel's face.

"Mothafucka I'll…" Chevel started to say but was caught in mid-sentence by a jaw breaking blow from Talon.

The two groups went at it until the gun shot rang out.

Monica thought that she was dreaming. She shook her head hoping it would jar her awake. But this wasn't a dream. What she was experiencing was real. She felt like Frankie in Set It Off when they asked her, "What's the procedure when you're being robbed." Monica froze up just like countless of people have. She couldn't move or speak. She took her eyes only to look in Stacks' face. Seeing the tears in his eyes she knew that whatever had happened to make him point his gun at her had to be serious. The only thing was that she didn't know what it could be. She hadn't done anything to make him react in such a manner.

"You got something you want to tell me?" he asked through clenched teeth. He tried to blink back the tears that were blurring his vision as he wiped his snotty nose. "Huh?"

"I-I-I don't know what you're talking about," she answered honestly as the words dragged out of her mouth. She was too scared to talk not knowing what might set him off and cause him to pull the trigger.

"You don't huh?" he asked not convinced. He threw the contents of the envelope at her. "Tell me what I'm lookin' at."

Monica cut her eyes at Stacks in short intervals as she gathered up the paperwork. Her face was one of confusion as she read the profile. "I don't believe this," she whispered in utter shock.

"Believe it. And you've known her how long?"

She thought for a while racking her brain to the time of their first encounter. "About five years or so. We met while seeing each other boosting out of the same store. And it says she's supposed to bringing down a boosting ring? Is she the one your people were talking about?"

"Obviously so. And you're telling me you knew nothing about this?" he asked, still not sure about the whole situation.

"How could I? You've read it yourself. She started on me and Cassie. Even suggested the credit card and forgery thing. I guess as soon as she found out I was messing with you she added it to her file." Monica said talking a mile a minute trying to convince Stacks of her innocence.

"Mo', please do not lie to me. Not now," he emphasized tightening the grip on his gun.

"Baby, I'm not. Why would I? I'm as knee deep in tis shit as you are. You think I'd jeopardize my life like that?" she pleaded on the verge of shedding her own tears.

"I don't know what to think anymore. All this shit is crazy."

"I'm about to have your baby. There's nothing I would do to hurt you. You have to believe me.

Her reminding him of the seed growing in her stomach was probably the only thing that was saving her. He lowered his gun to his side then lifted the bottle to his lips to take a much needed swig. "I can't believe this shit. How did I let this happen," he said still in disbelief.

Monica was more at ease now that she wasn't staring death in its eyes. She eased off the bed and hugged Stacks to her stomach for a split second before pushing him back and slapping him hard across the face. "Don't you ever point a gun at me again. That's the second time you've done that, won't be a third," she stated pulling his head back to her before he could react. "Now, what we need to do is fix this problem before it gets any further out of hand."

"Do you think Cassie knows about this?" he asked trying to forget that she just hit him.

"I doubt it. She doesn't really like Misty, or Danyel. She always felt that something wasn't right about her."

"And she was right. You should've listened to her."

"Yea, I should've."

"So you know what has to be done right?"

"What?" she asked pulling back to look him in the eyes. She didn't want to misconstrue anything he had to say.

"You and Cassie gotta take care of Misty. And this isn't up for debate," he made known before getting up and walking out the room.

Monica had seen Stacks in action yet had never experienced him show her any ill treatment. But the way he walked off gave her a glimpse at what might happen if he felt that the hundred percent loyalty she vowed to him started to lower.

Kinko was true to his word and shut the club down. He also knew that Talon would be right by his side letting his pole go. What he didn't know was that one of Chevel's people had made a call for more of their crew to show up at the club. People were screaming, running, and ducking as the bullets flew through the air. Kinko was big on the saying that "It was the man in the fight but the fight in the man that made the difference." So when he saw Chevel's back up doing more running than anything he wasn't surprised. What did surprise him was the chopper Jevon pulled out of his trunk and unloaded on the car hiding Chevel's people.

The sounds of police sirens caused the shooting to cease. Cars were jumped in before speeding off. It was crazy how people didn't care about shooting someone for something as simple as stepping on their shoes, but ran from those who wanted to put you away for the rest of your life. None of this mattered to Kinko. All he thought about was how he had to end this before it got out of hand. That meant taking out Piko's workers.

CHAPTER 33

It wasn't until a week later. Monday to be exact, after hiring three drivers, that Piko got the call from Chevel about the confrontation at the club. He let him know that he wasn't like Bokeem. He wasn't going to backdown from Kinko. He was only telling Piko out of respect, but nothing could be said to change his mind.

Piko understood where he was coming from. The whole ordeal was beginning to become a thorn in his side. He still thought about it and told Chevel to call him back in about an hour before he did anything. Stacks was still his brother and needed to talk to him in hopes of preventing an all out war.

He walked in his home and threw his keys on the kitchen counter along with the mail. He grabbed a Corona out of the refrigerator and took a sip before flippin' through the mail. Everything was addressed to Iris being that he has no way to prove his income. He couldn't wait for his company to take off. He hoped to have all three of his trucks on the road in the next couple of weeks so he can have some clean income rolling in. That was another reason to keep things at bay with Stacks. He needed his help with the process of cleaning his money.

He continued looking through the envelopes until an unmarked one caught his eye. Opening it he immediately recognized the handwriting. He knew he had to take a seat before he attempted to read the letter.

I know you're wondering exactly who this is sending you an anonymous letter. Maybe not, but I felt it was the only way you'd get to hear what I have to say. It's been six or so months since we last seen each other. One of the hardest things I've had to do in my life. I told you that I had to get away in order for me to clear my head and decide where I wanted to be. Jakeem, I love you and always will, but the pain and hurt you've put me through has been unbearable, yet I've forgiven you for every indiscretion you've done against me. All I've ever wanted and needed was you. The fact that I wasn't for you I'll never understand. All those times I was lonely, and I needed you to be there. To tell me I had nothing to worry about. That you would protect me from whatever demons I was facing, you were nowhere to be found. I left because I was tired of pretending that the neglect and constant cheating didn't affect me. The hole you left needed to be filled. And in my most down and vulnerable state someone filled it. I could have easily told you this to your face, but I couldn't tell you that in that time I became pregnant.

Piko read the rest of the letter in disbelief. He no longer wanted to read another word. He never thought that with all his sleeping around that his childhood love would let anyone else enter her let alone get her pregnant. He was now inflamed with emotions wanting to know who violated his lady's womb. His thoughts were interrupted by the ringing of his phone. "What!"

"Damn yo. You tell me to hit you back and you scream on me? What type of a shit you on?" Chevel questioned.

"Yo, I ain't even in the mood right now. Do what the fuck you wanna do," he said ending the call. He cut his cellphone off so that he couldn't be interrupted again. Cuing up a song on his stereo he went in the kitchen to grab the bottle of Everclear off the top of the cabinet. He was ready to drown out his sorrows.

Dropping down onto his lay-z boy at the same time the song began to play. "Sorry didn't notice you there/ but then again you didn't notice me…" Piko sung the words to Beauty off key along with Sisqó. He felt he was too much of a man to shed a tear, but on the inside he was crying his heart out.

CHAPTER 34

"Why the fuck this nigga not answering his phone?" Stacks wondered out loud with frustration. He was trying to give Piko a heads up on what was going on. On how they were under investigation.

Monica sat at their kitchen table nervously tapping her foot. Stacks had given her a week to figure out how to handle the situation. Today was the last day and she was scared to death. It wasn't the part of killing someone but having to do it intentionally. Any other time it was more of a survival thing, but the ultimatum Stacks had given her left no room for negotiation.

"You talk to Cassie yet?" Stacks asked.

"Yea. She said she think she saw Misty downtown talking to the DA."

"When was this?"

"A couple days before you showed me that information."

"What the fuck was she doing downtown?" he questioned feeling another twinge of anxiety hit him. He couldn't take all this stress coming his way.

"She was paying for a speeding ticket. Not everyone is out to get you Stacks."

"Yea, aight. Better not be," he stated as some of the tension eased off. "Look. Take my car, go pick up Misty then Cassie. Take a ride to the next county or somewhere and do what you have to do."

All Monica could do was nod her head in agreement. She was too afraid to speak. What was there to say when someone so easily spoke about death as easily as fixing a sandwich?

"Where Kinko at?" Chevel asked walking up to the group of people sitting on the bench in Douglas Park. He wasn't alone. He had a shooter on each side of him.

"Who wants to know?" one of the workers questioned. He was one of the replacements of the four who were relocated after the shootout with Bokeem's brother.

"Don't worry bout who, just tell me where he at."

"He ain't here," he answered now gaining the attention of the other workers stationed throughout the park. They were told to be on the lookout for anyone that seemed suspect.

"Aight then," he responded looking at the guys beside him. " I got a message for him."

"Well, say that shit and bounce nigga 'cause we trying to get this bread and you ain't doing nothin' but holdin' us up ya dig?"

"Oh yea?" Chevel grilled the slick talker. "Tell him paybacks a bitch," he said pulling his gun out along with his boys.

The slick talker's mouth gaped open and eyes got big. He wish he could have been more on point instead of being arrogant with his approach. If he had been listening to Kinko they wouldn't have been so close together and such an easy target. But that was an afterthought as bullets riddled their bodies and left them splayed out on the concrete while their pockets got ran through.

Chevel didn't know how many blocks he'd have to run up on before he found Kinko. It didn't matter for he was on a mission and had no plans to stop until he accomplished it. Either that or someone stopped him first. Little did he know that nobody had a clue to his whereabouts. Nobody but Stacks, who had sent him to Tennessee to set up shop and get out of Greensboro for a while.

Cassie walked out of her condo after hearing the honking horn for the fifty-eleventh time. She didn't like that Misty was riding shotgun or why they were in Stacks' SUV. She could see them talking, about what was beyond her. When Monica told her about the information they came across she let her know about what she thought she saw when she was paying for her speeding ticket. She didn't know what she had in mind when she said she was coming to pick her up. She was even more curious when she was asked to bring her gun.

"What's up?" Cassie greeted them as she eased into the back of the car.

"You," Monica replied.

"What's up *Misty*?" she asked with an attitude hoping to provoke her so she could say what she really felt.

"Nothing much. What's up with you?"

"Damn Mo', you done got all lazy and shit since you got pregnant. You can still come to work the fuck."

"Why'd you stop anyways?" Misty asked.

"Because my baby doesn't want me to be on my feet putting any stress on *our* baby. But look who's talking. Besides the jobs we go on we don't even know where you work." Monica mentioned not letting on to knowing exactly what she did for a living.

"Yea, she like Tommy off Martin," Cassie joked.

"Ya'll know how I get mine."

"We most definitely do," Monica stated with a sneaky grin.

"Where you got us going anyway Mo'?" Misty asked.

"We haven't been out together in a while, so I figured we'd have some girl time. Plus, I needed to get out the house."

"So, where we going?" Misty asked again.

"Damn ho, just relax and enjoy the ride. You'll see when we get there. Ungrateful ass," Cassie said sarcastically.

"Cassie don't start. She just wants to know. Shit I would to. You know most people have to be prepped to go certain places."

"Right. Damn, what I do to you for you to be coming at me like that anyways?"

"Don't even worry about it Misty. It's this new spot I've been hearing about that I wanna check out."

"Ok. I'm wit it. And you must be staying with Stacks because every time I go by your house you're never home."

Monica quickly cut her eyes to the rearview mirror to see Cassie's face. Misty was only confirming how she been watching them because she never tried to come by her place uninvited before.

"Yea, I spend the majority of my time with Stacks. Who wouldn't want to stay up under someone catering to their every need? I don't know why you popping up at my spot anyway. You know we don't do that. Must be bored. What's wrong your man treating you like every other he's been with? Or has he found someone else?"

Cassie chuckled knowing that that's exactly what it was. He was the one who had gotten her car out of the pound and copped her a Dolce & Gabbana, which she happened to put on to spite Misty.

"What you laughing at?" she asked turning in her seat to get a better look at Cassie.

"Oh nothing. And I do mean *nothing*," she said rolling her eyes at Misty.

"What, you still mad you ain't got him?"

"Nah boo, I don't want him. All he's good for is a few *accessories*," she emphasized by brushing off her shoulders and holding her hand out to look at her nails. She was hoping Misty caught on to her gesture.

"If you trying to say something then do it don't beat around the bush."

"Unlike you, I don't kiss and tell."

"Whatever. You's a silly ho," she said turning back around.

"Ya'll need to quit.," Monica said. Nobody paid attention when she turned down a dirt road and parked. "This shit has got to stop. Everything!"

"Where we at? Thought we were checking out a new spot?" Misty inquired.

"And we are. I just pulled over so we can settle all tis bullshit that's been going on," she stated cutting the are off.

"What you talking about?"

"You know what I'm talking about," she said reaching for the door where the .380 Stacks had given her to use. "We were supposed to be girls. All three of us, but you've been playing us all along," Monica stated as the emotions began to well up making her fight back tears.

Misty wasn't sure what Monica was talking about, but her gut was telling her that her cover was blown. Yet, she didn't flinch or break. She didn't want to jump to conclusions and expose herself. She saw the tear starting to form in the corners of Monica's eyes and understood that whatever it was she was talking about had to be serious. Because, from what she observed, she was the master at masking her emotions.

"Tell me what you're talking about, because I'm like real confused right now," she said glancing at Cassie hoping to read something in her expression, but nothing was there. Now it all made sense. How Monica, who'd been MIA all of sudden wanted to get up and demanded she sit upfront knowing she never offered that seat before, ever. That slight hesitation cost her as she felt the hard steel slam against her face causing a deep gash to form on her cheek.

"You police ass bitch!" Monica screamed after hitting her with the gun. She didn't give her a chance to recover as she pointed the gun at her. She wasn't sure if she had some special training for situations like this and wasn't trying to find out.

"What?!" Cassie asked in disbelief. She thought that Misty might've been working with the police but not an actual cop. Her own anger overcame her as she pulled the .38 out of her purse and aimed it at Misty's head. And even though she never shot anyone before, she knew that they were all in and there was no turning back.

Monica had forgot about Cassie being there for a second until her sudden outburst. "Yea, she's been working undercover. Was setting us up, but that wasn't enough. She caught whiff of Piko and Stacks and decided to go after them as well. But the dumb bitch didn't do her research. She thought Piko was the top dog that's why she been all up under him," she said. Then she thought about what Stacks had said the day he found out about Misty. She then pointed her gun at Cassie.

"Mo' what the fuck?"

"Did you know about her?"

"What?! You know damn well I didn't. As much as I don't like this bitch?"

"Then prove it."

"What you mean prove it?" she asked with an attitude not feeling how Monica was coming at her .

"Shoot her."

"Huh?"

"Please Cassie, don't make me do something I don't want to," she said as tears began to slide down her cheek. The predicament she was in was causing all of her emotions to rush out at one time. She was in self-preservation mode. She didn't want to kill her best friend, but her back was against the wall with only one way to get it off.

Cassie knew that Monica was on the verge of becoming hysterical and didn't want to be on the receiving end of that type of outbreak. Cassie's hand began to shake as she pressed the barrel to Misty's head.

"No wait!"

Those were that last words out of Misty's mouth before her brains were blown against the window.

"Again."

"She's dead Mo'."

"You have to make sure. Now shoot her again."

Cassie complied knocking more bone fragments from Misty's head.

"Good. Now we get rid of the evidence."

It wasn't long before Chevel found out that Kinko wasn't even in town, but not before almost losing his life. Some weren't as easy to run down on as those in the Dust Bowl. Still he felt that he made a big enough statement that would reach him as soon as he returned.

"Grab those bags out the back," Monica instructed Cassie motioning to the plastic covered clothes. After getting everything out oof the car she walked towards Cassie. "Give me your gun. I'll get rid of it for you."

Cassie wasn't in the right state of mind to resist as she handed over her gun. She watched as Monica wiped it down and put it in a shopping bag. Even though she was doing as Monica asked she was still in shock over killing someone.

Monica began to strip down to her underwear and had Cassie do the same. They put on the clothes that were in the plastic bag and threw their discarded ones into the back of the SUV.

Dousing the car with two cans of gasoline making sure a majority of it covered Misty's body, Monica set the car on fire. She waited until she walked a ways down the road before calling Stacks to come pick them up.

Cassie looked at Monica and wondered how she was able to turn her feelings off and on the way that she did. She realized that Monica had shed tears at the thought of possibly having to kill her best friend, but was back to her normal self after killing Misty. They were both put in a life or death situation and were forced to do what was in their best interest. She just hoped that she wasn't put in anymore of these types of predicaments. What she didn't know was that this wasn't even the tip of the iceberg. Things were about to turn up in Greensboro and her loyalty would be tested again.

CHAPTER 35

"Detective Lawrence, I need to see you in my office," Captain Scott requested.

"What is it cap?"

The homicide captain walked back behind his desk and threw a three inch thick file on top of it before sitting down. "Have a seat," he said then waited for Lawrence to comply. "What do you know about two individuals going by the name Piko and Stacks?"

"Hmm. Haven't heard those names in a while. They dibbled and dabbed in the drug game but nothing major from what I've heard. Why what's up?"

"This is what's up," he said pushing the file towards him.

"What am I looking at?" Lawrence asked before opening the folder. He sat it on his crossed legs and began scanning the pages.

"Remember I told you awhile back about an operation going on and how we weren't to get involved?"

"Yea, what about it?" he asked looking at his captain so that he caught everything he had to say.

"Well, that's it right there."

"Oh, *now* they need our help?"

"Not really. Their inside man, or should I say *woman*, was found dead in a burned up SUV. All they had to identify her with was her teeth.

"So now homicide is involved?"

"Exactly."

"Do they have any suspects?"

"Not to my knowledge. She was undercover. Supposedly investigating a credit card fraud and boosting ring. But also was gaining info on the two I mentioned."

"Hold up. You said credit card fraud and *boosting*?"

"Yea."

"Ok, how does that tie in with two guys who dealt in drugs?"

"Well, she was giving weekly reports, which didn't seem much as you'll see when you finish reading. But according to some of the reports she was close to this Piko guy who's been running this big drug operation along with his partner Stacks. But there's nothing in there on Stacks. No birth name, place of residence, nothing. It's like he doesn't exist. She was using Piko to get to Stacks.

"The old Coffee Syndrome."

"The what?"

"Coffee Syndrome. It's what I call a person who sleeps with the enemy in hopes of getting information out of them. "*Coffee*" is a Blaxploitation movie starring Pam Grier, but you wouldn't know nothing about that," he joked.

"Whatever."

"So, basically they feel that she was killed due to her investigation?"

"Right, and without her they lose all leads. They were about to close the case but remembered you were working on something that probably can help them connect the missing dots."

"You mean that murder in Claremont?"

"You'll have to get all the details from them."

What's that supposed to mean?"

'They wanted to meet with you in about," Scott pushed his sleeve back to look at his watch. "An hour. That's if you'll do it."

Detective Lawrence thought it through for a minute before making his decision. "After I solve this case and bring these two in, I want a promotion," he stated standing up with the file under his arm.

"I'll see what can be done. Just take care of this first and show them why you're the best in our department.

"Don't worry about that. Just start that paperwork," he mentioned walking out of the office. He had an hour to prepare for his meeting. He began smiling happy to know that he was needed in such a major way.

"Detective, it's good to meet you. I'm Agent Munrow and this is Agent Gaffney," Agent Munrow greeted extending his hand to give the detective a shake. "You come highly recommended by your department and was hoping you could help us."

"What is this all about?" he asked not giving any clues as to what he already knew. He didn't want to give up anything without first knowing all that they knew.

"I take it you've read the file and have been briefed on the situation or you wouldn't be here. Basically we want the people responsible for what happened to our agent."

"That's not a problem."

"Don't play with us. This is a serious matter," Agent Gaffney spoke up looking like Jesse "The Body " Ventura.

"Who says I'm playing? See there are avenues and elements that you failed to cover or looked over."

"What is that?"

"Eleven months is a long enough time to have gathered at least some type of information enough to warrant an indictment for at least one of the targets. Letting me know that the lady leading this operation was either misleading you or never had anyone in the first place."

"I see why you'd say that, but we can't let this go because our agent lacked the proper tactic for this task."

"I understand full of your concerns, but I was just pointing out the difference between her and I."

"Ok I see. So you'll help us?"

"With a few stipulations, yes."

"Like?" agent Munrow asked.

"I want full cooperation from your department. Meaning don't get in my way in any shape, form, or fashion."

"That's not a problem," Agent Gaffney said repeating Lawrence's earlier remark causing them all to laugh a little.

"Alright," Lawrence shook his head in acceptance. "I need to have a look at the crime scene as well as any evidence collected."

"I'll drive you myself. By the time we get back all you need should be available."

"Thank you, but like I said. I don't want any interference. I'll follow you to the location with my own team and we'll take it from there."

"If that's how you want it."

"That's exactly how I want it," he said getting up to let them know his business with them was complete. He was now focused on the case.

CHAPTER 36

Chevel wasn't no dummy. He knew that word would get back to Kinko about all the havoc he was causing to his crew. That was the point. He had to draw him out somehow. He figured to get the best results was to go at the head and watch the body drop. He was about to make a risky move but felt it necessary in order to get the results he was looking for.

He had been following Eve around town for about a week in hopes of being led to Stacks and eventually Kinko. When she pulled up to the train station he thought it was to pick Kinko up and made a call for some shooters to pull up asap.

Eve sat in her Denali that was a birthday gift from Stacks. She took his advice and started putting her money towards something she enjoyed. Stacks helped her open an art gallery. 'Consider it a loan,' is what he said when he gave her the money. She displayed a lot of the area's local talent as well as her own. She also did some freelance work here and there. She loved her brother to death and understood what he was doing when he sent someone to make a purchase from her. That or hire her to do job. He wanted to give her money but wanted her to earn it. At the same time, it drew people to her. The inquiries became so frequent that she became a small success in little to no time. It helped her get over the fact that her child's father had pulled a disappearing act on her twelve years ago leaving her financially distraught. She looked at her watch to make sure she wasn't late.

She was at the train station to pick up a man she hadn't seen a while.

"Yo, who the fuck is that? You said she was pickin' up Kinko," one of the guys Chevel had called demanded over the phone. He was parked off to the side with another shooter. These little episodes were getting out of hand. Instead of getting to the money they were out here acting like they were in Cali going through turf wars.

"I thought it would be him too. But look this what we gonna do," Chevel said then explained his newly derived plan.

"Damn boy you done got fat," Eve said hugging Devante.

"Everybody keeps saying that. I'm the big brother dammit, how I look being smaller than ya'll?" he joked.

"Whatever. And why you take the train instead of damn plane? Got me waiting out here all day."

"Knowing you, you just pulled up not too long ago. Talking bout all damn day. And you know I don't travel light," he mentioned lifting up the small duffel bag.

"Uh-uh. Tell me that's not what I think it is."

"Why not? You know why I left. Ain't no way I'ma let these niggas think they gonna get famous off me."

"Well, you staying at mama's house 'cause you not bringing nothing like that around my baby," she said getting in the car.

"What?! Are you crazy? Mothafuckas might try to get at you just because of me. And I know wit Tony, niggas hatin' even more. So if you don't have anything in your house to send a nigga away from here, you better get something," he stated after getting in the car.

"It doesn't matter what's in my house, you still staying at mamas," she made known pulling out of the parking lot.

"Why? You got a man living with you now? Don't want me hearing ya'll fuckin'?" Devante joked.

"Ha ha very funny Earthshake."

"Damn, you ain't gotta keep talkin' bout my weight. Shit at least wait 'til after I fuck this Thanksgiving food."

"Listen to you. Don't let me catch you on My Hundred Pound Life."

"Man, I like to eat but hells nah. Why do women like watching that show is something I'll never understand. But I do miss that home cooked food. Especially aunty's pies. Damn I can't wait."

"Damn, you got *me* hungry now."

"I know that's right. Stop at Wendy's right quick then."

"Ok," she said taking the next highway exit.

"Get me two four for fours and super size my size to a larges."

Eve looked over at Devante and let out a laugh while shaking her head.

"Whaat?" he asked innocently.

"Nothing. Nothing at all," she answered then placed their order.

When they pulled up to the window to collect their food , Devante leaned down between his legs and pulled two Glock 17s out of his duffel bag, loaded, and cocked them.

"what are you doing?" Eve questioned nervously.

"What I say? Because of me and Tony mothafuckas might try to get at you? It's either that or you done gave the wrong mothafucka some pussy," he said trying to make light of the situation.

"That's not telling me shit. What the fuck is going on?" she asked hysterically.

"There's been two cars following us since we've left the depot. Now they're behind us looking like they're bout to get out. So what you'll do is when I get out is head towards the highway and wait on the side by the exit."

"What you gonna do?"

"Just do as I say," he said looking back and forth between the side and rearview mirrors. As soon as a couple guys exited their car he went into action.

When Devante opened the door Eve pulled off almost catching his foot. He didn't let it slow him down as he began shooting at their pursuers, who were caught off guard by his actions. He was focused and determined. He wasn't aiming to hit but to buy time. You'd think that a person his size couldn't move as fast as he did, but he'd been toting his weight around along time so moving it was never a problem. He easily took off through the parking lot and headed towards the highway exit where Eve was waiting like he asked.

"What the fuck you waiting on? Go before the cops come," he gasped trying to catch his breath.

Eve didn't know who was worse, Devante or Tony. At least she never seen Tony do any dirt nor was his name in the streets like that. Devante might've left town, but those who remember him still bring his name up from time to time. If they heard he was back, what just took place was only a taste of what he was capable of. Like he said, they knew why he left, and how he did it wasn't a pretty sight. She figured that no matter how criminal minded her family was they always supported and loved one another whole heartedly. So dealing with their street life is what came with being a Knight.

"Ay, where's my food at? I'm hungry for real now," Devante mentioned rummaging through the Wendy's bag.

No matter how serious the situation was Eve couldn't help but laugh as she drove down the highway to their mother's house.

CHAPTER 37

Piko locked his office's building door then made his way to his car. Before he could get in his Tahoe he was swarmed by police cars. The gas began to build up in his stomach and seeped out silently.

"Put your hands up!" one of the officers yelled as he stepped out of his vehicle with his gun drawn.

"What's this all about officers?" Piko asked hands raised clearly above his head.

"You'll find out as soon as you get downtown," the officer answered placing the cuffs on him and putting him in the back of the squad car.

Piko felt his world come crumbling down. All the dirt he ever did was coming back to retrieve its debt.

Piko was sitting in a conference room leaning over the long table with his head in his hands. The door opened and in stepped a man in plain clothes. Piko looked at the tan khakis with extra starch creases in them. The brown belt that held them up. The rose colored dress shirt was tucked inside, but open at the top revealing a black turtleneck. He thought how he hadn't seen one of those in a while. The low cut and brown face that looked at him was that as someone who was the same age as him. Might even had went to school together. But that was irrelevant. They were on two different sides of the law. Led two separate lives. Their circles would never intermingle, therefore they could never be more than what they were. Good guy, bad guy.

"Mr. Fuller, or should I say Piko," Detective Lawrence quoted before taking a seat across from him. He was sipping coffee out of a white GPD mug. "I'm Detective Lawrence. Can I get you anything? Coffee? Cigarette?" he asked trying to use the kind tactic. He knew who was sitting in front of him and wasn't trying to drop the ball. He didn't tell his captain all that he knew about Piko and Stacks. Why would he? They held back from him he was just returning the favor. Plus all the information he knew was gathered from his own observation and conversations with people who dealt with them. If he hadn't straightened up he'd probably be knee deep in the streets himself.

"How 'bout my lawyer?" Piko knew that this request was supposed to put an end to all questioning. His brother had made sure he understood this if nothing else.

"Yea, I thought you'd say that. It's the most expected response, but what you're facing right now is more than you'd expect."

"I still want my lawyer."

"Okay, but let me run something by you. In fact let me tell you what you're actually facing and then you tell me if you rather talk to me or your lawyer."

Piko thought about it for a second figuring if anything he'd come out on top by picking Lawrence's brain. He'd just use it to his advantage if they really had something on him. "I'm listening."

"Let me start off with what *I* know and go from there. You probably thinking that this is something that just all of sudden happened. But it isn't. At least not in my book. You have a partner named Stacks, who you've been friends with what twelve, thirteen years now?"

Piko eyed Lawrence suspiciously wondering what was his reason for mentioning Stacks name.

"Don't look surprised. I know all about you two and how ya'll entered the drug game. For some reason your name has been ringing bells while no one is even mentioning anything about Stacks. Now this could mean one or two things. Either you're the head honcho between you two or it's him. Playing the puppet master where he's letting you shine and draw all the attention to you so when shit hits the fan it's you that takes the fall. Is that what's going on?"

"Let me stop you right there. You asked me to give you a chance to speak about what's goin' on concerning me and you have yet to do that. Then you insult me by assuming that I sell drugs. Then you mention some guy named Stacks that I've never heard of. I don't know what kinda game this is but I'm not trying to play it. So either charge me, get my lawyer, or let me go."

"Alright. I see how you want to do this. Well take a look at this and tell me how you want to proceed," he said pushing the FBI file towards him.

Piko leaned forward and pulled the file closer to him. The first thing he saw upon opening it was a picture of Misty a.k.a Danyel Smith. Along with numerous pictures of them together. He quickly read through the file then sat back letting out a deep sigh.

"I take it from your reaction that you knew nothing about this. And more than likely you two had some intimate encounters. And that intimacy kept her from doing her job. I gotta give it to you, you made sure she didn't have much to tell."

"Have you ever thought that there was nothin' to tell?"

"Maybe you're right. Maybe there isn't anything to tell. Or maybe that's what you want people to think. But that s been you guys forte. Discretion. That's how you've survived so long. But you're not fooling anyone. See, I was the one everybody ignored in school. The one that did shit to impress mothafuckas like you and Stacks. But I was also the one who paid attention to everything that was going on around me. So don't act like I don't know what I'm talking about. See, your Federal lover there was found dead on the outskirts of the city. She was shot twice in the head at point blank range while sitting in the passenger seat of a SUV that was set on fire. They say the way her body was positioned was as if she was facing the driver."

"And you're telling me this, because?"

"Because this particular vehicle is registered to one Jakeem Fuller."

CHAPTER 38

When Kinko walked into his home in Woodlea Lakes he heard the soft murmurs of his girl consoling their son. He'd been gone for close to a week and had experienced firsthand what it felt like to be homesick. The euphoria that swept over him was indescribable. He carried the two large suitcases passed the living room into their bedroom where he placed them on the bed. He walked back towards the bathroom where Keisha was on her knees giving their son Tey'von a bath. He looked at her round ass raised in the air as she bent over the edge of the tub. He grabbed his dick through his pants and licked his lips realizing how much he missed his lady.

"Dada," Tey'von yelled as soon as he saw Kinko standing in the doorway.

"Boy be still. Your daddy won't be home until next week. I can't wait either, 'cause you starting to get on my nerves."

"Damn, he's been that bad?" he asked walking into the bathroom.

"Oh my god! You scared me!" she exclaimed placing her hand over her heart. She stood up to give him a hug. "When you get back?"

"Not too long ago," Kinko pulled her tight while she held his face in her soapy hands while giving him a passionate kiss. He snaked his tongue in her mouth and gripped her soft ass in both of his hands. They both began to moan as he began to get hard.

"Dada," Tey'von broke up their intense greeting with his arms in the air.

"Ok, ok lil man I got you," Kinko said wiping his mouth, then bending down to pluck his son out of the water. He gave him a kiss on the cheek and lifted him high into the air. "What you been up to? Driving your mama crazy?" he joked and smiled knowing he wouldn't get no more than a toothless smile as a response.

"Yea, that's exactly what he's been doing."

"Well daddy's home and I'ma take care of both my babies," he said reaching out to rub on Keisha's breast.

"Boy stop, not in front of the baby."

"Shit, this my lil man. I ain't got nothin' to hide from him. That's what's wrong wit family's today. Always tryin' to keep shit from people. He gonna find out one way or another, and I rather it be from me."

"But he's only a baby K."

"And babies store all that info too. Look, I'ma raise my son like he's supposed to be raised and if I can't teach him what he's supposed to know about life then he won't learn it."

"Men, always trying to prove a point," Keisha said rolling her eyes.

"But you love thus man. Look there's two suitcases on the bed. Don't mess with the one on the left. Can you unpack the other one for me, I got this in here."

"Oh really? Just turn me into a Molly Maid huh?"

"Can you just do it please," he said then knelt down to put Tey'von back in the water. Upon doing so he caught a whiff of himself and thought how he needed to get in the water himself. He added more water to the tub and began to strip out of his clothes. "Yo, Keish you might as well come get these clothes too."

"Look, I understand you just got back, but this is not the Jeffersons, and my name is not Florence. And you couldn't wait to wash your ass? That boy needs to be in the bed," she said snatching bis clothes off the floor.

"Huh? It's only six o'clock you trippin'."

"Am I? Who's clothes is in them bags?"

Kinko laughed, knowing that that's where her attitude stemmed from. She was the most jealous stricken female he ever dealt with, but he wouldn't give her up for the world. "What clothes?" he asked deciding to mess with her.

"You don't know? What you mean you don't know? You know if…"

"Girl shut up, you know damn well them shits yours."

Keisha ran out of the room like a kid on Christmas. She was wondering who the numerous items belonged to when she unzipped the suitcase and saw the plastic bags on top of Kinko's neatly dirty folded ones. She never understood why he did that. Taking the Russian Sable out of its plastic covering she placed it on and began modeling it in front of the closet door mirror.

Kinko cut the water off after rinsing the bath water from him and Tey'von's bodies. Drying them both off he walked into the bedroom with two towels. One wrapped around his waist and the other around Tey'von. Keisha was finished playing super model and put away her clothes as well as Kinko's dirty clothes.

"Here," he said handing Tey'von to Keisha so she could get him ready for bed.

He was still in his towel pulling stacks of money out of the other suitcase. "Help me count this."

"How much do you think it is?" she asked pulling the bundles of money out of the bag.

"Shit, I don't know. I stopped counting after I got rid of the second joint. I was only expecting to make a hundred at the most, but I made that so fast. Can you believe them dudes paying fourteen a zone? I don't know where that ten a ki shit came from because it sure as hell isn't in Tennessee. I just need to count out Stacks cut, and the rest is ours to invest."

"When you gonna stop doing this?"

"Come on Keish, don't start this shit. I just got back, let me enjoy myself while I can. Plus, Me and Stacks been speaking on that already. So we have to find a business to start up by April."

"Are you serious?"

"Very. Let me hit up Stacks get him his money and get back to my baby."

"He's sleep."

"I'm talking bout you punk. And there's something in the side pocket for you too," he said before walking away.

CHAPTER 39

"What?! I don't have *any* car in my name. My credit won't even get me a Honda Accord."

"Well, records show differently."

"Wait, what kind of car you said it was?"

" An Infiniti QX80," Lawrence answered looking at his investigation notes.

"Champagne colored?"

Lawrence looked again at the notes. "Yup. Thought you didn't know anything about it?"

"I don't. Doesn't mean I don't recognize the cars that roam the city."

"So if it isn't yours, who's is it?"

"Yo, where the Infiniti at?" Kinko asked sliding into the passenger seat of Stacks' Jaguar.

"Long story."

Kinko handed Stacks the bag of money and waited for him to examine its contents. "That's sixty-five right there."

"So I'm taking it you did pretty good over there."

"What? That spot is a gold mine. The only reason I came back was 'cause I ran out of work."

"Yeah?"

"Straight up. But I can't lie, I was missing my son somethin' serious," Kinko mentioned as he felt his phone vibrate. "That's wifey tight there. Probably found my gift," he said answering the phone to a bunch of screaming. "Yo, what's the matter?" he smiled he went back and forth with Keisha about what was found.

"What's that all about?" Stacks asked when Kinko hung up.

" I left a ring and note asking her to marry me."

"Word up? That's what's up."

"Thanks. So what's good? Something not right? Your whole vibe is fucked up right now."

Stacks was only five years older than Kinko, but still regarded him as a much younger person. "My brother is back in town."

"Who Devante?"

"Yea, Devante."

"Ah, man. What the fuck happened?"

"He not on that type of time. We getting together for Thanksgiving. He only here now because I told him shit had died down and we had everything under control. But after my sister picked him up they were followed, and he ended up laying three niggas down. Now everyone's pointing at me wantin' to know how I'm a handle the situation."

"Do you know who it is?"

Stacks stared at Kinko for what seemed like an eternity. No more words needed to be exchanged as the understanding came across clearly.

Kinko leaned back in the plush seat and let out a deep sigh of frustration. "You got a blunt in here?"

"Nah."

"This shit is fuckin' crazy. This is what I was tryin' to tell you a while ago. You should've just let me take these mothafuckas out. So now they like some fuckin' roaches that you can't get rid of," he ranted pulling out a pack of Newports. "But don't even worry bout it big bruh I'm a handle it."

"What you gonna do?"

"Right now? Go home, get some time in with my wife then kiss my son goodbye."

"Whoa, whoa. What you mean goodbye?"

"I'm playing for keeps this time bruh. I'm not stopping til all of them are gone. And you ain't gonna be able to talk me out of if this time."

"Whatever you do leave Piko out of it. He knows better than to try my family like that his hands are clean."

"Well you better make sure he stays out of my way," Kinko made known as he opened the car door.

"I love you lil' bruh just be safe."

"I just want you to promise me something."

"Anything."

"If something happens to me , make sure Keisha and Tey'von are taken care of."

"Say no more," Stacks promised as Kinko closed the car door. He hated for either of them to be in this type of situation, but that's the consequences of the street life.

"So, what does all this mean?" Piko inquired.

"As you can see, nobody actually knows who Stacks is. But I do. I don't know his actual name, but that face is very familiar. Yet with murder of a government official lingering over your head..."

"I have to give you Stacks to make it all go away? Nah I ain't no rat. I rather die first."

"Oh, that's not a problem. Shit, I doubt you even make it to trial. Knowing you killed one of their own, the guards might not like having to look at you. They could find you hanging in your cell. Or you can help yourself because it seems like that's what your man did. Everything is pointing at you. I wonder why that is? So what I'm a do is walk out of here to give you some time to think about it then hopefully when I get back we can work towards putting this matter behind us," Detective Lawrence stated then got up and headed but not stopping to add more to his interrogation. "Oh, one more thing. There's been a lot of killings going on lately that the streets are tying to you. So if this murder doesn't stick we always have the RICO to fall back on. Either way," he said leaving the unspoken words to linger so Piko could let his own imagination wonder about what he was facing.

Kinko steered down Randleman Rd. on his way home. One hand on the wheel while he scrolling through his phone for the proper number to call.

"K, that you?" Talon picked up on the fifth ring.

"Who else would it be?"

"Yo, where the fuck you been? Niggas thought you got bagged."

"More like getting' to the bag. But I'll hold court in the street before I let 'em put me in a cage. But yo, we got some shit to handle."

"I take it you heard about what's been goin' on?"

"Yea, that's what we gotta handle. I want all the heavy hittas to meet me at the spot around two," he said looking at his watch. It gave him about four to five hours to spend with his family.

"Aight."

"And Talon. Nothing but choppers. This shit ends tonight," he made known before hanging up. He pulled up to his house and leaned back in his seat to take a moment to get himself together before getting out and heading inside.

As soon as he walked through the bedroom door Keisha jumped on him and showered him with kisses. As they undressed Kinko had to stop her from getting on her knees. He shook his head letting her know that it wasn't about him this time. He cut the radio on to let the late night slow jams play. Lifting her up and laying her on the bed he made slow love to his future wife. He figured if anything happened to him tonight he might can leave his son a sibling.

Piko couldn't figure out how it came to this. From the day he got in the game it never crossed his mind that his right hand man would set him up to take the fall for anything if shit hit the fan. All his own little misdeeds had come full circle. The days he used to get over on Stacks thinking he was none the wiser. He thought that since he never spoke on it he didn't notice. Stacks was always trying to guide him down new roads and avenues, but he ignored him. He chose the streets over his brother. The fast illegal life over a possible legitimate one. He was still living in an apartment that was in his exes name who had left him. Not only left him, but got pregnant while away from him. On the other hand Stacks had accumulated a house, property, and businesses. Yea, he turned him on to a lucrative business, but what good was that when you're facing capital murder and the RICO. He felt betrayed. It didn't matter what he'd done, you weren't supposed to do it to him.

Kinko stared at Keisha's sleeping form. She was stretched out with her new engagement ring in full view. He scanned the room not knowing if it'd be the last time seeing it. He got up and walked into the baby's room. As he stared down at the face of his son, he thought about how innocent he looked. Not knowing what was going on around him. What his father did on a daily basis to provide for him and keep his family safe. His mother passed when he was ten years old. That was the last time he shed a tear. Thoughts of him not being able to be there for his son caused the flood gates to open. They were tears of pain, hurt, anguish, and of heavy burden. For if he didn't do what he set out to then all the work he put in would be for naught. He bent down and kissed his son then headed for the garage.

In the garage he slid a false wall to the side to reveal a slew of weapons. He pulled down his newly acquired bulletproof riot vest, a Draco, and two Rugers. He put those along with a few extended clips in a duffle bag then slid the wall back. He walked over to his midnight blue Porche 911 Carrera GTS that Stacks got him for an early Christmas present. He wasn't supposed to drive it until then, but there might not be a then. These were his thought as he got behind the wheel placing the bag in the passenger seat.

As he pulled out of the garage and drove to meet his boys, he felt like the Ghost Rider, who sold his soul to the devil and was being called on to fulfill his request.

Chapter 40

"Yo, this shit is getting' old as fuck," Stacks said while laying on Monica's lap. They were on the couch watching the evening news.

"What's that?" Monica inquired rubbing on Stacks' chest.

"All this shit," he answered looking at the tv screen as it showed the latest crimes around the Triad. "I'm tired of the streets. The shooting, backstabbin', lies, and deceit. You can't even turn a dollar without havin' to kill a mothafucka."

"Well you don't have to be in them anymore."

"Easier said than done. You don't even know how deep I'm in these streets. And not that block hustlin' shit either."

"I know what you're saying."

"Even if I wanted to I couldn't get out. The things I've done," he said shaking his head.

"Like what?" she asked but was cut off by the ringing of his phone.

"Yea."

"What's going on?"

"Before you even start that shit was a coincidence. It had nothing to do with you. They were more than likely trying to get at me through Eve."

"That's beside the point. How we gonna handle this?"

'You still at mama's?"

"Yea, why?"

"Tomorrow's Thanksgiving. That's what you came down here for, so that's all you need to worry about. That turkey and Aunty's pies."

"Nigga, who the fuck you think you talkin' to?! This shit ain't no goddamn game! I'm the one who got this town like it is! I gave ya'll these streets! So don't try to handle me like some lame! Now somebody tried to get at my family so this needs to be handled," he stated aggressively.

"We should be leavin' around eight, nine-thirty. You can ride wit Mo', sis, and me. It doesn't matter. Just be ready to pull out around quarter to eight," Stacks said calmly. He didn't raise his voice because he understood the situation and had no reason to argue about it.

"Bro. Did you not hear what the fuck I said?!" Devante yelled into the phone.

"I run this shit now bruh. So when I say we leavin' tomorrow it's for a reason. You think I'm a let a mothafucka disrespect my family? If you do, you got me fucked up. Everything's bein' taken care of. So I'll see you tomorrow."

"That's all I wanna know. You know I love you right?" he said trying to salvage his sudden outburst.

"Yea, me too. Now take your fat ass to sleep so I can spend some time with my wife."

"Aight baby boy," Devante said laughing then hung up.

"Wife? Where that come from?" Monica asked with one eyebrow raised.

"What you mean? We've been together for over a year now. You about to have my baby *and* live together. If that ain't close to being husband and wife I don't know what is."

Monica smiled and wiggled her fingers in front of his face.

"You don't need a ring to be my wife," he stated then watched her face frown up. He never understood the sentimental value of something so simple as a piece of jewelry. You could buy a female a million rings, but they meant nothing once you presented them with that one that was linked to the title of wife. He didn't understand it nor if he was ready for all of the extra that came with it.

CHAPTER 41

"I guess you're getting a divorce," Detective Lawrence stated after being summoned back into the interrogation room.

"What you mean by that?"

"Well, you know how you guys like to say that you're married to the streets. Wasn't it Jay-Z said, 'The only life of mine/is a life of crime'? that does kinda hold true huh?" he said sipping on a fresh cup of coffee as he stood looking at Piko with one hand in his pocket. He jiggled the few coins that were in there out of habit. "That is, until shit turns sour and self-preservation kicks in."

"You know what you're asking me to do is damn near impossible. You think that that nigga gonna get caught slippin'? Or let someone set him up? He been preparin' for shit like this from the beginnin'. As you can see."

"Then how you get caught on the ass end of the donkey?"

Piko leaned back and looked at the ceiling as if that's where the answer was. "I wouldn't listen. He always told me to stay ten steps ahead of niggas. I was only one," he said with acceptance to his ignorance.

"Look, I understand I can't ask you to go doing things you wouldn't normally do. That's too obvious. So in hopes that you would help us help you, I thought of everything that needs to be done. I want you to meet somebody," he said then opened the door and motioned for someone to enter.

Piko watched as the person entered the room. He squinted his eyes at the familiar face trying to place where he knew him from.

"I want you to let him use you to get close to Stacks. And while we're getting things in order how about letting me in on all these shootings lately."

By the time they finished letting their guns off they knew that there was nothing else to do. But Kinko wasn't done. They hadn't gotten Chevel and he felt that that was the only way to end things. He told his people to lay low for a couple of weeks before parting ways.

Driving down McConnell Rd. he headed to A&T farm's pond and threw the black duffle bag filled with all but two guns in it. He figured no one would look there as he jumped back in his car and drove down Franklin Blvd. He parked in the gravel beside the NOI temple facing the store beside Legacy Crossing. The name had changed so many times he loss track. When he was a little snotty nose kid it was called Creekbend a.k.a Crackbend. Mr. Kim was the store owner then and would look out for the kids in the neighborhood. It was crazy that he was now dead. Shot in 2001 by a man trying to rob him.

Kinko shook the thought out of his head as he eased out of his car. He left the door open and engine running. He knew that it wouldn't take long. If it did it would be because he himself had taken a bullet.

Cutting through dirt paths, over gates, and yards, he stood in front of the home he'd been looking for. It was the last one on the street. What they called deadman's land, because you had no business being there if you weren't invited.

He checked and cocked the two guns he kept from the earlier shootings before walking up to the front door. He went into his normal regimen that he did whenever he went on missions by himself. Eyes closed, head to the sky, guns by his side as he took in two deep breaths. When the last one was released he opened his eyes in a different zone. He raised the guns to the died of his head as if he were a boxer with their guards up. He bounced from one foot to the other before lifting his right tight laced Tim boot up and kicking the door off its hinges.

Jogging into the front room he was highly alert while bouncing on the balls of his feet. He knew they heard the front door crash open and was probably hiding. He didn't care. The average shooter didn't aim for the head when shooting their gun. Kinko did and knew that that's what it would take to stop him. He eased deeper into the house while an old DMX song played in his head. "X is comin' for ya/can't do nothin' for ya/run hide duck duck/we don't give a..."

"I don't know shit about that. I ain't kill nobody. I know that much," Piko stated.

"But you're worried about the connection to you or would've never said anything about it."

"Be happy you got as much as you did. I need a fuckin' cigarette, can I get that?"

"Sure, *partner*," Lawrence said jokingly while tossing a pack of Newports in his direction.

Piko shook one of the cancer sticks loose and was quickly provided with a light. "Them lil' niggas don't listen to me yo.

Think they in Cali or Chicago somewhere," he began jabbering with smoke coming out of his nose.

"What you talking about?"

Piko kept going ignoring Lawrence's questioning. "You say you use to pay attention to what was goin' on right? Then you should know that niggas didn't get into this because they thought it was cool. It was because they got tired of wearing holey clothes, borrowin' food form neighbors, getting picked on at school. But now. Now you got mothafuckas in the suburbs while getting' block money. Hangin' wit the have nots hopin' to fit in, be known, shit like that. Niggas got the game fucked up."

"So you're admitting to having something to do with the killings?"

"Hells no! I'm just tellin' you how it is. I have no control over the next man. I'm a businessman all that other shit has nothin' to do with me. But what's crazy is how you're standing there all dressed up tryin' to pin this on me."

"I didn't do this to you, you did."

"Yea, yea, so you say. But how many people have to suffer for you to be happy? That's the question," Piko stated letting another stream of smoke escape through his nose as he looked off into the corner of the room.

The first room that he entered was occupied by a child as he saw the small sleeping figure on the twin bunkbed. He didn't understand why someone would leave their child alone knowing there was danger in looming. He figured that they were huddled up in another room hiding. He had to laugh at that thought. 'And they said they gangstas.' He walked over to the bed and knelt down to wake the child up. He was wasting too much time trying to be conservative and the child's presence almost took him out of his zone. He quickly got his composure back. Putting one of the guns in his waist he snatched the girl up by her hair and guided her to the other room.

"Yo, Chevel, I got your baby girl. Don't do nothin' stupid or you already know what it is," he yelled out then tapped the master bedroom door open with his boot. His gun was pointed at the girl's head as he walked into the room. "Cut the light on," he told the girl feeling a draft coming form an open window. As soon as she did he saw Chevel halfway out the window. "Pussy ass nigga," he said baring his teeth before shooting him in the ass.

Kinko let go of the girl and walked over to Chevel to pull him back into the room. "Where you think you're goin'?"

"Ahhh," Chevel yelled after Kinko kicked him the face. All that gangsta toughness was gone.

"Shut up. You weren't hollerin' that bullshit when you were making the city hot lookin' for me. Well, here I go," he said kicking him in the face again. "I'm a show you how it's supposed to be done."

Kinko walked over to the bed where his daughter and lady were huddled together. He snatched his lady by the front of her nightgown. She tried to put up a fight and caused the gown to rip down the middle revealing her breasts. "Damn you got some big ass titties," he commented before grabbing her by the neck. "Fuck over here. Look at this bitch, she a fighter. Remember you did this not me," he said before shooting her in the head.

"No! What the fuck! She had nothing to do with this."

"Mommy!"

Kinko grabbed the screaming girl by her hair as she ran to her dead mother's body. He lifted her in the air as she tried to wiggle free. "Did you think about all the people you killed who had nothin' to do with this? They were just out there tryin' to make some money to feed their family. I don't think so. Everyone becomes involved when in this life."

"No please," Chevel begged as Kinko put the gun to his daughter's head.

Kinko closed his eyes. "Forgive me father, for they know not what they do," he whispered before releasing a bullet into her brain. He didn't hesitate to shoot Chevel as soon as he let go of the girl. He shot him two more times to make sure he was dead. He went through the house to see if he left any evidence. He was ready to leave when he spotted the cellphone on the floor and 911 on the caller id. That's why they were so quiet. They were buying time in hopes that the police would get there in time to save them. The only thing is, the police never rushed to a black neighborhood which is why they had yet to arrive. He quickly ran out of the house and to his awaiting car as he heard the sirens in the distance.

"All I need for you to do is act like everything is normal and let me handle the rest."

"And I need to see that I don't get caught up."

"Trust me. You'll be given total immunity for your cooperation."

"You the fuckin' police. The fuck you mean trust you?" Piko said holding on to what little dignity he had left. "I want everything in black and white wit *your* signature on it or everything you *think* is in your favor will disappear."

"What…"

"Black and white or no deal."

"Ok, ok. Now let's go over our strategy."

Kinko spun out of the graveled parking area and turned left on Franklin Blvd. He easily weaved around the cars that had no business out that early in the morning. He started to turn left on Market St. and speed through the city but changed his mind. That would be too easy. They could put up roadblocks and shoot him to death or catch him and have him rot in jail. Neither was a good idea. Turning right on Old Burlington Rd. he began to accelerate. He saw one police car jump behind him and that's when the chase began. He didn't care how souped up their cars were, he had over five hundred horses under his hood with a top speed of two hundred mph. "Catch me if you can mothafuckas," he said to himself as he switched gears. He looked around for a cd to pop in but could find none. He decided to use his phone.

When his playlist cued up, he began to bob his head at the familiar beat and began to sing the hook. "If I should die, don't cry my niggas/ just ride my nigga/ bust bullets in the sky my niggas/ and when I gone don't mourn my niggas/ get it on my niggas/ Say word to K my niggas." he sung along. His hand and feet worked the gears like he was Tony Stewart or Dale Earnhardt Jr. as he sped down the road. As much as he tried to drown out his thoughts with the music it wasn't working. He knew now that he couldn't go back home to his family. If he could turn back the hands of time he would, but he couldn't.

He reached over to grab his phone. He wanted to hear his lady's voice and speak to his son one last time before it was all over. Grabbing his phone out the cubby hole he noticed that there was a police scanner. "Damn, my nigga must've known I was gonna act a fool in this bitch," he mumbled cutting the radio on.

"10-4, we have the suspect in sight going down Old Burlington Rd. headed into Burlington," the officer came over the radio.

"Burlington police have been notified with plans to box him in."

"Nah baby boy, not today," Kinko said as the trees and houses zoomed by as he sped down the street.

Being he was on a regular street he knew it would begin to narrow and needed to find the best route to take. An unmarked car pulled up beside him ready to slam into him to know him off the road. He never understood this method nor how people ever got caught like this. He had two advantages in his favor. The element of surprise, because they didn't know where he was going or if he even had a destination. Another was that they didn't have the big city budget where the helicopters could follow them.

He became a bit nervous as he was about to do something he'd hate. But when it came to freedom nothing was too big, crazy, or stupid. Going at a high speed he sent his car into a side drift while opening the door. He knew he'd feel every bit of pain he endured from the impact he made with the road as he tumbled and rolled out of the car. This wasn't the movies but real life and in real life it hurt. Hurt bad. But he was driven by the thought of incarceration and a lot of adrenaline pumping through his veins. He bounced to his feet and disappeared into some woods. He moved as if he had on track shoes instead of boots as the low branches scratched at his face. The cold winter morning air cut into his lungs causing hm to start breathing heavily, but he kept pushing on.

After what seemed like miles of woods and hours of running, he came to a clearing behind some apartments. He rested his hands on his knees to catch his breath, but not for long knowing they'd be on his trail. His pants were covered with sticky briars. Boots scuffed up and muddy. Face red from the scratches. He already knew what their next move would be and that was to let the dogs loose.

Jogging through parked cars and around buildings until he came to a wooden fence that separated the complex, he was in from another one. He easily hopped over it and ran between the buildings not knowing where he was going. He did know that he couldn't run forever.

Seeing an elder lady getting into her car he quickly approached, but not so much as to frighten her off. "Ma'am, can you please give me a ride. I'll pay you."

The lady looked at Kinko's rugged appearance from head to toe. Cocking her head to the side as if that would help her comprehend better of what he just asked her. "Are you in some type of trouble young man?"

Kinko watched the lady's movements as she dug her cotton gloved hand into her purse. He saw the crow's feet under her bifocal frames. Her pasty white face was topped with brunette hair that had streaks of gray flowing through it. Her calm demeanor was given away by her shaking hand. "No, I just need a ride home. My car broke down a few miles back."

"Then call an Uber or Lyft."

"No phone. Are you gonna help me or not?" he asked getting frustrated. He saw her hand come out of her purse holding a can of pepper spray.

"If you don't get away from me, I'll mace you and call the police," she said pointing the can in his direction.

"What?! And here I was tryin' to respect my elders," he said pulling his gun out. "I hate you fuckin' Karens," he stated grabbing the mace out of her hand before hitting her with a shoulder shove knocking her to the ground. He ran for thirty feet and started spraying the ground behind him until the can was almost empty. By that time he was at a concrete barrier wall which could only mean one thing. A highway. That's exactly what he needed. He sprayed the remaining mace onto the bottom of his shoes and the gloves he still wore. Throwing the can over the wall and one strong leap he followed suit. He still didn't know where he was and was hoping that in a few the police wouldn't either.

CHAPTER 42

Kinko didn't expect the drop from the wall to be so far down, but it was understandable. You didn't have any type of break to prevent one from being hit by an oncoming car. He let out a loud grunt as he landed on his ankle, twisting it. He didn't stay down long as he hopped up and hobbled over the highway before getting hit by a Mack truck. He made it to the other side only to realize that it too had a cement wall. One he knew he couldn't shimmy up, especially with a twisted ankle.

He made his way down the highway until he saw a guardrail that overlooked a narrow stream. He hopped on top of it, but because of his ankle almost slipped and feel headfirst to an early death. Gripping the top of the wall he pulled himself up. he waited a few seconds contemplating how he was going to land without messing his ankle up even more. Taking a deep breath, he jumped down.

"Shit!" he yelled as he twisted his other ankle. He laid there rolling back and forth grabbing his ankle, as he cursed the boots he had on for the cause of his sudden injuries. Slowly getting to his feet he adjusted his guns in his waist then limped on. He figured that he was in the projects as he saw the spaced out units, dark jeans, and hoody wearing guys scattered about trying to catch the early morning sales. He cracked a smile feeling a bit safer that he was back in his element. Safer, but not comfortable.

Kinko still didn't know where he was or where he was going. He relied on his instinct to tell him when to stop and relax. Until then he made sure to push forward.

He stepped around a dumpster bumping into a dude taking a piss. The vapors could be seen rising as the hot bodily fluid hit the cold cement.

"Yo, what the fuck," the guy voiced cutting his release short.

"My bad bruh," Kinko said and kept walking.

"Ayo, ain't you the one Denise be braidin' hair?" the guy questioned seeing the end of his braids dangling from underneath his skully.

"Nah, wrong guy," Kinko answered placing his hand on one of his guns as he kept walking. The guy fell in step behind him.

"You sure?" he inquired. He wasn't sure if it was the guy Denise owed her money, but he fit the description. The money he owed was owed to him and he needed his money. Them sacks of weed were starting to add up, but now wasn't the time to act on it.

"Yo man, I said it ain't me. Now unless you want me to empty this clip into your ass, I suggest you keep it pushin'" Kinko stated pulling his gun out. When he saw the guy wasn't with that type of drams he turned and walked between two buildings.

For this part of the season the weather wasn't matching up. Around this time of year you'd expect some kind of snow to be in the forecast. This is probably what was meant by global warming. As Kinko walked by the apartments on the sunny sixty-degree afternoon, people sat on their front stoops like it was summertime. The gossip line had just logged in as he felt the eyes followed his every move. He no longer heard the sirens, so he felt he might've lost the police and their nosey ass dogs. He had to laugh at the little metaphor that popped in his head.

"Who was that?" he heard a female voice asking. Who she was asking, he didn't know, but he knew they were asking about him.

"I don't know. Shit," a guy answered.

"Ask him."

"I ain't askin' him shit. Let him go where he goin'. Why you bein' so nosey for anyways?"

"I'm trying to look out for the nigga. I think that's the one they were talkin' about on the news this morning."

"Shit!" Kinko whispered catching the faint conversation as it travelled through the air. He picked his pace up until he came to an opening with a wide road in front of him. He turned to go back into the apartment's maze of buildings and bumped into an elderly lady who seemed to be wearing a nest of coats with a gray toboggan pulled tight over her head. Her matted hair escaped into her collar. What you could see of her face was one that was leathery and worn. From the looks of it she was homeless.

"Excuse me," he said then tried to make his way around her but was stopped by a firm grip. One that was unexpected from her.

"Come with me," she said not once looking him in the face.

"Hells no lady, you ain't gonna get me that easy," Kinko said thinking that she was a retired police ready to turn him in. Or better yet trying to make a citizen's arrest.

"Either come with me or go to jail."

Kinko eased up a bit after hearing what she said. He looked at the side of the lady's face since she wouldn't look at him. He thought that she might be blind.

"I'm not blind. Just follow me, before one of those kids call the police hoping to get some type of reward money," she said letting go of his arm and walking around one of the buildings.

Kinko's gut didn't tell him to flee so he followed behind her. She got into a Lincoln Town car and he quickly ran around to the passenger side and got in.

"You're lucky I got to you before the wrong person saw you," she said pulling off.

"How'd you know I was in trouble?"

"Besides being all over the news? You stick out like a sore thumb walking through here. If I wasn't visiting my friend you'd be about ten minutes from getting arrested. Luckily they don't know what you look like or who you are. That car you were driving wasn't in your name was it? Never mind, I know it isn't."

"Who are you?"

"Your new friend. But we'll talk amore when we get where we're going."

CHAPTER 43

Piko stumbled into his apartment exhausted. He'd been held at the police station for fifteen hours of questioning. He couldn't believe what he had agreed to do. It literally made him sick to his stomach as he ran to the kitchen sink and threw up. he wiped his mouth on a dish towel as he turned the water on to rinse the undigested food down the drain.

As he made his way to the bedroom the events of the past fifteen hours came rushing at him all at once. Danyel Smith aka Misty Jones was an FBI agent. An ex-FBI agent. Dead by who knows. They say she was found in a SUV that fit the description of the same one he saw Stacks drive from time to time. What he didn't understand was why was the car in his name? How'd it even get in his name in the first place? Did Stacks already have this planned? His mind was filled with a whirlwind of thoughts.

"Damn my nigga. What I do to deserve this?" he spoke into the empty room. He went into the bathroom to take a shower still thinking about Misty. He wondered if everyone knew besides him, and for how long? Getting in the shower his thoughts drifted to Iris, his one and only true love. Her getting pregnant was the reason she said she left. He wondered how it could've happened. Who was he kidding. It could've been anytime while he was entertaining different women. Tricking and getting tricked. As the song said, "Who's making love to your old lady/ while ya'll out here making love..." Stacks told him she wanted to have kids and that's another way to keep her sticking around. But he was hardheaded. He barely listened to Stacks advice and always suffered when he didn't. 'Fuck Stacks!' He was the reason for his current predicament. With those type of friends, he didn't need enemies.

Cutting the water off he stepped out of the shower and grabbed a towel to dry off with as he made his way into the bedroom. He turned the tv on to catch the ten o'clock news. If he did nothing else, he always watched the news. His mind was on being labeled the head of a crime enterprise. He was quickly brought out of his pondering by the news being broadcast from his tv.

"A carnage of murders has plagued the streets of northeast to northwest Greensboro. Who the police believe to be a suspect fled the scene of the area of the last multiple murder took place. Taken on a high-speed chase down Old Burlington Rd. into the outer city limits of Burlington where the suspect's vehicle crashed into a pole. But not before vacating the car. According to the officers involved in the chase he then ran into a wooded area and then into Brightwood Crossing Apartments where he seemed to disappear. He's described as a black male of medium build, between five -ten to six feet in height, wearing dark clothing. If you have any information on or about this person, please contact the Greensboro Police Department."

Piko watched as they flashed through the scenes and recognized as all being his trap houses. He knew that only one person could pull this off and wouldn't be surprised if Stacks orchestrated it as well. He probably been lying the whole time, trying to make him believe he had no control over what had been going on ever since he came up with the zoning format.

"You think you're so smart, but we'll see who gets the last laugh," he said to himself. He tried to laugh thinking how if anyone was to see him now, they'd tell him he was certified.

Looking at the tv he caught a glimpse of the wrecked vehicle. 'Damn, he smashed a new 911,' he thought before turning the channel.

Kinko had never been this paranoid in his life. He kept tightening his grip on his guns not knowing if the lady was helping him or tricking him. Those thoughts piqued especially when she paused too long a t an intersection in front of the police station. His heartbeat was loud enough to hear it in his eardrums. His breath didn't return to normal until they pulled up to a log cabin sitting on top of a grassy hill that was surrounded by woods. He was taken by surprise when they pulled into a two car garage.

"Never judge a book by its cover," the lady said.

Kinko didn't know that when he stepped out of the car and walked through the side door, that he was in the lower level of the house. There were two bedrooms with a connecting bath and a twenty-nine by twelve-foot rec room. He tried to take in as much as possible as he followed the lady up some stairs that opened to a kitchen and dining area. To his left was the living room and you could see the sun shining through two double doors which he figured led to a patio. Later he'd find out it was a sunroom, that had a deck attached to it. Two more bedrooms with baths as well as a study room finished off the floor plan.

"Take a seat," she said nodding towards the living room couch as she went into the bedroom down the hall.

"Yo, what's your name?" he asked not liking the anonymous treatment.

"Francine," she replied. Her voice no longer having the raspiness from the cold air that tainted it. now it sounded as if she was mimicking a foreign song. "You need to take those clothes off. I doubt if you'll want to keep them anyways," she stated coming back into the room carrying a terry cloth robe and handing it to him.

Kinko stared in disbelief at Francine, whose whole appearance had changed. The hidden hair wasn't matted at all but combed bone straight framing her face. The strands were coal black as if they were dyed that color, but it was all natural. Her skin, which he mistakened for being leathery, was a smooth coppery color. Her doe like eyes and hypnotizing light brown irises, held a foreign descent. With the absence of her coat, you could see her well proportioned body. Nothing of the old lady he took her for was present. What stood before him was a woman of pure beauty.

"What's wrong?" she grinned draping the robe over the back of the couch.

"N-nothin', just caught off guard a little bit."

"I get that a lot. But I told you not to judge a book by its cover. What size shoe you wear?" she asked in an accent he couldn't place.

"Look you don't…"

"Shhh, don't. I know you want to know why I'm doing this, and I'll explain it all to you. But you have to get rid of those clothes and get situated. There's a bathroom down the hall that you can shower and change at. There are some clothes in the closet that should fit you. And if you're a size eleven, some shoes are there too. Put your things in the trash bag that's in there. Quit staring at me and do what I say."

Kinko came out of the bathroom after soaking in the tub for about an hour trying to come up with some type of plan to get back to his family. He figured that that wouldn't be a problem since his face wasn't known. But he wasn't sure if it would be safe. People might be out to do what Francine said, 'Get a reward.' Looking at the clothes laid out for him, he wondered what her agenda was. He felt like James Caan on Misery, except he wasn't bound to a bed.

Putting the clothes on he saw all that his accessories were on the nightstand. Money, phone, and guns. He quickly grabbed his phone and punched in some numbers. It rang a few times before he hung up. As soon as he did it started ringing. Looking down at the caller id he smiled.

"Yo, what up?"

"You, my nigga. I ain't know if that was you or the police callin'. Especially after seeing your car on the news wrapped around a pole," Talon explained.

"I feel you. Glad you remember the code."

"Where you at?"

"Man, I don't even know my damn self. I think somewhere in Burlington. But yo, I need you to handle somethin' for me."

"Whatever you need, you know I got you."

"Ya'll still gotta lay low, but you gonna have to step up and hold shit down til I'm in the clear."

"That's not an issue bruh. I got you."

"Nah, listen there's more to it than that. You gonna have to get with Stacks. I'm a hit him up and let him know to deal with you."

"Aight. Anything else?"

"Make sure my wife and son are good."

"You don't even have to ask."

"I'm a holla at you," he said before hanging up and calling Keisha.

After listening to her go hysterical before calming down he let her know what now needed to be done. Next, he called Stacks to let him know he was safe, and that Talon would be contacting him. He then made his way into the kitchen to find out exactly what Francine knew.

CHAPTER 44

It had been two weeks since everyone's world came crashing down and the effects of it was felt on every block. The funeral homes saw a great uptick in business. It was a bittersweet moment. The news wasn't needed to know what happened. Word hit the street grapevine immediately. When the bodies popped up and Kinko disappeared it wasn't hard to put two and two together.

Through it all Piko did as he was told and acted as if nothing had happened. He was told that the undercover would come up with his own strategy to get close to Stacks, he just had to vouch for him if need be. While waiting for things to take place he drunk himself into a slump. He went from popping E pills to doing Xanax's, oxy's, and percocets. He stayed rolling to keep from thinking about how much pressure was on him.

He was now at his office desk trying to stay focused while going over his books when the phone rang. He jumped at the unexpected sound.

"JF's Trucking," he answered in his best voice. He was far from the receptionist. He lacked the patience and knew he had to hire one soon.

"Meet me at Barber Park."

Piko recognized the voice as the undercover who was supposed to get close to Stacks. He didn't know how this was going to play out and needed to know beforehand. "For what?"

"You're going to see Stacks at his barbershop/salon called Kurtesy Kuts in an hour and I need to discuss some things with you before you go."

"Are you goin'?"

"Just come to the park and we'll talk then," the detective said then hung up.

Piko replaced the phone on the receiver then rubbed his face. 'This is it,' he thought as he gave a deep sigh, stood up, and headed out the door.

Kurtesy Kuts was a bright shop. Staffed with half stylists and half barbers. Set up to be diversified so they could capture all aspects of the hair field. It was one of, if not the cleanest shop in Greensboro. It was family friendly, but also a great atmosphere for adults to relax and enjoy their time. Hair wasn't the only thing that was done there. Many small community events were held there as well.

Stacks was laughing and joking with the stylists as he got his hair done. He could easily get Monica to do it, but he liked to support his businesses especially around Christmas time. Plus, he liked the overall hair treatment he was given. That and picking up on the latest gossip. It was better than any tv show hearing the bizarre things people in his city were doing.

"Sheena, how you always the one to get to do Stacks hair?" Tasha asked feigning jealousy.

"If you want the best you go to the best," Sheena joked back.

"Is that right Stacks? Is that why you don't go to the rest of us, you don't think we're good enough?" Tasha asked walking around the chair to look at him while waving a rat tail comb in his face.

Stack looked at the short voluptuous Puerto Rican standing in front of him. She was pretty but wore too much make-up.

"Tell 'em I'm your one and only," Sheena said boosting the tension up. She was standing beside Tasha with her arms folded and eyebrow raised daring him to say that she wasn't.

Stacks watched as everyone stopped what they were doing to hear his answer. He was glad he hadn't slept with any of them, or he'd really be in a some bs. He looked from face to face a bit confused. He didn't favor any over the other, because he didn't want to cause discord in the work environment. But Sheena was the only one who did his hair unless she wasn't there. He was trying to figure out what to say without hurting anyone's feelings when he caught Raven's expression out the corner of his eye. She was a black and Italian stylist who helped bring some more flavor to his establishment.

The way that the corner of Raven's mouth was turned up let him know that she was suppressing a laugh. Looking around he noticed most of them were holding in their laughter. That's when he realized it was a joke. "Man, fuck ya'll. And ya'll niggas were in on it? Ya'll let the women gang up on me? That's what's up. Finish my hair Sheena," he laughed leaning back in the chair.

"Gurl, you see the look on his face? He ain't know what to say," Tasha laughed slapping hands with Sheena.

That was the type of atmosphere you got at Kurtesy Kuts. Love and laughs. Everybody was like family. If you couldn't get along with everyone, then you couldn't work there. Most grew up in the hood doing hair or cutting out the kitchen. Stacks helped them get license and out them to work immediately after. They loved Stacks because he gave them an opportunity no one else would nor was trying to.

Sheena finished with his hair and he walked over to the nail tech for his weekly cleaning. The door chime sounded, and it got silent. He didn't know what was going on and when he looked up Piko was looking down at him. Now he understood why it got so quiet. The rumor was that Piko and him were feuding. If they knew the truth though they'd all be shocked. "What up bruh?" Where you comin' from?"

"The job site," he replied trying to mask his nervousness.

"Aight. That shit poppin' like I told you huh?"

"Yea, especially since its holiday season. Got her up and running just in time. But them books are a fuckin' headache," he stated pulling up a seat.

"Shit, get you a bookkeeper. That way you won't even have to go to the office unless you want to."

"I've been thinkin' about it."

"What you come to get you a cut or somethin'?" Stacks asked glancing at his head and facial hair knowing that he didn't need a cut. He thought that he was a Tyrese look alike except he didn't rock a bald head and needed to get a cut whenever his waves didn't lay down right. Plus, he had a barber across town that he'd been going to since they were kids and wasn't switching up.

Stacks was a great body reader and knew that Piko showing up at his shop wasn't a coincidence.

"Yea, since you still tryin' to make light skin niggas relevant," Piko joked hoping to keep Stacks from noticing anything be off about him.

"Ah, you got jokes huh? You must be feelin' good lookin' like Kool Moe Dee standing by that white Jeep Wrangler before

LL crushed him like a jellybean. But fyi. I'm not a fad, I'll always be relevant."

"Aight El DeBarge. Let me go get this shit tightened up."

"I never thought I'd see the day you let someone else touch that bean head?"

"Might as well since I'm here."

Dropping into one of the chairs, Stacks could still feel the tension in the air. "Yo, why the fuck everyone so damn quiet? Ya'll talkin' bout a nigga or somethin'?"

Piko cut his eyes at Stacks. He wasn't use to this side of him. He knew about it, but never witnessed it firsthand. He was always soft spoken and calm. This small glimpse let him know why he was respected and got things done so easily. It also let him know that he was capable of doing everything he suspected him of.

Nobody answered Stacks' inquiry as he got lined up. he didn't take being ignored to the heart yet wasn't liking it either. When he was finished, he paid the barber a hundred and waited on Piko. A customer got his attention and they spoke away from everyone else. The whole time their eyes focused on Piko.

Piko watched the guy speaking to Stacks out of the corner of his eye. He knew it was something serious the way Stacks' face balled up in confusion. His expression suddenly turned to anger. An expression only recognized by someone who knew him. As the barber dusted him off, he went into his pocket to pay with shaking hands.

"Ayo P, where you 'bout to go?" Stacks asked still standing with the customer he was talking to.

"To the crib. I might go to the club later tho. Why what's up?"

"I need to holla at you right quick."

"What up?" he asked walking towards them.

"Nah, not right here. Come to the back. Everybody don't need to hear this."

Piko followed them to the back and out the back door and outside where their breath could be seen vaporize through the cold air. Stacks, who left his coat inside, didn't seem fazed by the freezing weather as he stepped into the alley. He walked straight to the back of the building facing his and took a piss against the wall causing steam to raise from the bricks. He shook the last drops off and zipped his pants back up. he pulled out a vanilla flavored blunt and lit as he turned around to face Piko.

"Now," he started pulling hard on the blunt until his lungs were filled to their capacity. "This guy here, who by the way name is Naheem, told me some very disturbing news."

"Like what?" Piko asked curious as to what was actually told by someone neither of them knew. At least he didn't. He looked from Naheem and into the eyes of his childhood friend as the weed smoke escaped from his nostril like a fiery dragon.

"Some shit that I ain't even tryin' to hear. I've been knowin' you too long to believe anything comin' out of his mouth. But like I told him, he wasn't gonna leave without sayin' the shit to your face," he stated.

"What the fuck you talkin' bout bruh?" Piko asked.

"You know what the fuck he talkin' bout," Naheem said pulling out a .32 revolver with tape around the handle.

"Nigga, you don't even know me yo."

"I ain't gotta know you to know you a rat," he shot back raising the gun.

Stacks looked from Naheem to Piko not believing the guy actually had the nuts to confront Piko about his assumption let alone pull a gun out on him. He wanted to see if he was going to deny the accusation or just stand there helplessly. He knew Piko wasn't a killer, but his life was now on the line and had to make a decision.

"P man, tell me dude lyin' and I'll off his ass right now," Stacks said with the blunt dangling from his lip. One of his eyes were squinted closed to prevent the smoke from getting in it. He had pulled his own gun out and cocked it.

Piko could feel the sweat glands open up under his arms as he began to perspire. He didn't say a word as he bowed his head out of guilt. He didn't know if he should let his life end this way. In the back of some alley. He could keep what he did a secret, but it would still eat him up being that he'd always know. He looked up and reached under his shirt for his gun, but before he could get it out Naheem instinctively pulled his trigger hitting Piko square in the chest.

"Nah man what the fuck!" Stacks yelled in disbelief. He couldn't think straight seeing his boy shot point blank. The blunt fell from his mouth as the rage flooded his eyes.

"Man, that nigga was gonna kill me what the fuck was I supposed to do? You said tell him what I said to his face," Naheem stated not understanding why Stacks was mad at him. He just helped expose a rat in his camp.

Just as Stacks upped his gun Sincere busted through the door.

"Yo yo, chill son."

"Nah, I'ma kill him. He just bodied my man."

"It ain't worth it."

"If this nigga don't die today, you will for getting' in my way."

Sincere looked at Naheem then shook his head. Opportunities came knocking every day and he wasn't about to let this one goo unheard. He felt if he showed Stacks his loyalty now it'll pay off later. Pulling a brand new .45 he pointed it at Naheem and fired three shots into him.

Stacks was standing over Piko's body trying not to shed a tear as others came out and were saying he had no pulse. From that point all he could do to keep his composure was walk back into the building.

"Sin get rid of the body and make it look like a robbery. Call it in and tell them you came out after hearing the gunshots and found Piko," Stacks said. He let everyone know that the shop was closed until further notice. He was in a daze not knowing how he was going to tell Piko's family of their loss. He wasn't handling it well and couldn't imagine how they would.

CHAPTER 45

2021 went out on a sad note and 2022 came in with new hope, so Stacks thought. First was the birth of his daughter Jakeema Solé in honor of Piko. People were still mourning his death, ruining the Christmas spirit. There wasn't a dry eye in the building during the service. His casket was closed, which at first he questioned, but due to a mishap by the mortician they decided to keep it that way. Even Iris popped up holding a three month old baby girl. He wanted to confront her to see about her wellbeing because regardless of what she was still family. But she left before the service ended.

Nobody attended Naheem's funeral. Stacks thought about going just to kick the casket over, but chose not to. After things calmed down he spoke to Sincere and let him know to get with Teflon about running Piko's old spots. He could find his own workers but there was to be no turf wars. If he caught a whiff of any type of beef he was shutting the whole operation down. He wanted things to go back to normal. Back to running smooth again. He thought about Kinko and wondered how he was holding up.

After a month of being shacked up with Francine, he knew it wouldn't be long before the inevitable happened. Kinko felt like a blow up doll the way Francine was using his body. She seemed to need the release more than him. At times it was like she was trying to pull his life force through his shaft. At the same time when she looked into his eyes he felt connected as if she'd jump through his pupils into his soul. Her orgasms sounded like a bunch of hissing snakes.

"Did you feel it?" she asked rolling off of him to sit on the edge of the bed.

"Feel what?" Kinko asked confused as he went in the opposite direction to put his boxers on.

"The energy exchange?"

"You losin' me. I don't know what you're talkin' about."

"Do you know a guy named Ifalolu?"

"Not that I can recall. Why?"

"You've been asking how I know you."

"Yea, and you still haven't told me."

"Ifalolu is your grandfather and how I know you. He's also the reason how you've been slipping the grasp of the law and… death."

"Hol' up. say what? My grandfather?" he asked turning to look at Francine. "I don't know about any grandfather."

"No one wanted you to know. This is your father's father from Ghana. He has been in your life since the beginning."

"And where do you fit in on all this?"

"I'm supposed to be only who I am. A help mate. If I hadn't seen the news and worked quickly the results could've been different."

"You're losin' me again."

"Your grandfather is a vey powerful man who knows and can do what others cannot. He is what some consider a witch doctor, and I am one of his many students."

"What?! You bullshittin' me right?"

Francine turned a blank face towards him to show how serious she was. "This is not a joking matter. I know all about the son you have at home and the woman you just asked to marry you. Does that tell you anything?"

Kinko couldn't believe his ears at what he was hearing. He was caught up in what felt like a Tales from the Darkside episode. He thought about the way she came on to him. How her exotic advances became overbearing until he collapsed under its pressure. The last thought that crossed his mind was the exchange she mentioned. "What was it you were doing earlier?"

"What you mean?" Francine asked with a smile.

"That wet kiss you gave me?"

She chuckled. "That was to seal our bond."

"What bond?" Kinko insisted jumping up.

Francine stood up and glided to the window where she stood for a few seconds before turning around giving Kinko a clear view of her naked body surrounded by the sunlight from the window. "Like I told you. Your grandfather suggested I assist you and in so doing we become united."

"What? I'm supposed to leave my wife and son? Ain't no way."

"You'll always have your sons, but the one you think will be your wife won't."

"Man, this fuckin' shit is bananas. I gotta get out of here," he said rushing to put his clothes on.

"Please, don't leave it is not time," she said approaching him.

"I don't give a fuck what time it is. I'm goin' home. I gotta get back to my family," he said misinterpreting what she said. "I'm a borrow one of your cars and bring it back tomorrow."

"Did you not hear what I said? It is not time for you to leave. Things are not yet ready for your return."

Kinko looked at her through squinted eyes as he now understood what was being said. "I'm a just have to take that chance," he let it be known as he walked out room.

Francine threw a robe on and followed Kinko down the steps to the bottom floor. She stood in the doorway that led to the garage and watched as he got in her Tahoe. "Be careful," she said no longer feeling the need to try and stop him. He was set on leaving and there was nothing she could do to stop him. She had grown to like him more than she expected. She didn't think she had let Ifalolu down. She did what was asked. She just hoped that he was still protected.

CHAPTER 46

The hustle didn't stop just because people died. That happened every day. It was unavoidable. All it did was help those like Stacks see that life was too short to be out there half-assing in the streets.

As Cassie maneuvered a black Nissan Altima around an eighteen-wheeler to the driver's side, two more flanked the passenger and front. Her passenger opened the door of the speeding car and skillfully hopped onto the rig. After politely asking the driver to pull over and relieved of his duties they continued to their destination. That was the whole agenda behind Stacks getting Piko to set up the trucking company. Copy the itinerary and logbooks to see worthy loads then set up the jacking. Cassie was an excellent driver, so it was a given to have her part of the team. It was supposed to be an easy lick, but not this time. Soon as they pulled up to the designated drop off spot the police were waiting.

Kinko felt that everything was everything since he came back home. Keisha was glad to see him at the same time how much stress he put her through let alone the danger. He couldn't argue with her because he didn't expect things to go the way that they did. At the same time, she was supposed to understand how this street life went. He didn't want to argue with her so the only thing he could do was go for a ride.

As soon as Kinko started to back out of his driveway, he heard sirens and screeching tires. He was stuck between just giving up and shooting it out, but when he realized he was in Keisha's car his second option was gone.

Opening the car door, he got out with his hands laced behind his head as he laid on the concrete. He wasn't going to make a scene especially not with his son in the house. His time was up and he had to go. As they placed the cuffs on him, he thought about what Francine said before he left. 'It's not time.' Now he understood. Once again he let his ego get in the way.

Keisha had come out on the porch holding their son as the police placed him in the back of their car. When they drove off, he didn't know who was crying more, his son, Keisha, or him.

"Ma, you sure you ok with watchin' Jakeema?" Stacks asked.

"Why wouldn't I be? I'm not too old to watch a baby."

"I didn't say that. I wasn't sure if you had plans or not."

"Boy just go. You and Monica haven't had any self time in a while. Just focus on having a good time I got this," she said pushing Stacks out the door.

Stacks hopped in his forest green Tesla and rolled the window down. "Aight now, don't hesitate to call if you need anything."

"Damn, would you leave already."

"Bye, Mrs. Knight," Monica waved as they pulled off.

"Bye baby. And don't worry about Jakeema she'll be ok."

Since the arrival of their daughter Stacks had transformed his entire appearance. He went back to the wavelength cut and didn't even attempt to hang out anymore. He was going on twenty-seven and didn't have the time, energy, or mental compacity to mingle with people at such spots. He rarely wore street clothes outside the occasional jeans and sneakers. It was now khakis, polo shirts, and suits. Right now, he was in his tan Steve Harvey suit with brown Stacy Adams shoes. His fedora was slightly tilted to the right so you could see the large diamond studded earring in his left lobe. He matched that with a clustered diamond ring. His eyes were hid behind a pair of Versace shades.

Looking at Stacks with admiration she still couldn't figure out why people did that. Wore shades at night. She was dressed just as immaculate as he was in her strapless Christian Dior bodice dress with square toed Paciotti boots. Her hair was in a silk twist that was pulled back into a French roll. The Chanel lip gloss drew the necessary attention needed to emphasize the fullness of her lips. Diamond chandelier earrings fell from her earlobes and brushed the top of her shoulders. The Shea butter she rubbed into her skin gave her a radiant glow. She didn't bother with makeup for it would only take away from her natural beauty.

They were headed to see the paly CATS. Stacks remembered his mother taking him to the see the same play when he was younger. Only because his sister had a part in it. The play had premiered in 1981 and forty years later was still popular. Even made a movie out of it. Their next stop was going to be to Cassie's club for open mic night to hear some spoken word. He hoped everything went smoothly this morning. Since he hadn't heard anything, he figured that it did.

When the play was over Stacks grabbed their coats and guided Monica through the theaters departing crowd. Once outside he helped put her coat on before slipping his own on. He took in the night's fresh air as they walked towards his car when his phone rang.

"Talk to me."

"Ayo, this Sincere."

"What up? Everything good?" he asked with his hand on the door handle

"Nah. Not good at all big bruh. I need to holla at you where you at?"

"Bout to head to Cassie's what's up?" Stacks demanded he wasn't trying to wait to hear anything.

"Cassie got bagged."

"What?! How?" he asked in disbelief looking over at Monica as they slid into the car and closed the door.

"I don't know and the reason I need to talk to you face to face."

"Aight. In the meantime, find out what her bond is and get her out and whoever was with her."

"I only got so much…"

"Nigga I'm not askin' I'm tellin' you."

"Ok, so you still going to the club?"

"Yea, somebody gotta keep it goin' til she gets out."

"Ok, I'll go handle that right now."

Stacks hung up the phone and let out a breath of frustration.

"What's wrong?"

"Cassie got locked," he answered starting the car then pulled off to get out of the parking lot so he could get to his destination.

"How?" Monica asked in the same disbelieving tone that Stacks had when he heard the news.

"I'm tryin' to figure the shit out myself."

"So, what's up?"

"Ain't shit up. And I'm not bout to start overreacting that's probably what whoever did this is banking on. We goin' to Cassie's and chill. In the morning we'll figure out what's going on," Stacks stated as he kept his eyes on the moving vehicles around him. He let out a little chuckle thinking about Monica's hood mentality. He didn't know how she could be raised in a good household as hood as she was.

"What's so funny?

"You."

"How?"

"You somethin' else. No matter what I do to keep you from this side of the tracks you always ready to cross back over."

"Who would I be not to? Remember, we in this one hundred percent, fifty- fifty. I'm your wife an ain't no way I'm a sit back and let nothing go down and I don't have your back."

"I can dig it."

"Shoot, I'll pull this dress up and go to war like I got on fatigues and boots."

"Aight G.I. Jane," he laughed. Their humorous moment was interrupted by another call to Stacks phone. "Damn, what now," he mumbled as he answered the phone.

"They locked my baby up! He ain't do nothing! He was, we was!" the voice screamed.

"Yo, hold up. I can't hear you wit all that yellin'. Now who you talkin' bout?"

"Kinko, they locked him up with no bond," Keisha said calmly.

"What's the charge?"

"You already know."

"Damn! Look, Ain't shit we can do right now. I'm a get wit my lawyer in the mornin' and see what we can do aight?"

"Okay."

Stacks hung up. Just as he was pulling up to Cassie's club, he made a U-turn and headed back out. "Change of plans babe. I don't know what the fucks goin' on, but it looks like shit's bout to hit the fan."

As Stacks turned out of the parking lot, he could hear the sirens in the distance getting closer. He didn't know where they were headed. His heart began to race nervously as he continued driving. Through his rearview he saw the cars flood the club's parking lot and his instincts told him they were there for him. His suspicions were confirmed a few blocks later when the police cars got behind him and flashed their lights. "Babe, you gonna have to switch with me."

"What you bout to do?" she asked, herself becoming nervous. All that tough talk was out the window.

"I ain't tryin' to go to jail. And I always told myself that if the cops ever came for me, I was holdin' court in the streets."

"That was before you had a family. I can't lose you Stacks."

"Just get ready to switch," he said knowing it wasn't the right time to have this conversation.

Monica did as she was told trying not to cry. The thought of losing him had never crossed her mind. And now that the possibility of something like that occurring, she was scared. Sitting on Stacks lap until he slid from under her. She began to pick up speed as Stacks hit a few buttons then hopped in the back seat. Lifting up the seat cushions he rummaged through the artillery underneath. He pulled out a double plated Teflon vest and a Draco with extended clip. He took off his hat and put the vest on. He grabbed the Draco and placed the box under before loading the chamber. He had Monica pop the hatch and as soon as it was high enough, he began unloading on the cop cars behind them. The 7.62 nato bullets ate up the front of their cars causing them to swerve and stop. After a while they slowed the chase and Stacks closed the hatch.

Looking over at Monica he saw tears rolling down her cheeks and felt her pain. "Baby, don't break on me now. We just gotta get home and we good."

"How Tony, huh? How will we be good? You don't think they know where we live?" she stated with a shaky voice.

"No. You know how everything goes when we buy things. We just gotta grab a few things and we'll get out of town."

"And what about Jakeema?"

"We'll send for her soon as we get where we're goin' ok?"

"Whatever *Stacks*, you got it all figured out."

"Look you can get mad at me later, but right now I need you to focus."

"I'm good," she replied wiping her eyes and nose.

Out of nowhere a Chevy Suburban came off a side street and rammed into them. The door on Stacks' side was bent in half pinning him in his seat and knocking him unconscious.

When he came to, he was being lifted onto a gurney and escorted to an ambulance. His eyes scanned the area and saw the totaled Tesla with a hole in the windshield. He began to panic wondering where Monica was. He tried to speak but couldn't find his voice. All he could do was scream out as the ambulance doors were closed and he was rushed to the hospital.

At first thought he figured the police had ran into them, but it was someone who had ran a red light. Asking about Monica's condition, he was told that he was the only survivor at the scene. His whole body deflated with the news. He felt that they might as well kill him too because he had just lost his other half.

Easing out of the raised bed he winced in pain as he shuffled to the room's closet. The cold linoleum floor and air condition assaulted his bare feet and body as he grabbed his clothes. He didn't see the vest and figured the police was notified so he had little if no time to waste. With Monica gone he was now on his own. He'd get Jakeema anytime, but for now she was safe with his mother.

"Not so fast."

The voice said startling Stacks and freezing him in place. He looked up from where he was putting his shoes on and saw two plainclothes officers standing in the doorway.

"We're glad that you're able to move about. Now if you'll so kindly submit to these cuffs, I'll gladly read you your rights.

Stacks looked at the officers then the window. He didn't know how high up he was, but he was ready to take that chance no matter the height. He quickly made his move ignoring the excruciating pain. He braced himself for the impact but was easily thrown back due to the window being an inch thick and unbreakable.

"Stupid mothafucka. Cuff this fool before he tries to slit his wrists next.

CHAPTER 47

Stacks was escorted to a conference room where he was handcuffed to a steel chair. Five minutes passed before Detective Lawrence and another officer walked in with their traditional cup of coffee. Lawrence held a folder under his arm as he sat down across from Stacks. Taking sips from his cup while flipping through the file was a tactic he used to get under his suspects' skin. He knew all there was to know about this case being he was the lead detective on it. So, reading the file was unnecessary. He was mainly buying time to strategize his approach. This wasn't Piko. He couldn't just scare this man with the threat of a long prison term no matter how hard he fought to get away.

Lawrence looked at Stacks over the steam that came from his cup as he raised it to his lips. He was trying to read the man that nobody knew about or nor could find dirt on. Yet, he was, according to Piko, responsible for just about every illegal activity throughout Greensboro. He couldn't believe that this was the guy behind Piko's notoriety. Ecclesiastes Knight. In school they called him Pretty Tony. He didn't talk much, nor did he pose any type of threat, but no one trusted him around their girl. He didn't have the gift of gab, he just knew the art of seduction.

Stacks felt the detective glaring at him and decided to lock eyes with him. "You're looking at me as if you know me."

"I do."

"Well, I don't know you so maybe you can enlighten me on where you recognize me from."

"Dudley."

"Over a thousand of people attend that school year to year and you expect me to remember you?"

"I don't expect anything and that's not why we're here for."

Stacks reached across the table and pulled back the pack of Newports and a lighter. He knew that this wasn't a friendly conversation that would benefit him and wasn't about to pretend that it was. He wasn't trying to accept anything he had to offer. He took the cigarettes for a reason. Not to smoke, because he had quit when Jakeema was born.

"Help yourself," Lawrence said sarcastically as he watched Stacks light a cigarette. "Can I get you anything else?"

Stacks leaned to the side and crossed his legs. He looked at Detective Lawrence through squinted eyes as the smoke wisped by. He was trying to get a feel for this guy. To know his angle. More importantly how he found out about him. "Tell me what you know."

"Huh?" Lawrence muttered, caught off guard.

"Obviously someone told you somethin' about me, so I want to hear what it is."

"That's not important. You were found with a military issued vest and high caliber weapon on you at the scene of the car wreck."

"Vest yea, gun? No."

"So, you're denying what was found?"

"I don't know what was found I was unconscious. For all I know that could've been planted. Plus, that vehicle doesn't belong to me, how am I supposed to know what someone has in it?"

"Then why the vest?"

"I've been getting' death threats. And I've always been the type that lives by the motto 'Better safe than sorry'."

"Then why you try to run at the hospital?"

"How was I to know if they were real police? Nobody identified themselves."

"That's a bunch of bull."

"And so are you," he replied putting the cigarette out. "Now we can talk like grown men or begin pointing out all the technicalities of this arrest."

"Sparks, give me. A few minutes with Mr. Knight. And bring me another cup of coffee."

"And a can of Sprite while you're at it. My throat is kinda dry," Stacks smiled.

"You sure you want to be left alone with him?"

"We good. I want to hear what he has to say."

"If you say so," Sparks replied leaving the room.

"Oh, so you think you're safe wit me by yourself?"

"Shit why wouldn't I be? You're cuffed to a chair that's bolted to the floor in a precinct."

"Slide those cigarettes back over here."

Detective Lawrence pushed the pack over to Stacks. This time when Stacks went to light the cigarette he didn't have to lean over. After taking a pull from the cigarette he slid the pack back along with the handcuffs.

"What the hell?"

"I've been underestimated my whole life. No one ever understood who I was or was capable of. Even 'til this day people wonder who I am."

"Who didn't know who Pretty Tony was?"

Stacks let out a short laugh. "Yea, but nobody *knew* me. Mothafuckas were so worried that I'd fuck their girl and didn't know I had already fucked their minds. And that's way more powerful than any physical contact," Stacks stated. He didn't know why he felt like talking. Maybe he just wanted at least one person to see things through his eyes. "But to understand me is like tryin' to understand God. So tell me, why are ya'll after me?"

When Sparks walked out of the room he immediately pulled out his cell phone and dialed a private number.

"Yes," a sultry Asian voice asked.

"Sparks here. Our boy's in custody and is talking to the Detective. I was asked to step out so I can't monitor the current conversation."

"Messaged is received," the voice responded then disconnected.

Sparks closed his phone then headed to get the coffee and soda.

"You want to take the gloves off or the simple police version?" Detective Lawrence asked as he loosened up his tie.

"I don't wanton half ass shit."

"Okay. Let's say this. You've been under surveillance for two and a half years."

"That's a long time with no arrest."

"I said the same thing when I was presented with the case. Piko's name continued to sound off throughout Greensboro.

Him and his partner *Stacks*. While everyone knew who Piko was, they didn't have a clue as to the position Stacks played. Me knowing of ya'll thought I understood it all being from what I saw back in the day. Ya'll were so close, I figured him being the bigger of you two that he was protecting you. But my mama always told me to watch the quiet ones, they sneaky. I guess she was right."

"If you're done reminiscing, I'm ready to hear why ya'll been after me."

"You were pinpointed as the mastermind behind all of this. Allowing Piko to take the fame while you stayed in the shadows," Lawrence stated as he stared into Stacks blank face hoping to gain some type of reaction out of him, but there was none. "You built an organization that dealt in drugs and money laundering. That there alone gets you life in the FEDs."

"I didn't ask for threats I asked for the cause of my arrest."

Lawrence hated to admit it, but he was intimidated by Stacks. His calm demeanor was overbearing. He was use to people ranting and raving by now, ready to spill the beans after hearing what they were up against. With Stacks it was like having a simple everyday conversation. "As I said all this was first aimed at Piko."

"So basically, you have nothin' but a bunch of suspicions. I'm very disappointed. The way you came in here with such confidence I'd at least think you'd present a phony video surveillance tape or some type of rigged wiretap. But this?" he stated shaking his head. He stood up and adjusted his clothes. " I don't think I need to contact my lawyer to be set free do I?" he asked looking down at the detective.

"You should sit down."

"For what? You have nothin' on me."

"Nothing but a live witness that worked in your operation and is willing to testify against you."

Stacks looked at Lawrence in mock confusion wondering who he could be talking about. Was it Cassie? Sincere? He highly doubted it was Kinko. He figured Lawrence had to be lying, but he sat down just the same. "Who?"

"Come on now. You know that's not how the game goes. You gotta give to get."

"Give what?" he asked trying to figure him out. This mental chess game wasn't supposed to last this long, but he wasn't going to give up that easy.

"Your connects."

Stacks started to laugh but stopped abruptly as if he never began. He had thought of using the detective to escape, but knew he'd never make it out of the station. His thoughts were interrupted by a knock on the door followed by Detective Sparks walking in.

"Everything alright in here?" he asked placing the coffee and soda on the table.

"Yea, yea, we straight. Just give us a few more minutes."

Once Sparks closed the door Stacks began to talk. "Have you seen the 'Usual Suspects'? he asked popping open the can and taking a much needed gulp.

"Who hasn't?"

"And everyone wanted to know who Keyser Sôze was?"

"And? What's your point?"

'Keyser is a misspelling of the word Kaiser, which is the German word for 'Emperor'. Just a little jewel I thought I'd drop on you."

"Thanks, but a history lesson won't get you out of this."

"It won't? Well, how about this one. See there was this kid once from around the way. I'll say his name is uh, Steve." Stacks started then watched how Lawrence seemed to react to this as he moved uncomfortably in his seat. "Yea, that's what we'll call him. Steve. Stayed in Dudley Heights. Two parent home. Good jobs. But this kid. This kid felt like an outcast even though he was an only child that was well taken care of. He tried to fit in with the bad boys, but they ignored him. Still, he went out his way to try to impress these guys. You could see the anger on his face every time he was pushed away. That all it would've taken was for someone to accept him and he would've done anything they said. He would've been loyal to that person. But that never happened. So, he grew up with a black heart and a vendetta to get those same people who pushed him away."

"Was that supposed to have some type of meaning?" Lawrence asked starting to feel the mugginess of the airtight room.

Stacks finished off the soda and slowly placed it on the table. "Meanin', nothin' gets by me. I know who you are Detective *Steven* Lawrence. The same kid I was talkin' about. I didn't talk much because I was watchin', analyzin' everythin'. It never occurred to you that we pushed you away not because we didn't want you to be down, but because we didn't want you liviin' a life you didn't have to. See what a little push gets you? Head detective doing real good for yourself. Cleaning up your community. Yet despite the good efforts you still have the wrong guy."

Lawrence didn't really have a comeback and felt cornered. He did have a trump card and was eager to play it. He pulled out a plastic bag containing a gold loop earring and tossed it on the table. "Maybe if I was like you, I'd feel bad about this whole thing, but I'm not so I have no ill feelings about locking people like you away. I love my job, and I'm damn good at it as you can see," he said nodding at the earring.

Stacks glanced down at the bag and nothing about it registered. "What's that supposed to be?"

"Oh, so you don't recognize it? Cool, well let me explain. Around say, October 2020, four people were found dead out pass Old Battleground Rd. And this earring was laying there at the scene of the crime. Of course, we ran tests, and nothing came back."

"Soooo, you're tellin' me this because?"

"Technology is something else. The lady found at the car crash is the owner of this fine piece of jewelry. And nine times out of ten she was with you. It can't be proven but..."

"It's irrelevant."

"Why, because you don't think we can place you there?"

"No, because you can't charge a dead person."

"Who's dead?"

"The lady you're speaking of."

"Dead? Nah. She's in a coma, and better stay that way because as soon as she comes out of it, she'll be charged."

Stacks sat in mere shock. He could easily manipulate his way out of this with a little help, but hearing that's Monica was still alive changed things dramatically.

"And I'll make sure you're living under the jail like Gotti. But I don't know if you'll be such a stand up guy. You might be like Alpo or Frank Lucas nah more like Nikki Barnes. How bout it?"

"Don't ever compare me to any fuckin' rat. I piss standin' up. So you can put twelve in the box anytime," Stacks made known standing up.

"Have it your way. I just thought I could be of some help. You know, for old times sake," Lawrence smiled satisfied that he finally had gotten under Stacks' skin.

"Enough of this small talk. Get me my lawyer before I do end up with a murder charge."

CHAPTER 48

Walking into the cell block Stacks glanced around. The cell doors filled up with inmates trying to get a glimpse of the new occupant. He could care less about being the center of attention he needed to use the phone. That was the only thing that the guards had sympathy about being he wasn't allowed one downstairs. His lawyer couldn't bail him out since it was late when he was arrested and there wasn't a magistrate at the jail.

He called his mother and explained what he could without saying too much. She picked up on all the talk being she was seasoned in this lifestyle. It didn't matter that his father was long deceased, he had taught her well and was there to oversee things when needed. Like now.

When he was finished, he was directed to his room. He wasn't expecting a cellmate, but he had no say in the matter. He figured that he had to take the top bunk. He didn't know who was on the bottom and could care less.

"Yo, who that?" the voice asked from the bottom bunk.

Stacks didn't respond nor planned to either. He wasn't trying to make any friends. His stay was going to only as long as it took him to make bail.

"Yo, I asked who that?"

Again, Stacks was silent as he laid down on the plastic mat using the folded blanket as a pillow. He could hear the guy raise up off his bunk. The shadow stood tall and glared at him.

"Maaannn, get the fuck outta here. Stacks, what the fuck yo?!"

Hearing his name Stacks turned to look at his cellmate and peered into the face of his right hand man. "Man goddamn. Kinko what's up bruh?" Stacks raised up to pound Kinko up.

"How the fuck they catch you and for what?"

"Bro it's a long story, but everything gonna be aight."

"I hope so. I miss my lil mans like crazy."

"Yea, I had just spoke to your girl before they started chasing me."

"That's crazy."

"But don't worry bout a thing. I got them top notch lawyers on standby so we good."

"Truthfully, I ain't sweatin' none of it. I know they don't have nothin' but some assumption shit. Once this is over though I'm out. NC too much. These niggas don't know how to mind their fuckin' business. They out here tellin' like it's a fad. Plus, they got the game twisted. It ain't about money anymore, they just want the fame."

"I feel ya. Where would you go?"

"I was diggin' that spot in Tennessee."

"Word. Have you heard anything about Cassie?"

"Nah, what's up wit her?"

"She got bagged too."

"Ahh, damn. Yea there's a Master Splinter somewhere bruh. But nah, I ain't heard nothin'. Shouldn't be too hard to find out tho."

"Just make sure she knows she good. Not to panic and I'm get ya'll out of here you hear me?"

"I'm already knowin' big bruh."

Around one o'clock the next day Stacks was called for a lawyer visit. He wondered why he wasn't called for a first appearance so he could get his bond and get out of there.it didn't occur to him that he was federally being sought after and the handling was different.

When he entered the small room he expected to see Mr. Korwinski, his business lawyer. Instead, it was a petite lady that resembled Kelly Hu from The Scorpion King movie. She was dressed in a floral 12th Street mini dress. Miss Sixty Tyler heels to give her five- two frame a boost. Her free flowing hair was bone straight with a part down the middle. The ends swayed at the top of her small breasts as she stood up and stepped towards Stacks with her hand extended.

"Mr. Knight."

"Yes," he answered switching to his professional tone. He didn't know what made him shun his street lingo. He blamed it on her beauty that caused him to want to be seen and heard as a regular man than a hardened criminal. He never did embrace that type of image. More of a seasoned crook that didn't indulge or waste time in petty crimes.

Gripping her hand, he felt the soft contours of her skin. It was like running your fingers across goose feathers or through a country spring. As he drunk in her beauty, he saw the red rise to the top of her cheeks out of embarrassment as if she knew what he was thinking.

"I'm Stacey Lin. You should already know who sent me, so there's no need to mention any names. Mr. Knight."

"Please, call me Tony."

"Ok, *Tony*. Listen, I'm the best at what I do, but in order for me to help make this go away you're going to have to tell me everything from right before the point of your arrest until now," Ms. Lin stated then listened as Stacks reiterated the last twenty-four hours.

"So, from what I gather they don't have anything on you except for hearsay. Well, that and the shooting out of the vehicle. But that's the least of our worries. There's someone working against you, do you have any idea who that might be?"

"Not that I can think of. Except two people, but one's in a coma and the other is dead."

"Are you sure about that?'

Stacks looked at Stacey as if she lost her mind. He also had to wonder if she knew something that hadn't been said.

"I'm sure of it."

"Ok, then that brings me to Cassie and Kevin."

"Nah, they wouldn't be around me if they were like that," he said and looked at the disdain look on Stacey's face. Listen, that was a minor mistake that slipped by me these people you mentioned are legit. Plus, they don't know enough to be behind this."

"Then why are you in jail with no bond and a federal hold on you?"

"I don't know. And isn't that what your job is?"

"Yes, it is. I'm a have to do some digging and find who this CI is then we'll know what we're up against," she stated then stood up to leave.

"Stacey, I need a favor."

"What's that?" she asked flipping her hair over her shoulder as she put her papers in her briefcase.

"I need you to represent Cassie and Kevin. I'll pay whatever."

"I'll run it by our people."

"Kinko needs it the most he's facing a multitude of murder charges."

"Hmp," she grunted as if what he said meant nothing. What he didn't know was that there wasn't a charge or case she hadn't seen or oversaw. Justus' arm stretched far and wide. "Let 'em know someone will be seeing them soon and not to talk to anyone," she stated then left the room with her hair swaying back and forth across her back like the pendulum on a grandfather clock.

CHAPTER 49

Stacks laid on his bunk with his hands behind his head staring at the underside of the top bunk. Kinko felt it only right to give up the bottom bunk. He had used extra sheets to make a curtain around his bed to enclose himself in from anyone who might try to get a glimpse of him. It had been eight months since his arrest and nothing seemed to be moving how it should be. Cassie was the only one who was able to get a bond while he and Kinko were still being refused one. At the same time this was part of the plan. He wanted things to stretch out as long as possible. For at least two years that would give his people time to take care of everything. The only downside was the wait.

He came to find out that a guy by the name of Felix Devine was behind Cassie's arrest. He was an undercover that was in the crew she used from time to time. He implemented her as their ringleader. It would've stuck had she been anyone else, but when Stacks let it be known of her importance to him Stacey worked her magic and had the charges dismissed on a *technicality*.

Kinko's situation was a bit more complicated, and Stacks had to keep convincing him that everything will work out for him. Nothing could be proven, but they wanted him to sweat it out in jail as if that would get him to confess to the crimes. They didn't know that he was use to the jailhouse politics. He could survive as long as he needed to but being apart from his son was starting to wear on him.

"Ayo Stacks," Kinko called from the other side of the sheet.

"Yea," he replied trying not to sound irritated from being disturbed from his deep thinking.

"I'm a do it yo."

"Do what?"

"Take the plea."

"Nah, bruh. That's what they want you to do. Get tired of bein' in here and cop out. If they had anything they wouldn't even offer you that short time. Let them lawyers work you gonna beat this."

"I feel you, but I'm missing my son man."

"Just like I'm missing my daughter but think about this. You take that plea and you gone for *seven* years. That's time you'll never get back time away from your son that you gonna hate that you missed," Stacks stated trying to keep Kinko from making a big mistake. He trusted in Justus and the team of legal people he sent to take care of them. Even though he was trying to help Kinko keep his composure his mind was elsewhere. Monica had yet to come out of her coma and her parents had her transferred to a private hospital that he didn't know the location to. It was like her parents were trying to sever ties to him, which would be impossible since they had a child together.

CHAPTER 50

Before the year was out Stacks had been relocated to the Winston-Salem jail. That's how the FEDs worked. They didn't allow you to sit too long in the jail of the city you were arrested in. He didn't mid, because he was basically by himself. The motions and pressure Stacey had put on the DA's office had caused them to drop Kinko's charges. He mainly spent his time on the phone, playing chess, and watching the news. He read a few books here and there and thought that maybe when this was all over, he might write one himself. Call it Diablo's Block.

It wasn't two years but eighteen months that passed before he went to trial. He didn't go all dressed up in an expensive suit. He didn't wasn't the jury feeling he was throwing it in their face by flaunting his wealth. He donned a regular suit and some turtle shell framed specs. He had a fresh cut shedding the long hair don't care image.

The courtroom was jammed packed with an array of people. It looked more like a celebrity viewing than a federal case being heard. Even though he was known in the streets, thanks to people like Justus he also rubbed shoulders with some major important people. This was a major case to be talked about amongst bloggers and hood viners.

Looking around he saw his mother and sister. Jakeema wasn't there and that hurt him just like the strain it was putting on his family. He had been good at shielding this side of his life from his family over the years, but when it came to the FEDs, they didn't spare anyone when they were after you. Even Phyliss was there smiling at him when they locked eyes. To his utmost surprised tucked away in the back was Justus. The man who pulled most of the strings in his world. Why he risked showing his face was beyond him. He figured it was more for support than a form of intimidation. As he stated before, 'The organization liked him.' He knew he was their biggest contributor and admired amongst those who had been doing this for years. Years when his father was in charge. At the sound of the bailiff he turned around to face his fate.

"Order in the court. Order in the court. Oyez, oyez, oyez. Please rise for the presiding Judge Clemmons."

Once the judge entered the courtroom and took his seat, everyone was instructed to take their seat as well.

"I take it that everyone is prepared?" the judge asked.

"Yes, your honor," the prosecutor replied and was echoed by Stacks' lawyer.

"Then we shall proceed as scheduled."

Opening statements were made and the prosecutor presented his evidence and witnesses that Stacey easily dismantled.

"This is nothing. If they keep this up, then you're guaranteed to walk out of here. I don't even know why they would present such weak evidence knowing it has no legs to stand on.

Stacks listened to what she said but wasn't really paying attention. He knew in order for things to be right again he had to follow through with his plan. As he watched the numerous agents give their testimony as to what they thought they knew, he sat listening.

"Is this your last witness?" the judge asked the prosecutor.

"No, your honor. We have one more."

"Well call them up. And I hope they're better than the others, because I can truthfully say that this case so far has no merit and unless some concrete evidence is given, I have no choice but to dismiss this."

"Your honor I guarantee that this last witness will rap this case up," the prosecutor assured.

"Very well then. You may proceed."

The prosecutor turned to Stacks with a smile as he announced his last witness. "The prosecution would like to call…"

His words were cut off by a lot of shouting as two burly men burst into the courtroom toting Dracos. It was like Columbine as they shot the prosecutor, bailiffs, and anyone that stood in their way. Stacks ducked under the table hoping not to catch any strays.

"Stacks come on!" one of the guys shouted.

Stacks eased from under the table and stood up only to feel a hand on his arm. He looked down and saw Stacey staring into his face.

"Relax," she said.

Stacks glanced around the room and realized that he was imagining the rescue squad. He had to see this out the hard way. The mirage was his denial of what he was putting himself through, but it was too late to turn back now.

"…Jakeem Fuller," the prosecutor finished his announcement.

The room seemed to erupt in chaos. The murmurs and gasps echoed throughout the room. People stood up to leave rushing to get to a phone to try and be the first to spread the news.

Stacks wanted to shed a tear, not because the only person who could take him down was about to take the witness stand. It was much deeper than that. He was in an emotional turmoil. A tug of war between love and hate. Honor and betrayal. Only a handful of people knew what had transpired that day in the alley that supposedly resulted in Piko's death. It would be in his best interest to have him really be dead, but he was a bit happy to see his childhood friend still alive. He could understand why any and everyone would be furious, but not Stacks. He knew this day would come. This was his plan. His big exit. He could admit that he didn't expect things to fall so easily in place like they did whether he orchestrated it or not.

Stacks started plotting and planning the day he was forced to kill Kareem. He needed a way to distance himself from the streets as well as Piko who felt he was the streets. He couldn't see the bigger picture or the end game. How people lasted for years, decades committing crimes. Forming underground networks around the world while staying behind the scenes. He presented the legit businesses to Piko in hopes he'd take the opportunity to avoid what he was attracting. The law. That's why he needed to part ways with him.

Stacks knew about all the side deals Piko made. How he tried to undercut him on payouts. History between them made him look pass it, but not to the point where he couldn't capitalize on Piko's arrogance. And to do that he needed to stack enough money to exit the game.

Regardless of the snake moves Piko made against him, Stacks still kept him in mind when making his own plans. He knew Kinko was a live wire and hated everything about Piko. Stacks was the only thing that kept him from acting out his feelings. But once he let him loose it put everything into motion. He just didn't expect anyone to get caught in the process. And definitely didn't plan on getting Monica hurt let alone possibly losing her.

Stacks was willing to do anything he had to to save his loved ones. Even sit down for twenty-five years.

EPILOGUE

As the U.S. Marshals placed the chains, cuffs, and locks on Stacks in preparation to transfer him to the prison in Bennettsville, SC. When he was done being shackled down, they started for the exit. Surrounded on all sides he carried nothing with him but his pride, dignity, and psp. He felt like he did in the beginning when he took on the task of getting involved in this life. Alone.

Detective Lawrence pushed off the counter he was leaning against and approached Stacks. "How'd you know?"

Stacks looked over at the guy, who did all he could to try and end his reign. His face gave away no form of emotion, but his body showed defeat. "I was doin' this for over ten years without so much of a glance from the police. The closest I've came to twelve was at a car auction. Then out of nowhere there are investigations, undercovers, and felonious arrests. It was too obvious Steve. Too obvious."

"Then why did you stick around?"

"It's called sacrifice. If you were really payin' attention to what was happenin' you would've caught on. Do you read the bible?"

"When I can why?"

"I beseech you therefore, brethren, by the mercies of God, that ye present your bodies a living sacrifice, holy, acceptable unto God, which is your reasonable service. And be not conformed to this world: but be ye transformed be the renewing of your mind. Romans twelve one and two," he quoted as he was pulled along by the marshals.

Lawrence looked at Stacks' receding back in bewilderment. He could no longer resent the man who seemed to have it all when they were younger. He was now left no choice but to respect him.

I.M. Heartfelt

Crime Family Pt. 1: The Sacrifice

Be on the lookout for

Crime Family Pt.2

"Justice"

Also by the author

"CheckMate: It's Your Move"
"Mirror Image"

www.ingramcontent.com/pod-product-compliance
Lightning Source LLC
Chambersburg PA
CBHW070628260626
47161CB00007B/2630